Conciliation Commitment

The Second Jack Prendergast Novel

1903 - 1914

John D Smith

Copyright © 2021 John D Smith

ISBN: 9798713392765

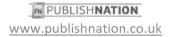

www.publishnation.co.uk

Acknowledgments and thanks

My thanks again to Publishnation and Scott Gaunt for their assistance in delivering this second book to publication.

This second novel is for our son, Greg and our daughter, Laura. ….that you may know a little more about your Great-grandad's life….xx

Love you both.

And with thanks to all my friends and family who have given me their support and enthusiasm.

And as always for Patricia…x

Enjoy……

PART ONE – CONCILIATION

"They gave me a thousand reasons to leave you, but I found a thousand and one reasons to be with you." -Matshona Dhliwayo

Chapter 1

(Ferry, Dublin to Liverpool, November 1903)
Michael Rafferty stood on the ferry and watched the mainland come into view. Despite his friends and family's caution about a rough sea voyage, he had recovered from the early waves and swell quickly and was comfortable on the deck, watching the sea.

England. A place he had long been told about, but never in a positive way.

His jet-black hair, dusky skin and gentle features attracting the looks of a number of the ladies travelling with their respective husbands. At over six feet tall and well-built from a life on the land, he carried a confidence and self-belief that belied his age.

He had been reluctant to move to a different world, but as his fare had been paid by Uncle Seamus, he'd decided to take a chance.

'Come and join me over here lad. Good work and plenty of opportunities.'

Michael was glad of the change this offered. His work in Ireland had diminished and his family had encouraged him to go and earn.

There was around thirty minutes of the journey remaining.

He glanced to see an attractive woman – maybe thirty to forty – looking directly towards him with a slight smile. She glanced to her side, and moved away from her husband who was deep in conversation with another distinguished character at his side.

She sidled towards Michael and spoke in a whisper.

'Come with me …quickly..'

He looked from side to side, and checking that her man was still engrossed in his discussion, he turned to follow.

Once they were out of sight, she pushed him into corner, obscured by the small lifeboat.

'Very little time' she said as she attacked him passionately.

'*My God*' thought Michael. *' England is certainly a land of opportunity…'*

Chapter 2

(Brawmarsh, December 1903)

Jack stood open-mouthed at the couple before him. His long-lost brother and sister?

'What the bloody hell…how did you find me? Well, I'm …you'd better come inside.'

They followed him into the room, and he waved his hand for them to sit. The youth was a thin, gaunt-faced fellow with a sallow complexion. He was dressed poorly, as was his sister. She was equally slight and unkempt. They both looked as if they had not fed or washed for days.

'So, tell me? How did you find me, for God's sake?'

Joseph cast a nervous look to his sister.

'We asked in our old village if anyone had seen where you'd gone. One fella said he saw you leaving, and that you'd taken the road to Yorkshire. We took that direction and kept asking if anyone knew you. We've walked for three days until we stopped outside this town and a shopkeeper gave us your address.'

'My God. You could have ended up anywhere! Three days on the road. When did you last eat?'

Mary eventually raised her head to quietly reply.

'We ate on the first day, Jack, but ran out of what little food we had. We had no money, so we drank water from the streams and coped as best we could.'

Jack shook his head as he looked at the young couple. *Why had they come all this way?* He jumped to his feet and turned to the scullery.

'I have a lot of questions for you two, but let's get some food in you.'

He skinned and gutted a rabbit from his larder and added potatoes, carrots and swede.

'Right, that'll take a while to cook, so first thing is to get you both cleaned up. To be honest, you smell like donkeys, the pair of you! You first, Mary. Go and clean yourself in the scullery. There's soap and towels in there. Sorry it's cold water, lass but needs must. Pull the curtain across while I talk to your brother Have you a change of clothes?'

She shook her head.

'We've only the clothes we're wearing'

'Well, you'd best wash your clothes out as well. I've no clothes for a woman here. I've an old nightshirt that you can wear while we dry them in front of the fire'

She slipped away to the scullery and Jack turned to her brother.

'I have to ask? How do I know you're my brother and sister? You could be anyone.'

Joseph nodded and put his head in his hands.

'We're the son and daughter of Brendan and Constance Prendergast. Born in Eddington on our smallholding. Moved out by the Earl of Worksop. I'm eighteen, Mary is seventeen. You left our home some seven or eight years ago.'

Jack stared hard at the young man and continued his questioning.

'And our younger sister. Where is she?'

'Celia passed from the fever five years ago.'

Jack felt the tears come to his eyes. His youngest sister dead. Christ, she'd be no more than ten or eleven years old. He drew a deep breath.

'Ah bless her. Poor lass. And my mother. How's she?'

'She passed a few months later, Jack. Never got over Celia's death.'

'Oh, my God.'

He'd put his family to the back of his mind since arriving in Brawmarsh, but had occasionally thought of his Ma. He sought to control his tears.

'They said her heart was broken, Jack but it was the fever again'

'I suppose I should ask about Da – the old bastard?'

'That's why we're here. He passed away last week. He drank heavily after Ma's death, and lost interest in the smallholding. I did what I could, brother but the land owners told us to leave when he died. No rights. We were evicted within days.'

Joseph paused and sought to cover his grief.

'Nowhere to go, Jack. That's when Mary and I decided to find you'

Jack stood and thought about what he could do. He had two bedrooms but, as yet only one bed. He had bedclothes, but only one decent set. They had no clothes, and nothing he had would fit Joseph, but he would have to make do tonight. He had no clothes for a young woman.

Mary returned to the room in the loose-fitting nightshirt. Joseph moved to wash himself and his rags. Jack found an old shirt and trousers for him to wear.

'Listen. You need food and sleep first. Then we'll talk about what's next.'

In due course, he returned to the scullery and poured three bowls of rabbit stew and rough bread. Unsurprisingly, his siblings ate greedily and he watched as they wiped the last remnants of the food from the bowls.

'You need to take some rest. Mary, take the small room upstairs at the back; I'll find you a mat and some covers. Joseph, you take my bed in the front. We'll talk tomorrow.'

They offered no debate, and after they had left Jack sat and pondered what he should do now.

Chapter 3

Jack had an uncomfortable night on his small sofa and slept intermittently as he mulled over the evening events.

He had two or three issues to address today. He needed to source more food to feed the new arrivals, provide clothes for a seventeen-year-old girl and her brother, and finally to determine what he did with the two of them for sleeping arrangements. God. yesterday seemed so simple!

He arose, letting the pair sleep on and walked to the village.

The food supply was straightforward. He bought meat, vegetables and bread and then wandered on to the second-hand shop.

Mrs Conway greeted him like a hawk.

'Morning Jack. What can I help you with today?'

'Morning. I think I need a couple of small beds and mattresses as a start.

He saw the woman smile to herself and rub her hands with the prospect of a major sale.

'Aw Jack, you're a pleasure to deal with' she laughed.

Jesus thought Jack. *I'm supposed to be a hard trade union negotiator and this bloody woman does me every time.*

After some twenty minutes or so he walked away having bought two small beds and mattresses and some decent second-hand, but clean bedclothes. He asked for any young ladies clothing, and shirts and trousers for Joseph.

'Not a chance, fella. Bought as soon as I have 'em. You'll need to be here very early doors to get them'

Jack arranged for delivery of his purchases and stopped to consider what he could do to find clothes for his siblings. He was left with only one option.

He walked reluctantly towards Emma's house. As he knocked on the outer door, he hoped that Florence would be at work to avoid any conflict or unpleasantness.

'Come in lad. A long while since we've seen you.'

Emma was looking tired and careworn. Jack was clearly aware that she missed her husband. He understood, from Thomas, that he and Florence contributed financially to her upkeep and she that was living relatively comfortably in her older age.

'What brings you here, lad?'

'Well Emma, I have a problem...'

He explained the arrival of Joseph and Mary and their circumstances.

'So, we need to sort clothes for the pair of them, Jack? I'll check with Thomas and Flo and see if they've got any decent cast offs. I can allus do a bit of sewing to make them fit reasonably well. If we can get hold of material, I can sort dresses and shirts. Can this lass Mary do any sewing or dressmaking?'

'Not a clue, Emma. I imagine she would have had to do a bit of that.'

'How have you found the two of them, Jack. Must have been a real shock for you lad?'

Jack reflected that he had not really considered his views on his siblings. He stopped himself from voicing any opinion to Emma.

'Early days Emma. They are both quiet. I've only had them with me overnight and I'm still not sure how this will all work out. I never expected to have responsibility for others. Well, I thought I might once with Florence....'

His voice tailed away and Emma touched his arm gently.

'Aye lad we all hoped for that, didn't we?'

'How is she, Emma?'

Emma smiled thinly.

'She's lost a lot of her get up and go to be honest Jack. She's still immersed in her nursing and hoping to progress, but she seems so serious and less fun these days.'

'She needs to live a little more, Emma. Get another interest away from nursing.'

'Funny you should say that lad. The one thing that seems to have her captivated away from her work recently is this 'votes for women' movement. Seems to be the only thing that captures her attention away from her work.'

Jack looked surprised and smiled.

'Aye, that seems odd. Never had Florence as having any interest in politics and such. Well at least she and I have one thing in common...'

'You've lots in common, Jack. More's the pity you both couldn't see it.'

'Emma, it wasn't my choice that we broke up. This bloody nursing was the cause.'

They both were quiet for the moment reflecting on what might have been.

Emma shook her head and broke the silence.

'Any road, mebbe best option is to bring your brother and sister here in the next few days and we'll see if we can sort some bits and pieces to put them on. What do you think?'

Jack displayed some reticence at this suggestion. He had avoided any meeting with Florence for some time and was reluctant to be party to any awkward gathering. Emma raised her finger and pointed to him.

'Listen Jack Prendergast. This is getting bloody silly, man! You and Florence will need to move on. I decide who visits my home, and I'm telling you that if you want help for your family you need to come here. We need to measure and sort any clothing and materials. Your brother and sister have never met us, so of course you need to be here. Florence has to be here to help me with Mary. For God's sake, grow up and get over it!'

9

Jack raised his hand in acceptance and kissed Emma gently on the cheek.

'OK I'll bring the two of them on Thursday, if that's alright. Gives me a couple of days to sort the house and find out a bit more about them.'

He turned and fleetingly raised his hand as he left.

Chapter 4

(Jack's House, Brawmarsh 15 December 1903)
It had been a few days since Jack had visited Emma and he had spent this time talking at length to Joseph and Mary. It became clear that neither had any form of education and lacked any capability to read or write. His father had not allowed any form of school education and had used both siblings as free labour in the home and on the smallholding.

Joseph was bluntly a scrawny young man who, despite having to work on the land, had not developed any significant bulk. He was nervous, tentative in his speech and lacked – in Jack's view -any attributes which would allow him to present himself as any sort of proposition to an employer requiring physical work.

He had – under pressure from Jack's questioning - admitted that his lack of strength and capability had resulted in both verbal and physical abuse from their father. He had tended the animals and appeared to have some enthusiasm and consideration for their care.

Mary – whilst initially quiet and allowing her brother to speak on her behalf – appeared to be a little more robust in her disposition. She too, had suffered under her father and, given her mother's failing health, had assumed most of the domestic responsibilities. She could cook and sew and was happy to take on some of the cleaning and tidying of the house as requested.

She still looked fragile and pale, but Jack saw an underlying strength of character that may surface given an increase in her confidence and association with others in the wider world.

Jack stood and addressed his siblings forcefully.

'Listen both of you. I can provide for you for a short while, but you both will need to find work soonest. Do you understand?'

Both nodded and Jack continued.

'I have no idea where I will find work for you, brother. You are not a great proposition for any physical work and you have no reading and writing capability. You know something about livestock so possibly we could look for employment there.'

Joseph sank his head and nodded.

'For God's sake lad, show a bit of fire! Tell me you disagree. Show some bloody spirit...'

Jack turned away and threw his hands upwards in despair as his brother continued to hang his head and say nothing.

'And you Mary. I will ask around the town and see if we can find any work cleaning, cooking or washing. Would you be happy with that?'

Mary gave a small smile.

'Thank you, Jack,'

'OK then. I'm going for a beer at the Club. I suggest you two look at a bit of cleaning and preparing some dinner for the three of us. There's food in the pantry. I'll be back by 8 o'clock'

He turned and pulled his coat from the door hook and left them to their tasks.

Chapter 5

Jack sat alone in a corner of the Club saloon and considered his options.

One, he needed to help his siblings find work.

Two, he needed to look at a long-term resolution to their living arrangements. There was no way he was prepared to share a cramped bedroom with his brother. The small attic was an option for Joseph, but he baulked at the cost and the ongoing situation of the three of them in the limited house space. He had some savings left, but they would be all but spent if he had to buy more furniture and bedding, plus continuing to feed the two of them.

He believed he could seek out work for Mary in the town, even if only for a few hours a day. Joseph was entirely another matter, given his nature and lack of any skill.

At least his work was undemanding at the moment. With no further meetings organised before Christmas and, unusually peaceful relations between employers and his members, he could focus his attentions on the family issues. He had a couple of sessions to attend with the local Labour Representation Committee but, with no impending elections, again the demands on his time were not significant.

'How are ya Prendergast?' shouted a voice from the bar.

He looked up to see Seamus and another younger man and waved a welcome as they walked over to join him at the table.

'Well enough Seamus. Not seen you in here for a week or two?'

'Busy fella. We've done at the foundry but we found a hell of a job at the big house. The old Lord is virtually knocking the place down and re-building. There's best part of a year's work for us so happy as Larry, aren't we, lad.'

He turned to the young man who nodded as he took a good draft of Guinness.

He leaned over to Jack.

'I'm Michael Rafferty. Seamus's nephew. Good to meet you, Jack. Heard a fair bit about you. I was hoping to meet you earlier but this old bastard has kept me hard at it as soon as I got here'

'And you, Michael. If it's Seamus been telling you, then ignore the worst bits'

Michael laughed as they shook hands.

'No, he's said you're a grand fella and so has Thomas'

Jack looked the man up and down. Good looking, and carrying a strong air of confidence in himself.

'So, Thomas is still with you Seamus. Behaving himself these days, is he?'

'He's fine lad. Since you sorted him out his drinking's under control and he seems to have grown up a fair bit. I think he's coming down here later'

'That's grand. Not seen him here for a spell so I hope he's learned his lessons.''

Jack turned back to Michael

'So how are finding the flesh pots of Yorkshire, Michael?'

'Ah to be fair I've not had much chance to get myself out and about but I don't believe there's a great social life to be had in the town. I'm a young fella with young fella's interests, if you understand me. Mind, I've seen a few pretty young lasses hereabouts. Are ya a single man yerself, Jack?'

'I am Michael, but not through choice. A long story...'

Seamus stood and offered refills making his way to the bar.

'And what is it you do Jack. I believe you're a trade union fella?'

'I am. Full Time Officer for the Steelworkers Union. Keeps me occupied.'

'So, you'll be a socialist then?'

'Totally committed, Michael. I get meself involved in the Labour movement a fair bit.'

'And what's your view on Ireland?'

Jack smiled to himself. It was always a leading question when he met an Irishman. He'd learned to be careful but he had heard enough of their cause from Seamus and Patrick to cause him to read a fair bit of the politics.

'I suspect you're a supporter of the Republican cause, like your Uncle and old Patrick God bless him?'

'Sure I am. They'll be a time when we break free, Jack. We'll do what we need to do to get there. Patrick was a grand supporter of our cause. Pity he missed....'

Jack grimaced at the strength and passion of the young man's view. Patrick had been an absolute extremist and his commitment – his attempted assassination of the King - had resulted in his incarceration in a lunatic asylum likely never to be released.

'Your friend Patrick was a bloody idiot, Michael. He wasted his life by a stupid action. He now cannot serve your cause where he is. For my part, I am sympathetic to your mission. I understand your motives and your hopes. But I don't believe you'll achieve what you wish for by violence. There's another way through negotiation and conviction.'

Michael stood and gestured aggressively.

'Pah fella!. You don't understand. Every time we talk, we are sold down the fecking river. The only way we'll gain our freedom is by fight, by rebellion. And trust me man, it's coming soon!'

He turned and walked away. With a brief conversation with Seamus, he stormed from the room and left.

'Well, you and Michael seemed to get along then Jack.' Seamus placed the beers on the table and sat back.

'Not so well, fella.' Jack shook his head.

'He's a bloody headcase Jack when it comes to our movement. He's young and passionate but it's all about violence and fight. No belief in the value of diplomacy. Mind I can understand how these youngsters are becoming frustrated. No concessions from your Government …just empty thin assurances about the future. He's right in one respect… there's a growing belief that conflict will be the only way.'

'I'm trying to understand, Seamus but the approach of your nephew doesn't help. He's as crazy as Patrick!'

Seamus took a long draw on his beer and looked directly at Jack.

'No lad. He's worse than Patrick. He's clever and more connected. I love his passions but I fear the worst…'

They drank together with their own thoughts before Seamus broke the silence.

'Any way, fella you've told me nothing about your life at the moment.'

Jack relayed the happenings of the last week as Seamus listened in amazement.

'So, you've got lodgers for the duration, fella. Are you happy with that?'

'Not at all Seamus. The house was never intended to be a bloody lodge house. I need to get them work and lodgings soonest.'

'Would the lad be any use to us Jack? We've some labouring work he could help us with for a few weeks or more.'

Jack shook his head, laughed out loud and looked directly at Seamus.

'Fella, I'd not drop this lad on you. He'd be a total disaster. I doubt he could deal with more than an hour of your work. And I don't think he'd fit your business.'

Seamus took a long draft of his beer and spoke.

'From what you've said Prendergast you've got some issues here. The lass seems as if she could find some work.

Your brother must be a worry lad. Send him to us if you wish and we'll see how he goes. What do you think?'

Jack sighed and stopped Seamus from any further comment.

I'll do that Seamus, but you've been warned fella. You've been warned!'

Chapter 6

Florence sat quietly reading some paperwork as Emma busied herself cleaning around the room.

'Quiet lass. Anything interesting in that?'

'It's some documents about votes for women Auntie. There's a body of women who are forming a group to try and get the Government's attention. The Woman's Social and Politics Union based in Manchester. They've a rally coming up in the New Year.'

Emma shook her head.

'Waste of time Florence. The authorities are run by men. Always been the way. I'm not convinced that it's the right way to go really.'

Florence laid down the document and reddened as she spoke.

'Then nothing will change whilst women like yourself accept the way it is. I work and contribute my efforts to this country and I deserve the right to decide how it's governed. If we sit back it will be men with money who decide. It's unfair and wrong, Auntie Emma.'

Emma smiled to herself and couldn't stop herself from a teasing comment.

'My God lass I thought I was listening to Jack Prendergast for a minute.'

Emma reddened further and waved he hand dismissively.

'I've no need to be compared to Jack. I'm my own women with the independence to think as I will. I don't need any man's politics to advise me.'

She gathered her papers and set to leave the room. Emma could not resist one more comment.

18

'Aye well, you'll have the chance to compare notes with Mr Prendergast. He's coming round tonight with his brother and sister to sort out some clothes for the pair of them. I did tell you we'd agreed to help.'

'Tonight...' said Florence clearly flustered. 'Well, I might not be available.'

'Oh yes you will, lass. I need you to check for any clothes you can pass on to the girl and to help me with any fitting.'

***

Emma and Florence sat waiting for Jack and his family to arrive. The latter was clearly uncomfortable and shuffled nervously, seeking to hide her discomfort from her aunt.

'Where's Thomas?'

'God knows lass. He's hit and miss most nights, isn't he? Depends how busy they are at the Manor I suppose. Why? Do you need your big brother here to chaperone you?'

Emma's eyes twinkled and she smirked quietly awaiting the anticipated response from her niece.

'Oh, stop it Auntie Emma! I'm not daft. I know you're trying to tease me and it won't work. I'm sure we can all be civil together.'

Emma turned away and shook her head. She believed Florence had never stopped having strong affections for Jack Prendergast. It would be entertaining tonight to see them in the same room again. She noted that her niece had appeared to make a limited effort to dress well but nevertheless had bathed and fixed her hair to set an attractive image.

She turned her attention to Thomas' absence. Whilst he had addressed his life-style, he seemed to have few interests these days other than his work. There was no sign of him returning to his drinking and apparently no female company in his life. He was however often late for his evening meal with no explanation or apology. She was lost as to what he was doing after his work.

'Evening Auntie, Flo.'

Thomas burst into the room, a bounce in his step and embraced Emma dancing her around the room.

'What the hell nephew? Have you started your bloody drinking again?'

Thomas waved his finger towards her and laughed.

'You'll have to wait for my news Auntie Emma. Trust me, I'm not drinking...and you'll be pleased to know there's no woman involved. Off to get washed and changed for our visitors.'

He disappeared to his room leaving Florence and Emma exchanging puzzled looks.

A knock at the door. Jack, Joseph and Mary entered the room to hugs and welcomes from Emma. Jack and Florence merely exchanged short pleasantries and avoided any physical contact.

Emma studied the two newcomers for a short spell. Mary, a slender lass but not unattractive – in need of some filling out she thought. Joseph – much as Jack had described. Thin and lacking in any presence. He stood to the rear of the group and, after the introductions, appeared uncomfortable and unwilling to involve himself in any social contact.

Joseph gazed around the room. He shivered at the thought of having to mix with a group of people. He knew no one at all, including his brother. He felt embarrassed by his poor clothes and his lack of social skills. He hoped that he could pass the evening quickly and without having to enter any significant conversation. Staying as far back as he could, he smiled thinly and hung his head to avoid any direct eye contact.

Mary was in her own haze. She had not benefitted from any company whilst at home – just her father and brother over the last few years.

'Come on and sit yourselves down.'

Emma fussed around the newcomers, clearly trying to abate their nervousness.

'I'll make you all a hot drink. Have you eaten?'

'Aye we're grand Emma. Had a bite before we left.'

Jack glanced surreptitiously towards Florence who was seated next to Mary and attempting to encourage her in conversation. She looked a little careworn since he'd last seen her and perhaps more intense. She seemed to have lost a lot of her vitality. More serious he felt.

'Auntie Emma, I'm going to take Mary to my room and let her try on some bits and pieces I've dug out. There's also some clothes from a couple of my work mates which might suit.'

With that she took Mary's hand and led her to the stairs almost colliding with her brother as he burst into the room.

Thomas stood aside to let them pass and took Mary's hand as he was introduced. He had expected to see a plain and ordinary young girl, but couldn't help noticing that she had a pretty face and the most captivating blue eyes.

'You can let the lass go now, brother' said Florence with a smirk.

Thomas with some embarrassment released Mary's hand and turned to join the others. Emma scurried after the girls.

'I'll come and help niece. We can look at any fitting and alterations.'

Jack introduced Joseph and he and Thomas briefly exchanged updates since they had last met. Joseph sat quietly until Thomas turned to him and gestured towards an untidy pile of clothes.

'Right then fella I've brought a couple of shirts and trousers that might sort you out. I've an old jacket as well.'

He looked Joseph up and down.

'I think you'll need to put on a bit of meat, lad. I feel they might all be a bit too big for you but perhaps Auntie Emma could try and sort that.'

They watched as the young man nodded his thanks and moved to the scullery to undress.

Over the next hour or so they watched as Joseph emerged with his new attire. It was clear that they would need some significant alteration, but at least they were clean and serviceable for a short time. The jacket, however was not an option as it hung loosely over his skeletal figure.

They were interrupted by the ladies returning to the room.

Mary was transformed and stopped their conversation in its tracks.

'My God, what have you done with my sister? Is this a different lady?'

Jack shook his head and laughed.

'You're a real beauty Mary. I'm taken aback....'

Florence raised an eyebrow.

'Never had an eye for what lies beneath have you, Jack?'

'Seems not Florence. Perhaps my perception of beauty was not as able as it should have been in the past.'

The group fell silent at these caustic and bitter exchanges between the two.

'We need to get back home Mary, Thomas.'

Jack grabbed his coat and ushered his siblings towards the door.

'Wait.' said Emma. 'What about the alterations on the lad's clothing?

'Thanks Emma but I'm sure Mary can sort that. Thank you for your help.'

With that he turned angrily and led his family away.

Chapter 7

(Brawmarsh, January 1904)

Christmas had come and gone and Winter had set in with vengeance. In the early morning snow, Jack walked briskly through the town to take the bus to his Rotherham office.

He reflected on the past couple of weeks. His brother had taken up the offer of employment with Seamus over the last week, inevitably returning exhausted. He had said little about his experience, and was brief in his response to any questions Jack had raised about what he had been occupied with at his work.

Mary, on the contrary, appeared far more buoyant. She had sewn and altered the clothing they had been given and seemed to revel in the opportunity to maintain the house and cook for her brothers. With Jack's agreement, she had on two or three occasions visited Emma's home and appeared to be striking up a blossoming friendship with her. It was clear that she was receiving some guidance on her personal care and presentation.

He felt unsettled about the way the two of them had got along. Perhaps, he thought it was a bit of jealousy. He had once wanted to be with Florence and share her hopes and aspirations. It seemed as though Mary was starting to replace him....

He shook himself from his thoughts and climbed onto the sparsely occupied bus. Always quiet after Christmas as people struggled with debt after their spend. The last meeting of the Labour Committee had raised this and Jack had agreed to participate in house visits in the community to seek to offer any help where they could. He was conscious that, despite his union role, he had little contact with his members away from their work. This was possibly an opportunity to broaden his role away from routine administration and meetings.

He had to admit to himself that his Union role had not proved as demanding or stimulating as he had expected. Occasional involvement in wage issues and the odd individual members problems had seemed to be the highlights, with the majority of his time in regional gatherings and procedural matters.

He arrived at the office at eight o'clock and settled into his chair to write a report covering activities in the last month.

He reached to pick up the ringing phone, breaking him from his paperwork.

'Is that Jack Prendergast?'

'It is. Who's this?'

'Jack, it's Bernard Catkin from Docketts and Worrall in Clifton. Need ya here sharpish, fella. There's been an explosion. Bad job Jack. Need ya here...'

Jack sat back in shock and was lost for words. His first major issue...for Christs sake, get it together man!

'On my way, Bernard. Any lads hurt or what?'

'Aye Jack. Looks like there's a few dead and some bad injuries ..bad injuries.'

'Alright fella. I'm on my way.'

He grabbed his coat and then stopped. He realised he needed to phone the Union Head Office and bring them up to date.

Frustratingly the call rang out and remained unanswered.

Bugger it thought Jack. *First priority is getting to Clifton.*

He ran to the door and locked the office. What next? Fastest way to get there. From his previous trip to the works, the bus route would take at least 40 minutes stopping along the way in a trundle.

He jumped to the middle of the road waving down a small automobile. The driver – a small moustached and well-dressed man – pulled the car to a halt and waved his hand aggressively towards Jack.

'Are you bloody mad, man! I could have killed you....'

Jack hesitated before jumping in the passenger seat.

'Listen mister. My apologies but I need to get to Clifton as soon as I can. There's been an explosion at the steel works....'

The driver looked in disbelief and pointed.

'You're a bloody madman! I'm driving straight to the police station now. Explain yourself there!'

He accelerated his small vehicle and focused on the road ahead seeking to ignore his newly acquired company.

'Wait just for a minute please' pleaded Jack. 'I'm a trade union officer and some of my lads have been killed, others badly hurt. I'm happy to pay for your petrol but I need your help to get there quickly.'

The man pulled his car gently to the roadside and looked reflectively at Jack.

'You could be a bloody murderer for all I know?'

'If I were, you'd be dead by now, wouldn't you?'

The driver tapped at his steering wheel for a few seconds before re-starting his engine.

'Alright young man, I'll take you at your word. If I'm wrong I can assure you that you will live to regret your actions.'

Jack nodded and sat back as the vehicle accelerated.

'What's your name anyway?'

'Prendergast. Jack Prendergast. Sorry, sir and you are?'

The man smiled briefly to himself.

'Not been asked that in a long time in this locality. I'm William Harcourt. I'm better known as Lord Rotherham.'

'Bloody hell!' Jack stuttered. 'Sorry for the bad language, Lord Rotherham.'

'Heard worse lad. Just call me Bill eh? I suppose you'll be a bloody socialist then?'

'I am. I suppose you'll be a bloody Tory?

Rotherham laughed out loud.

'Good response, young fellow. I am a Tory, but don't tar me with the same brush as some of those stuck-up bastards in the party'

Jack smiled and pondered for a moment.

'I'm aware of you by reputation, sir…Bill. It's said that you're a good employer amongst the miners. A bit of a social conscience compared with other pit owners.'

'I try to be fair, Jack. Not always easy. You look at the likes of me and see a wealthy landowner with mines reaping profits. I'm the first to say I live comfortably, but the bloody property taxes will hit the estate heavily on my death. There will come a time, young man, when the likes of Rotherham Hall will be untenable to maintain. No doubt you socialists would enjoy the effect. but trust me you will come to regret it. Property such as mine will be lost, fall in to disrepair.'

Jack listened intently and, conscious of the benevolence of his driver, chose his response carefully.

'I have a simple view Bill. The working class do not have the monies to live as you live. They have to look at the pennies every day and most weeks struggle to find enough to feed and clothe their families. I doubt that is the main issue for yourself and others of your class. My belief is that we must change society to remove this poverty and deprivation. I don't seek to haul you to financial ruin. I simply look to remove the inequality and unfairness between those who have and those who do not. I know there are those who would see you and your like dragged down and eliminated as a class. I share their passion, if not their extreme views.'

Rotherham turned briefly to look narrow-eyed towards Jack.

26

'I should throw you out on the road now as my enemy! However, you are entitled to your views, despite the fact that I find them unpalatable. Whilst you were talking, I have recalled where I heard your name before. You were the instigator of a strike at Cartwrights works a couple of years ago, were you not?'

'I was involved in the strike, Lord Rotherham, but the instigator was Frank Cartwright. His disregard of the safety of his workers and greed for profits caused the problems. I – with others – sought to change his attitude for the better.'

Rotherham chuckled to himself.

'You have a way with words, Prendergast. Change his attitude indeed! Let's be candid, shall we? Frank was an arsehole. Bloody incompetent and arrogant. His father was cut from a different cloth. Were you aware that he passed last month?'

Jack was shocked. He reflected on his meeting with Sidney Cartwright which ended the strike. A straight man and true to his word, albeit a tough old bugger. He and Arthur – his good friend Arthur Davies now gone – had reached a sound agreement for the workforce. He felt himself respectfully hanging his head.

'He was a good man, Jack...a good businessman. A friend of mine and one of the last I had. I miss him.'

Jack found the situation strange. Both he and a Lord of the land experiencing strong emotions for their lost friends. The moment ended as Rotherham swung his vehicle to the front of the burning foundry.

'My God lad, this looks bloody bad!'

Jack stood from the car and stared at the building. One complete wall had been demolished and blackened machine debris was scattered across the surrounding area. Men everywhere were digging with shovels and bare hands amongst the still burning fires and embers, seeking any hope of finding their friends and workmates. The inside of the building was literally a furnace – unapproachable still

27

and spitting fragments of flaming ore at the workers seeking to find their colleagues.

Jack ran to the scene, watching the blackened men beating the incidental fires from their bodies and turning regularly to clear the smoke and fragments of material from their eyes, noses and throats. He saw bodies being hauled from the remains of the building and turned sickened by the sight of the burnt carcasses.

'Where should I dig?' he shouted to one of them as he found an abandoned shovel.

'Lad it doesn't matter. We've no clue where the men are. Dig gently and hope fella. Just dig and hope....'

Chapter 8

(Steelworkers Union office, Rotherham, Late January 1904)
Jack re-read the letter before him for a second time.

Hand delivered that morning to his home it was enclosed in an expensive envelope addressed to *'Mr Jack Prendergast, Esquire'*. He knew no-one who would use that term so, with some trepidation, he tore it open to reveal a handwritten letter on high quality vellum paper headed by some form of heraldic crest.

'Dear Jack,

Please excuse the informality of my contact but I am aware that we parted company – unsurprisingly given the circumstances – with some haste after you commandeered my vehicle. Under the circumstances, I completely understand the urgency of your journey and was pleased to assist.

Despite my best efforts, I have been unable to obtain any detailed understanding of the outcome of the terrible incident at Dockets and Worrall's Foundry. I am given to understand that tragically, there were a number of deaths and additionally serious injuries amongst your work colleagues.

I would welcome the opportunity to meet with you at your convenience. I recognise that you will inevitably have significant demands upon your time, but if practical I shall be at home in the afternoon of Saturday 30th January.

Should you be available, your attendance at any time in the afternoon of the above date would be appreciated.

I am respectfully.

Yours sincerely'

The letter was signed with a flourish *'Bill Rotherham'*.

Jack pushed back his office chair and sat thoughtfully seeking to determine the purpose of such a meeting. The 30th January was tomorrow. He had no major plans for the day, but equally was reluctant to spend his time satisfying the curiosity of the local aristocracy.

He had been shocked to the core by the aftermath of the explosion and still shivered as he reluctantly brought to mind the sight of not just corpses, but limbs and other body parts being dug from the debris. Worse still – and not credible to Jack was the vision of smaller bodies – children – being pulled to one side. He had discovered later that lads as young as twelve and thirteen were employed to carry out some of the routine cleaning and clearing tasks.

Jack had subsequently confronted the foundry management on this and other issues. He was told, almost dismissively, that there were no restrictions on employment of young workers, that the legislation only covered textile workers, that the children were sent by their parents to supplement the family income. He was told that as far as they were aware the young men attended the required school hours and that it was not the responsibility of the Company to monitor this.

Sadly, they were in the main correct. The government appointed factory inspectors were happy to undertake their inspections in a cursory manner and accept the assurances of the management that all the requirements were fully met.

He had held long discussions with Company representatives and it became clear that they had broadly fulfilled their safety obligations. The furnace had been inspected less than three months earlier and given a clean bill of health.

Nevertheless, the carnage had resulted in eight deaths – three of them youngsters under the age of thirteen. A further six men and one child had been brutally damaged with lost limbs and other severe injuries. The Company had waived any liability in the absence of evidence suggesting their shortcomings.

Jack had visited all the families of the deceased and injured in the subsequent days and had returned home in despair and frustration. Widows left in their darkest time without any future income, tearful and desperate and dreading the future. A mother who had lost her eldest boy for the sake of a shilling or two each week.

A child who had lost a limb and would forever be subject to rejection in his community. His young life was over, and he would never know a life with opportunity and joy. He had been unable to offer any help other than emotional comfort, which felt totally inadequate and insufficient.

He had sought the benevolence of both the foundry owners and the union hierarchy seeking some support, compensation and financial assistance. He found only gestures and faint promises of how this could be addressed in the future.

'Look Jack. We don't have the funds to look after all our members. We would like to lad, but it's not practical.'

'Of course, we want to help our employees but we can't throw money away when we are not responsible for what has happened.'

He threw the letters to one side.

Since Christmas, he had also – as part of his commitment to the Labour Group – visited areas of Brawmarsh to understand how the community were coping after the demands of the festive celebrations. The answer was not good.

Some had answered his knock on the door and shut it in his face when he announced his purpose and politics. Some had been polite, but with the children around their feet had asked that he come back at another time – he knew that was an indication that they were disinterested in talking to him.

A small number had invited him into their houses. Jack had entered and sought to cover his despair.

A family of four or five or sometimes more. The children dressed poorly – some naked in the absence of any clothes for bed. All the properties lacked other than the most minimal heating, if any. Most of the houses had damp dripping across the walls. Many of the homes had religious icons and photographs of the King, which Jack found incongruous – the wealthiest idolised by the poor.

He recognised that several of the families suffered as a consequence of the father's drinking – monies earned or given never reaching the home.

Jack broke from his thoughts and thumped his fist to the desk. Things had to change. The lack of compensation for workers, the indifference of the Company owners, the need for a stronger focus by the Labour movement on basic social deprivation rather the current emphasis on political presence. He would drive this as his prime agenda with the union, the businesses and his socialist colleagues.

He drew out a piece of writing paper and began to write......

Chapter 9

(Rotherham Manor, 30th January 1904)

The building was imposing, set in extensive lawned gardens with land extending as far as the eye could see. To the left stood a stable-block and garage. To the right outbuildings presumably housing staff quarters and storage areas. The building itself was built of Dorset Stone and some three floors high. Matching wings sat on either side of the central house.

Jack could not explain to himself how he had chosen to attend this appointment. He had made a minimal gesture by shaving and dressing in his best jacket and trousers. It completely contradicted his principles and beliefs in presenting himself at the arched oak door of the manor house. Maybe he should just turn and walk away down the half mile driveway and forget the invitation from Rotherham.

'Bugger it. I'll spend ten minutes out of politeness and thank him for his help.' he said to himself.

He pulled the large bell ring at the side of the door. He laughed out loud. *'Should I bow or salute or what?'*

The door swung open to reveal an elderly man in formal dress who disdainfully looked him up and down.

'Yes?'

'Jack Prendergast. I've a meeting with Bill.'

The butler grimaced at the informality.

'I assume you mean his Lordship/'

Jack decided to have some fun at the expense of the man.

'It that's Bill, then aye. It's him I've come to see'

He could almost feel the sense of outrage pertaining from the man and found himself smirking at his discomfort.

'Please wait here Mr Prendergast.' He turned, closing the door as Jack attempted to follow him through the entrance.

Jack waved a crude gesture to the door. 'Miserable old bastard'

He stood in the winter chill for minutes, convinced that the delay was deliberate and ready to walk away as the door re-opened.

Lord Rotherham stood before him. A man of average height and heavy build, dressed in a heavy tweed jacket and corduroy trousers. A ruddy complexion complemented by the standard well maintained military moustache of his time and well-groomed salt and pepper hair. He looked to be in his late fifties or so, but had an upright stance which suggested a military background.

'Jack, come in. You've met Blewitt I believe? Total pain in the backside but served my father so I feel obliged to keep him on. Come in and follow me to the library.'

The hallway was cavernous. The walls covered with ornate and detailed paintings. Decorative tapestries laid on heavy wallpaper. Ornamental vases and figures freely distributed on pedestals and small tables. Heavy carpeting which felt as if his feet were unable to move freely.

'My God. There's some money here Bill.'

Rotherham turned and smiled.

'There's a good bit of money here but it will never be mine to spend. Heritage lad. For the future…though I suspect much of it will be sold to meet the taxes.'

He led Jack to the Library.

The younger man was stopped in his tracks. He owned some ten books but laid out on shelves were possibly hundreds and maybe more. He wandered away from his host and stroked the volumes across their spines. Novels, history, biography and – he noted with some surprise – political tomes and documents ranging across the political divide.

'You have copies of Marx, Bill? And I see some other socialist material?'

'Yes. Written as 'Das Kapital' and subsequently translated. I suppose Jack it's a question of 'know thine enemy. You'll note that my tastes range across the political divide so to speak. I believe it's necessary to understand all points of view before forming an educated opinion. I can recommend it to you as an option....'

Rotherham held Jack in a hard stare before bursting into laughter.

'Listen young man, you must develop a sense of humour and appreciate the benefits of seeing both sides of any argument. You are welcome – indeed I encourage you - to loan any material from my library. You will of course need to return this after consumption.'

Jack nodded his thanks.

'I may take you up on that offer, Bill. But I can't imagine that's why you invited me to meet with you. I'm grateful for your help with my journey.'

'A very terrible event Jack. I understand with tragic consequences/'

Jack outlined the background to the explosion and the resultant death and injury toll.

Rotherham listened intently shaking his head as he heard of the loss of life and mutilations. After Jack concluded he stood and looked through the window clearly distressed by the detail.

'And what of the families? How are they coping, surviving this catastrophe?

'For the dead, paupers' funerals in most cases. They have no savings and no income where the man of the house was killed. The injured are being dealt with at the local hospital or in Sheffield when the damage is severe. Many will never work again and they and their families may end up in the workhouses.'

'But surely your union will help them? And the Company? Have they not assisted?'

Jack looked at him and shook his head.

'Our union does not have the funds to do much. A token gesture which will provide some assistance, but we are unable to do more. The Company management have offered nothing. They fear being accused of a liability and until a full investigation is completed, they will not compromise their position.'

'And the men had no personal insurance, I suppose?'

Jack stood and faced his host.

'You really have no understanding of their finances do you, Lord Rotherham? The majority can barely live from day to day, let alone spend on such luxuries. There is recent law covering compensation for workers but it still requires proof of negligence. It's totally useless in addressing incidents like this, even though the dead and injured were not at fault.'

Rotherham walked back to his seat and opened a desk drawer.

'If acceptable, I would like to offer a little financial help to the people affected by the incident?'

He produced a cheque book and completed his notations before signing with a flourish.

£30, Mr Prendergast. To whom would this be payable?'

Jack gave details of a fund which the Union had established for voluntary contributions extending his thanks and assuring the generous sum would indeed provide relief to the affected families.

'This is kind of you, Bill. My apologies if I was a tad short but the issues of poverty and insurance are high on my priorities and frustrations at this time, as you may understand.'

The man waved his hand languidly dismissing Jack's concern.

'I have realised that I am far from the perfect host. Can I offer you tea or perhaps something stronger? Of course, you may need to return to your wife and family?'

'I'm fine Bill. I'm no hard drinker so I'll resist. As for my wife and family I'm unmarried. I was betrothed once but sadly it was not to be. As for family I have recently been joined in my home by a brother aged eighteen and a sister of seventeen. They are a sufficient problem without adding any further responsibilities.'

Rotherham rose and strode to an ornate sideboard. He drew a half full decanter from within and poured himself a large brandy.

'You sound somewhat disturbed by your family obligations, Jack?'

'Both are well enough, Bill but they have yet to find any appropriate work and the liability for their food and lodging rests with me. Joseph is a frail lad and far from outgoing in his character. He was employed on your estate by the Irish builders, but lasted only two days incapable of dealing with the physical demands. My sister is a better proposition in that she cooks, sews and cleans well but there is little call for her skills in the community.

'Does your brother have any redeeming qualities? Every man has some capabilities.'

Jack shook his head.

'He worked with livestock on my late Father's smallholding so he may have some application in that type of occupation, but again most farms have their family and can't afford the cost of additional hands.'

Rotherham pursed his lips in thought and laid both hands firmly upon his desk.

'Send them both here lad. Tell them to ask for my son George…I'll tell him they're coming but be aware he can be a snobby little bastard. Second thoughts…ask them to speak to Blewitt. I'll sort him to ensure they have no issues.'

Jack sat back in surprise.

'You don't need to do that. I can't pass my issues to you.'

'Jack I'm short of a couple of staff over the last few months. A kitchen maid lost to illness and a farmhand being offered work at a better rate at another estate. Trust me my generosity and funds are not so charitable. We have simply not had the time to replace the leavers.'

He reached across and shook the man's hand. Rotherham clung to his grip as if seeking some comfort from their newly established friendship. Jack realised he knew little about the man other than his public persona.

'And you Bill? Other than your son....?'

'As you may have observed Jack, I'm no longer a young man. I married late after a career in the Army, serving predominantly in the Crimea. My wife – the beautiful Susanna – I lost in childbirth. It would have been our second. Lost them both some twenty years ago. So, I carried on and – as best I could - raised George. I suspect I was not particularly successful in ensuring he was equipped to take up his future responsibilities.'

The man's eyes saddened and he looked wistful and stopped deep in thought.

'George is frankly a disappointment, young man. He is, in principle, the manager of my estates but bluntly he has neither the motivation or capability to fulfil the position. Too intent on his social life and – how shall we put it – the pleasures of the flesh. Privately Jack I suspect the likelihood of him providing a successor and heir is entirely unlikely. I will say no more.'

His eyes reddened and he stood to refill his tumbler. Jack felt he had now overstayed his welcome and stood indicating his intention to leave.

'Thank you for your company Bill. I will, with appreciation, take advantage of your offer for the loan of books and materials.'

They once more exchanged a handshake.

'You are welcome young man. Both to enjoy my library and to visit again should you choose to do so. It has been a pleasure.'

He escorted Jack, clasped his back firmly and raised his hand, closing the door as he returned to his solitude.

Chapter 10

(Brawmarsh, Spring 1904)

Florence gazed in her mirror. My Lord she thought *'you are looking tired and weary girl.'*

She sat on her bed and became lost in her thoughts. *'What a few months it had been'*

She returned to her placard and assertively corrected some of the wording amending *'Votes For Women'* to *'Votes For Women Today*!'

'Better' she thought.

Winding her hair into a tight bun, she stepped down the stairs and met Emma's jaundiced and sceptical face.

'And where is it you're wasting your time and money tonight, niece.' she spat.

Florence pushed past her Auntie and waved her sign before Emma's angry face.

'I'm to Bradford. There will be hundreds there. We're taking twenty alone on the train. Our movement is growing, Auntie.'

'Your movement is pointless lass! You will all come to your senses soon. You will never get a vote for women, silly girl. Do you not realise that men – aye wealthy men - will need to support you? They will never give up their power, their hold on the community.'

Florence flushed with anger at this further exchange with Emma.

'And women of your time will always accept that the men are right, won't you?'

Emma swung around aggressively with a ladle pointing towards her niece.

'Listen to me lass. You are young, you have no property, no assets, nothing to bargain with the monied men. Why would they allow you to influence the country and the

Government? The day women get any say is a long many years away. You are wasting your bloody time girl!'

Florence glared, threw on her coat and turned to disdainfully to leave.

Emma drew close to her and grasped her collar.

'And what's more, girl you are misleading young Mary. She idolises you and you are taking her along a road that you both will regret. She's not yet eighteen, Florence. Do you want the lass to have police record along with yourself because your behaviour will take you there? Trust me.'

She stood in tears as Florence shrugged her away and threw the door to a forceful close.

Chapter 11

Jack walked to the Club; his head full of mixed emotions. On the positive side, Lord Rotherham had been as good as his word and the estate had found employment for both his siblings.

Joseph had undertaken a position as a junior member of the staff looking after livestock. He had been given responsibility for exercising, grooming and stabling the horses but with a further requirement that he supported the local wildfowl shoots and assisted the summer monthly fox hunts. He had admitted to Jack quietly that he loved the former and hated the latter. He remained a sensitive boy, but had buckled down and seemed to be equipped to meet his responsibilities. He had been told that – if he continued to fulfil his employment tasks competently – accommodation could be available in the stable block on a permanent basis.

Jack smiled at the thought of his brother moving on from the house. Joseph – whilst an unprepossessing individual - seemed to cast a negative presence, and his moving on would undoubtedly lighten the atmosphere in the home.

Mary had been engaged as a chambermaid cum assistant cook cum whatever jobs she was required to undertake. Clearly Rotherham utilised his staff efficiently. There was no room for her to live on the estate and Jack found himself comfortable with this situation. She would turn eighteen in the next few months, but he still felt that she was too naïve and innocent to be let loose without his continued influence and direction.

She continued to meet regularly with Florence and they clearly had become close friends. He had conceded Mary's request to accompany Florence to emancipation events and protests – how could he argue given his belief in their cause?

The incidental benefit had been that Mary had kept him up to date with Florence's life. He had gathered that she had more passionately embraced the agenda of female emancipation – now attending the local meetings and recently being elected to a Committee role for her fervour. More importantly, he had noted that she had little time for any male company given her current priorities.

Jack was happy to maintain his sister at the house. She was generally good company and helped to maintain the home and provide very substantial meals on occasion – he did not ask from where some of the provisions had been derived....

The investigation into the explosion at Docketts and Worrall's Foundry had been inconclusive. A view of 'accidental death' had been announced and consequently no liability for the Company. It was suggested that a worker had cast an illicit cigarette aside amidst inflammatory material and that this had in turn combusted with sufficient strength to cause a small fracture in the furnace. This had expanded sufficiently to create the breach and release of the molten ore.

He found the conclusion to be, to say the least unconvincing, but, as the team who had investigated was deemed to be independent, he found no route to challenge their judgement.

He had re-visited the families of the bereaved and injured victims on several occasions but was angered by his frustrations and incapability to offer any significant help, beyond the paltry gestures offered through the charitable donations.

Jack stopped and sat for a brief moment on a small bench.

The park was full at this time of day. Young families enjoying the late spring evening, their children running freely and laughing and screeching in affected terror as they were chased by their father. A couple wandered by, hands held clearly in love and ignorant of any others within their world.

He dropped his head in his hands. He wanted their world. He had hoped for, and almost presumed, that his future with Florence would have created this scene. Instead, he felt he had become a sad young man in his early twenties with no relationship and his only focus on bloody politics.

'My God man, get a bloody grip. This can't be your life.'

A smart smack around his head caused him to re-awaken from his thoughts, jump up and confront his aggressor.

'Well Prendergast. Are you coming for a beer or what?'

Thomas Davies grasped him around his neck and laughed at his disposition.

'Bloody hell man, you've the weight of the world on your shoulders. Come on. Let's sort you a drink.'

Jack raised a brief thin smile and nodded as he was steered toward the Club.

They eventually found a table away from the hubbub of the bar and snooker tables and Thomas raised his glass.

'Will you join me in a toast, fella?'

'What? To celebrate me being a sad miserable bastard?'

Thomas reached across again and they clinked their beers.

'Jack, you've always been a miserable bugger. Why would I celebrate that? No, I've some news about my future. I've bought myself a business, lad.'

Jack sat back and looked curiously at Thomas.

'What sort of business? If it had been a few years ago, it would have been a pub and you'd have been dead in the year, so tell me it's not a pub?'

'It's a building company, fella. I've bought old Thompson's yard and all his equipment. Deposit down and the rest a loan from the bank.'

Jack sat back and was lost for words. Thomas was disappointed by his bland response

'You're not enthused by the idea then....'

They drew on their beers as Jack puzzled over his response.

'No Thomas. Pleased for you, but concerned how deep you're getting yourself in debt. What's wrong with working with Seamus? He's plenty of work.'

'Aye well that's the clever bit Jack. I'll still be working with Seamus, but I'm at liberty to take on other work. Gives me a bit a freedom from being dependent on the Irish lads. And to be honest, it means I don't have to work alongside bloody Michael every day. I'm fine with the debt. Used my savings to pay half and the rest is paid monthly, so it drives me to find work. I can get by on money from Seamus for a short while yet. And, what's more, I've a couple of rooms above the workshop. I'll either move there meself or rent them out for income.'

'So, you're thinking of moving from Emma's then. Will she cope without your money?'

'No plans to move yet Jack. She'll be fine and I'll keep an eye on her. She'll still have Florence's money and Uncle Arthur tucked a bit away. It's always been tight but they'll be right.'

Jack baulked at the mention of his ex-fiancée. They had not met for a good while since their last confrontation and he had generally avoided Emma's when he thought she'd be at the house. Mary had provided a commentary of their emancipation activities and he understood that this had become a significant and increasing passion for Florence.

'Deep in thought again lad? I've noticed that mention of my sister always quietens you.'

'Aye Thomas. Have to admit I miss what might have been, but so be it.'

Thomas took a long draw on his beer and glanced away uneasily.

'Whilst we're alone Jack I want to ask you something..,;
He stopped and clearly was uncomfortable and nervous.

'I've taken a strong affection for your sister, Jack. Not that I've told her or owt. I've been in her company several times when she's visited Florence and…well…I suppose I'm asking if you'd be alright if I walked out with her?'

It was a bolt to the heart for Jack. The fact that his sister was of an age for any man to be interested in her was unexpected, but of course, at nearly eighteen and a blossoming beauty, she was bound to create that attention. However, it was the thought that, should Thomas and Mary build a relationship, he would have the brother-in-law he expected to have through his marriage to Florence.

'And how do you know she'd be interested in a ne 'r do well like you, Thomas Davies. You've just told me you're in debt, you've risked having no future employment and lucky not to be in prison, given your past record. Why would I let you near my sister? And how do you know she'd be interested in you?'

Thomas sat open-mouthed and lost for words at the strength of Jack's response.

'Well…I don't know…just that Florence has said…' he stuttered

Jack held him in a long hard stare before breaking into a broad smile.

'I'm joking with you, man. I'm not going to stand in your way, but do you believe she'd accept your suggestion?'

'To be honest I don't know, Jack. My sister has teased and said that maybe I should ask Mary before others take an interest.'

Jack smacked Thomas hard on his shoulder and raised his beer.

'Then, good luck lad. You've no problem with me.'

The two men tapped glasses before Jack continued.

46

'So, you're not finding Michael Rafferty to your taste then?'

Thomas grimaced and pointed to his head.

'Mad as a bloody hatter, Jack. Never shuts up about the bloody 'cause' except when he's bragging about his conquests. He thinks he's God's bloody gift to women. Nasty piece of work behind all the Irish blarney. I thought Patrick was bloody mad – this one is dangerous, fella…bloody dangerous.'

Jack nodded in agreement.

'That's my view, Thomas. Best keep clear where we can.'

Jack purchased more beers and sat quietly musing on his next question before tentatively speaking.

'And how is Florence?'

'Took your time asking me, fella' Thomas grinned.

'She's OK. As you'll probably know she's committing a lot of her time and effort into this vote for women thing.'

'Aye. More than a bit surprised by that, Thomas. Never had strong political views in the past.'

'I think fella, that she's getting a bit disappointed with her work. She's not said much, but it seems she hasn't gained a couple of opportunities for more responsibility at the hospital. Seems like any promotions are about how long they've worked at the place and whose face fits. I know she's applied for other posts in Rotherham and Doncaster, but no luck there. I'm guessing she's putting her efforts elsewhere as a result.'

Jack smiled thinly and pulled out his pocket watch.

'Right, I'm away Thomas. Bit of work to do.'

Thomas stood and shook his hand warmly.

'Thanks for your understanding about Mary, Jack. I'll not push my luck if she not interested.'

'Aye, no doubt I'll find out, lad'

Chapter 12

(Brawmarsh, August 1904)

It had been a glorious summer. Day after day of sun with little rain. As always, the smoke and smog from the foundry hung over the town, but was soon burnt away by late morning.

There was an air of excitement, particularly amongst the children. The fair had arrived with a promise of the smell of candy floss, brandy snaps and toffee apples. The threat of the switchback and galloping horses with loud and raucous music to match. The chance to see exotic animals – someone had said that the fair had a snake nearly six feet long!

The men and women too looked forward to their half day holiday, albeit without pay. Nevertheless, they had scrimped and saved to have some money to treat their families and – for the men – to take a beer or two.

Over the last few months Thomas had escorted Mary on several walks – usually accompanied by Florence at Mary's suggestion. His sister was at work and had said she may be there later. He had hoped that they might go to the fair unaccompanied but Jack had decided he might enjoy the opportunity to join them…..

Inevitably some of the younger men had consumed ale beyond their capability and were now showing off by jumping on and off the rides to demonstrate their bravado to groups of the local lasses.

Jack stood by as his sister and Thomas climbed on board the switchback. He noticed that Mary had allowed him to take her hand clearly – he believed - pretending to be frightened by the speed of the ride. He stood back and took in the scene and then, from the corner of his eye, caught the arrival of Seamus and Michael. By their gentle stagger he could tell that they had taken a drink or two before their arrival. Standing to one side, he sought to blend into the crowd and the Irishmen passed by without noting his presence.

Michael leapt forward and joined the ride hanging loosely to the rail around the edge. He stepped off stumbling into a group of girls and, in doing so, fell into one of their number knocking her to the floor.

It was inevitable that two of the local lads ran towards them and Michael was soon the subject of flying punches and kicks. He wiped the blood from his face and confronted the two men.

'Are you ready yer bastards? Two to one is it? Well come on, both of ya.'

Once again, the boys moved towards him neither seeing that he drawn a knife. Others in the group saw him pull the weapon from his waistband and shouted a warning.

Jack watched as the knife was slashed towards one of the young men cutting his shirt and drawing blood through a deep wound. He moved quickly alongside Seamus and gripped him firmly by his arm.

'Don't get involved fella. He started the fight and you'll get yerself hurt bad.'

He was unable to hold the man's bulk as he broke loose and flinched as Seamus threw himself on the second man.

Predictably the rest of the local young men joined the melee and Seamus and Michael, despite their strength, were thrown to the floor and subjected the delivery of repeated fists and boots to their heads and bodies.

Thomas dashed over to Jack's side.

'Should we help them, Jack'

'No fella. Leave em! They both need a message, especially that bloody Rafferty. He pulled a bloody knife! Hang on here's the police...'

Three of the local constabulary ran toward the fracas blowing their whistles and waving truncheons above their heads. Most of the group scattered and ran leaving the victims well beaten on the floor.

'Anybody see what happened.' The first officer on the scene turned to the audience. 'What? No one saw owt then?'

The observers quietly one by one moved away. It was clear that the knife had disappeared. Seamus and Michael were raised to their feet.

Another policeman confronted them.

'So, do you want to tell us what happened here gentlemen?

Michael, his nose and cheeks bloodied, waved him away.

'We were dancing and we slipped officer. Probably too much beer and we got a tad excited on the roundabouts.'

He was eyed up and down.

'Aye. Well, you'll be on your way home now the both of you. If we catch you out any later, you'll be in the cells to calm down. So, go on and bugger off sharpish. We don't need your types causing trouble here.'

Seamus grasped Michael by the arm and pulled him away as he thought to respond.

'We're away. No problem.' He hauled his nephew by the collar and they disappeared with Michael still shouting abuse.

Jack and Thomas watched the scene in disbelief.

'Told you he was bloody mad.'

'Correct fella. Off his bloody head.'

They both turned as Mary and Florence joined them. The latter pointed and shook her finger in her brother's face.

'Causing trouble again brother. You escort a lady and can't behave….'

He threw his arms up in defence against her unexpected tirade.

Jack turned aggressively towards her.

'Oh, for God's sake woman shut up! You weren't here and you didn't see what happened. Thomas did not start it or get involved. You are a bloody pain in the backside, girl'

He turned and threw his hand angrily in the air as he walked away.

Chapter 13

(Jack's House. Brawmarsh, October 1904)
He sat and reflected on the last couple of months.

Joseph had, to his surprise, settled well into his job at the Manor and had moved to a small room above the stable block at the Manor. He had said little other than to indicate that he was happy and had taken to accompanying George Harcourt on horse rides across the estate. His absence from the house was not particularly noticeable.

Mary's relationship with Thomas appeared to be flourishing. She spoke about him with a strong affection, and his occasional meeting with Thomas at the Club indicated the attraction was more than mutual. Despite his concerns, it appeared that her man was making some success of his business and had acquired a contract to refurbish a number of properties in the town. He seemed to have reduced his work at the Manor house; clearly to his relief.

Seamus and Michael had not frequented the Club since the incident at the fair. He had heard they now used the Royal pub in Lower Parkgate as their watering hole. He was pleased that he no longer had to suffer Rafferty's company although he missed the company of Seamus.

Jack returned his attention to his part-drafted speech. He acknowledged to himself that this could not be other than notes…. prompts. He performed more effectively when he was 'off the cuff' and spoke from the heart.

He had taken to Lord Rotherham's offer and drawn books and pamphlets from his library – both libertarian and conservative. He hoped he had formed a more balanced perspective, but simply saw the former as the better argument. The butler, Blewitt had taken a very jaundiced view to the liberty and requested – demanded - that Jack record any withdrawals and a date for their expected return.

The meeting of the Labour group was a week away, and was shortly followed by the annual conference of the Steelworkers and Blast Furnacemen's Union. Both – given what he wished to say - would be difficult and contentious.

The former group was occupied by long-standing males with fixed views. The latter, long-standing males with fixed views. He was determined to shake up both of the meetings with his perception of how the future should be shaped – he expected strong opposition from both.

His concentration was broken by Mary returning from her work. She, as usual, had a bright smile on her face and – nowadays – a skip in her step. Her income, though limited, had allowed her to buy new clothes and she looked now so different from the girl who had arrived at his door in rags almost a year ago.

'Later than usual, sister. Stopped on your journey home again, I suppose.'

She blushed and looked away shyly as she always tended to when teased.

'I called to see Florence when I was passing.'

'Passing lass. It's a bit of a long way home if you're passing Thomas's home.'

They both burst into laughter.

Mary stopped and held up her hand.

'Listen brother. You are going to find this difficult, but we've been invited to Emma's birthday next week. She's sixty so a big celebration. There's no way you can refuse to be there.'

Jack pursed his lips and rubbed his forehead. Much as he loved Emma, the suggestion that he and Florence should be in the same room was too much to consider.

'When is the party Mary? I've a fair number of commitments over the next few weeks.'

'Not on a Saturday though, brother. Am I correct? The party is on the 22nd at the Village Hall.'

Jack shuffled his papers and, clearly uncomfortable with his lack of any reasonable excuse for avoiding the event, responded abruptly.

'I'll turn up to give my best wishes to Emma, but it's just before the Union Conference so I'll need be away after a quick beer.'

Chapter 14

(Labour Group Meeting, Rotherham, October 1904)
The room above the Green Man was rudimentary but served its purpose. The landlord was sympathetic to socialist principles and offered the facility at no cost, notwithstanding the fact that the ale consumed contributed very well to his income on a monthly basis.

A single battered oak table and mismatched chairs and stools were occupied by the nine Committee members who were undifferentiated in dress – all wearing plain collarless shirts and waistcoats, some jacketed, others sleeves rolled to their elbows as if ready for combat.

At the head of the table Charlie Hall sat with his fingers entwined. A large bearded man, gruff in tone and, with a reputation for demanding brevity of contribution and adherence to the set agenda.

He banged his fist to the table to bring the members to order. Turning to Jack Prendergast he pointed to the paperwork before him and spoke tersely.

'Right brothers. Simple agenda so we'll keep it short and succinct, shall we?' A statement rather than invite.

'Main focus tonight is on next local elections and fundraising for our candidates. I know it's a few months away, but facts are that there's bugger all in our coffers. We need ideas, gentlemen. Ways we can raise money. Any thoughts?'

The usual suggestions – raffles, approaching local like-minded benefactors, pub collections – were offered. Requesting more trade union funding was also proposed

Hall banged the table with the flat of his hand.

'They'll fetch nowt – never have. Now I believe it's time we looked at membership subs. They've been 2 pence a week for a couple of years. If we added a penny a week with our hundred or so members that'd sort most of what we need. No doubt the trade unions will moan but they'll need to cough up as well.'

The committee members, reluctant to face the wrath of their Chairman, all murmured their assent.

Jack fidgeted uncomfortably but knew he had to voice his disagreement. He stood nervously and addressed his colleagues.

'I have to tell the Committee that I do not support this proposal.' He raised his palm towards Hall as he sought to interrupt.

No, Mr Chairman. I'll have my say. It seems to me that our political agenda is constantly prioritised. I understand that representation is our aim and I don't dissent from that as our objective in the long term.'

'Aye well, I glad you grasp that young man. Now sit down and let's move on....'

Jack once again raised his hand.

'No Charlie. I will have my say.'

He glanced around at each of the men who sat in stunned silence at manner in which he had spoken to and overruled their Chairman.

'As I said I appreciate the need for our body – now the Labour Party – to increase representation. However, I believe we are putting the cart before the horse. We have two members of Parliament, so some success at national level but frankly insufficient to radically change the political direction of the country. The lack of a universal franchise in this country is the cause of our weakness. We will never progress until we obtain votes and the current system does not lend itself to our support.'

He paused and noted that at least two or three of the group were more attentive. Taking a draw from his beer he continued.

'Men who pay an annual rental of £10 have had the right to vote for nigh on twenty years, yet a vast number have not registered. Ask yourselves why, brothers?'

'Can't be bothered' shouted one man.

'Aye George, you are correct. But why? I'll give you my view. I've visited many homes in Brawmarsh and Sparkgate over the summer. What I've seen is poverty, gentlemen. Pure and simple – poverty! The men I meet there don't have the enthusiasm to sign up to vote. They have enough of a problem keeping their families under a roof and barely fed.'

Charlie Hall stood and pointed his finger at Jack.

'Listen, young Prendergast. You're trying to teach granny to suck eggs. I've been a Labour man for twenty years – afore you were out of the bloody cradle! I know about elections. I've run many and what I hear from our people is 'get elected and change things'. Every week in the Club and the pub that's what I'm hearing, lad'

Jack narrowed his eyes and sought to control his temper.

'The bloody Club and pub, fella! So, you're talking to men who either have some money or them who are pissing their wages up the wall depriving their families. Get your arse out into the town and meet the families who suffer as a consequence...'

The Chairman banged his fist repeatedly on the table.

'We've had the vote on our spend. Need to move on.'

George Frankley was normally a quiet and moderate voice who followed the party line. Now he stood and pointed directly at Hall.

'I've sat and listened to you for a few years, Charlie. I want to hear what the lad is saying. Shut up and give him the floor!'

The members looked to one another in disbelief.

'Aye' said another. 'Give him a chance. I'd like to hear what he's proposing.'

There were voices of support and Jack smiled quietly and continued.

'I'll get to my points. Here's what I'm proposing.

Number one. We cut back our spend on the election this time and look to offer some funding to the needy in our communities. That will help them seeing that our movement has their interests at heart.'

'Two. Every member of this Committee gets out and visits – encourage and help the men who have the right to vote to register;'

'And three. To support the campaign to get votes for women with our voices and any funds we can spare.'

He was interrupted by another member Harry Harris, who was known to be a misogynist.

'Votes for women, lad. Waste of bloody time. It'll never happen and, if it did, what do our women know of the world of politics? Better looking after the bairns and leaving the running of the country to men.'

Jack clenched his fists and leaned over the table towards Harris.

'And you, Harry are exactly why Labour will never be successful. You need to look at the facts, fella. Half of the population are women. That half of our population suffer the consequences of poverty and deprivation, have to deal with feeding and clothing their children with bugger all money. If we get out there and push this, we – if we are seen to be their best option – would have votes coming out of our ears. I'm not saying we throw bundles of money at their cause, but a bit of funds and our support will win their hearts and minds. And finally, Mr Harris, my ex-fiancée would tie you in knots in any debate. There's a lot of very clever women in our community and by the sounds of it, smarter than you!'

He went to resume his seat but stood for one more comment.

'And don't expect my trade union to donate more. I have yet to tackle them on their priorities too…'

The room fell silent.

Frankley was the first to speak.

'Mr Chairman. This lad makes a lot of sense. I'm withdrawing my support for your proposal. I suggest we do what he's suggesting and talk again next month'

Jack watched in amazement as one by one – with the exception of Hall and Harris – the Chairman's motion was overturned.

Chapter 15

(Village Hall, Brawmarsh 22 October 1904)
Jack found his best shirt and trousers and smoothed himself down before he left the house.

His sister had already left – beautifully attired – collected by Thomas who had equally made the effort. He understood Emma would be accompanied to the event by Florence and that the night was a surprise for the former.

He left the house, still uncomfortable, but accepting that he was duty bound to attend. He stopped as he passed by the Welfare Club.

'Bugger it. I need a quick beer to set me up.'

At this time in the evening the place was busy and he nodded to a few of the regulars. As he looked for a quiet space, he saw Seamus sitting alone in a corner.

'Well fella. Long time since I've seen ya. What brings you here tonight?'

Seamus stood and embraced Jack warmly.

'Good to see ya lad. Aye, I've kept me head down for a month or two. Been drinking down the road.'

'And your nephew, Seamus?'

'Oh, shite knows where he is Jack. As long as he's not with me he's fine. Appears he's gone to some sort of meet with his bloody idiot friends in Sheffield. Fecking nightmare he is.'

They sat and exchanged banter for a while before Jack checked his pocket watch and hurriedly stood.

'Bloody hell! Lost track of the time. Emma'll be arriving at her party in ten minutes. Need to run, lad.'

'Do you think they'll mind if I join you, Jack?'

'I'd think that, as long as your bloody nephew's not with you, you'd be welcome fella.'

They reached the venue and had just bought drinks as Emma and Florence arrived to cheers and shouts from the party. Emma was quickly surrounded by friends receiving hugs and kisses. She was clearly stunned by the surprise and was escorted to her seat by her niece. A schooner of sherry was placed in front of her which she raised as a thank you to the attendees.

Jack and Seamus made their way across to add their congratulations and, as they moved away, could not avoid encountering Florence in their path.

With some awkwardness, they briefly exchanged gestures of acknowledgment before she slipped past to re-join her aunt.

'What's happened with you two, fella? Betrothed one minute and avoiding each other the next. Seems bloody stupid to me so it does.'

Jack shook his head.

'Seamus, I can't explain either. I still find her attractive; I still have strong feelings for her but we clash and bicker on the odd occasion we are in each other's company. I think all that's in the past now – whatever we had has gone....'

Seamus drew Jack towards a table in the corner.

'Sit yourself down lad. I'll get another drink.'

Jack watched him step in the direction of the bar, then stop and turn, walking instead towards the group containing Florence. He saw him speak briefly in her ear and then draw her gently from the group guiding her, somewhat reluctantly, back towards him.

Florence was clearly flustered and hesitant. Jack was equally disconcerted by the situation. Seamus ignored their responses and drew a chair for Florence waving her to sit.

He leaned across the table and spoke quietly but firmly to both of them.

'Now, the pair of you will listen to me for a minute. Everyone who knows you believes you are right for one another. You're both behaving like bloody idiots. Whatever has gone on, whatever's been said it's time you sat down and talked. I'm a single man and have never been lucky enough to find the right one for me. You two are right for each other and likely you'll never find another one to match each other. I wasn't supposed to be here tonight so perhaps it's fate that I am to knock your bloody heads together. Now sit here and talk. I'm away for a beer and to see if I can get Emma tipsy!'

He walked away leaving the two of them open-mouthed at his tirade.

Initially they sat in an uncomfortable silence until Jack laughed aloud.

'Well lass, that's us put in our place. Mebbe we do as told and catch up?'

Florence smiled uneasily.

'I suppose there's no harm in that, Jack. How have you been?'

They sat and exchanged respective accounts of their recent endeavours. As Florence commented on her work, Jack listened intently before responding.

'It seems that you expected to have progressed, Florence. You seem a bit disillusioned.'

'Frustrated, Jack. I would have hoped to move up by now but it's not happened. There's a pecking order it seems regardless of your effort and capability.'

Jack felt that he was stepping into a delicate area given their past issues with her career and sought to change the subject.

'And has that led to you devoting more time to the women's vote activity?'

Florence appeared to brighten at this topic and started to speak with a strong passion.

'I think I would have become involved regardless of work, Jack. I really believe in the movement. I'm going over to Manchester next Saturday to join a protest march. I was hoping Mary could come with me?'

Jack nodded his assent.

'Aye, as long as you keep an eye on her. I can hardly argue when I support your group and what they are fighting to achieve.

He went on to tell her about the Labour Group meeting and how he had sought to bring emancipation to their agenda.

'I suspect I've put a few noses out of joint, Florence. There's no doubt that Charlie Hall and I won't be sharing a pint for a good while, if ever.'

She smirked and pretended shock.

'Well, fancy that. Jack Prendergast causing trouble!'

They both burst into laughter until they heard the party assemble around the dance floor with shouts and excited cheering.

Initially they both feared the worst.

'It's not my brother causing trouble again is it?'

Jack stood and shook his head with a broad grin.

'No, it's worse Florence. He's trying to dance! Our Mary'll never be able to walk tomorrow the way he's treading on her feet.'

They joined the circle around the pair, watching Thomas' inept attempt to maintain a rhythm whilst appearing to haul his clearly anxious partner in a clumsy sequence of twists and swirls. Then to their astonishment, Seamus led Emma to the floor.

'Oh my God, no.' cried Jack. 'This will be a disaster...'

The Irishman turned and performed an expansive bow towards his partner and, as he gently held her in a formal dance pose, proceeded to glide Emma around in a tempo perfectly in tune with the music.

The audience watched with amazement.

'He's bloody good.' Jack said. 'Almost professional.'

Seamus overheard his comment and drew his partner to their side.

'That's a shock for ya fella then. It's what comes of being the only brother with five sisters. They never let me sit down when I was younger.'

He swirled Emma away and then stopped breaking away.

'And what's more you should see more perform a jig.'

The audience applauded and cheered as he burst into a perfect Irish jig.

Still laughing Jack turned his attention back to Florence.

'Look, Miss Davies I've enjoyed chatting with you again tonight. Would you be up to me taking you for a drink one evening.....no intention other than we talk about our mutual interests?' he ended hurriedly.

Florence looked pensive for a moment and then nodded.

'I'd like that Mr Prendergast...without any obligations on either.'

There was a further flurry behind them as once again the party surrounded the floor. They pushed their way to the front of the group.

Thomas was on his knee gently holding Mary's hand. He gazed up at her and in a hesitant voice said.

'Mary Prendergast. Will you do me the honour of becoming my wife?'

Chapter 16

(Trade Union Conference, Sheffield, 29 October 1904)
The major meeting of the year would be attended by around 200 delegates from around the South Yorkshire region. Many of the attendees arrived to hear the speeches and form their opinions on the strength of the debate. Others saw it as an opportunity to meet with old friends and allies, privately planning and scheming to drive their group and personal agendas. Others simply saw the event as an escape from the drudgery of their work and home life and a chance to enjoy many beers, without being nagged about their spending.

As usual, the event was held in a large and well-furnished room at one of the finest hotels in the area. The Union offered food and some measure of free drink in the belief that the attendees would both require and expect these temptations to increase the numbers present. Set with a top table for the officials the remainder of the hall was furnished with a range of chairs from various eras, some more comfortable than others.

The head of the Union, Regional Chairman Norman Braithwaite, presented himself to a lectern.

'Brothers, I welcome you to the 1904 Conference. As is our practice we will agree last year's minutes and then invite reports from each of our Regional and Area Officials.'

The mundane elements of the agenda were quickly dealt with and were followed by a number of reports which were received with moderate applause.

It was clear that the majority of the representatives had attended previously, and were hoping that the meeting would conclude at a prompt pace to allow their return to the bar. Much of delivery was uninspiring and tended to regurgitate the propaganda of previous years.

Jack stopped himself from a yawn and scribbled on a short pad, particularly noting the financial report from the Union Treasurer.

He listened to the three other Area speakers. All bragged that they had increased their membership, all declared that they had supported and defended their members, all claimed that their approach was in line with socialist principles and their commitment to the Union body.

Jack strode to the stage. He noted the impatience of his membership as they presumed another repetition.

'Members. My numbers have increased by some two hundred this year. I have faced no significant disputes over the last twelve months.'

He took a deep breath and continued.

'But today I don't wish to dwell on the routine report as provided by my colleagues. I believe it is time to give a different view.'

He saw Braithwaite and the senior team suddenly prompted from their slumber.

'Today members I have a stronger message for you all. I have listened to the various report and like a number of you have lost the will to carry on...'

Several members from the conference cheered and shouted their laughing encouragement.

'I heard the Treasurers report. It appears that one tenth of our members contributions are granted to the Labour Party movement.'

'Here, here' shouted a voice. 'Support the Socialists.'

Jack paused and looked for the speaker.

'Aye, fella. Let's support the Socialists. Regrettably, that's not where our interests are to be served at this time. I'll come back to that shortly'

'In my view, we will need to change our approach, gentlemen. Earlier this year we lost eight lives as a consequence of an explosion at one of the foundries. A further six were left infirmed – limbs lost and their lives changed forever. We – as a union – frankly contributed bugger all in practical terms. Four of the dead and injured were aged under fourteen years. The families suffered badly, both from their losses and the loss of income.'

'I'm proposing that we create a Union Compensation Fund with monies to be allocated from our coffers supplemented by a weekly contribution from employers for each of their workers. We can sell this to them on the basis of potentially reducing their liability, where any employee is killed or injured at work. The Union contribution to be taken from funds we currently allocate to the Labour movement. Where our members can afford a small weekly contribution, their cover will be increased appropriately.'

There was clearly a division in the support from the audience. Some murmured or shouted their backing for the approach. Others were vociferously against the withdrawal of the political funds and called their disapproval.

One man stood and raised his fist towards Jack.

'We already have the Workmen's Compensation Act of a few years ago. Get your bloody facts straight. That covers our members who die or get injured at work. We don't need owt else.'

Jack continued above the noise.

'What you say is true, fella. The Liberal Government introduced that law, but they managed to ensure that the employers didn't have any routine liability. How many of our members have the capability or money to challenge and prove this? How many claims have been successful? I'll tell you brother – next to bugger all. My proposition would compensate the employee or their families where there is no evidence that that employee was at fault. The incident at Docketts and Worrall was found to be the fault of another employee, so they got away without any compensation.'

He took a deep breath and ploughed on.

67

'Back to our political funds. The way we continue to support our Labour friends is to encourage our members to sign up their right to vote where they qualify and, gentlemen, to support the campaign for increased suffrage, including the 'Votes For Women' campaign.'

As he had expected this comment was not widely popular and a number of the delegates stood hurling abuse towards him.

Jack held up his hands in defence.

'One more point. We have to stop the employment of children under the age of fourteen. They are ill-equipped to deal with the demands of the foundry work. Bluntly, they should still be undertaking education to prepare them for a better future than most of us have experienced. I'm calling for the end of the employment of bairns under fourteen'

'I've said my piece, brothers. I urge the Union to listen'

He stepped away from the podium and Braithwaite announced a short break in the proceedings.

The Chairman approached Jack and moved him gently to a corner of the hall.

'Quite a speech, young fella. Certainly stirred up the Conference, that has. When we re-convene, we've a few routine proposals to address but I intend to put your suggestions to the meeting for a vote. I have to tell you that I don't think you'll get support for reduced political contributions, nor for specific support for the women's vote option but I've an idea how to frame it. Bear with me, Jack.'

The conference delegates re-assembled some twenty minutes late. Norman Braithwaite led them through the series on minor amendments and the turned his attention to Jack's intervention.

'Jack Prendergast has made a series of propositions which I believe we should consider and then conduct a vote.'

He allowed the various grumbles and exchanges to conclude before outlining his thoughts.

68

'We heard a proposal for a compensation fund which, after consideration, I feel is a very good suggestion. I'd like to take this a step further by proposing the appointment of a Compensation Officer for our union. The appointee would take responsibility for the fund-raising through employers and members, with the assistance of all our Branch Secretaries. Given he raised it, I'm recommending we ask Jack to take on this responsibility in addition to his other full-time officer duties.'

He asked for a show of hands and the majority of the representatives assented to this proposal. Braithwaite turned to Jack with a broad smile.

'That'll teach you to open your mouth, lad. Now, to continue, there's no way that we can withdraw our funding for the Labour movement, so I'm not putting that to the floor. I'll look at again with our Executive over the next few months.'

He glanced around to see a number of nodding heads amongst the major political activists.

'I do however think that we can help push the initiative to get members to sign up to vote. I'm asking our Regional Secretary to undertake a campaign, again with the help of our officers and Branch officials, to encourage our eligible brothers to have their names added to the voting register. This will be a main pillar in our general support to widen the electoral franchise. We need no vote on this issue, brothers'

'Finally, I cannot disagree with brother Prendergast on the employment of children. I demand that every officer of this union acts to prevent any engagement of underage juveniles. Go back to your employers and insist this stops now!'

He stood down from the platform and gave Jack a clandestine wink. Jack smiled and shook his head in admiration. He was a cunning old bugger. He'd not only delivered on the compensation agenda, but had also removed any decision on political funding to the Executive, a body where he had substantial influence. Braithwaite had also – without mentioning women – committed the Union to every aspect of increasing the voting population.

He approached Jack.

'You are a bloody operator, Norman. I suspect there's very few who realised how you manipulated the decisions.'

'Jack Prendergast, that's a terrible accusation to make to a man of my integrity. Years of practice, lad, years of practice.'

He patted Jack on the shoulder and, with a broad grin, suggested they meet in the next week or so to sort out his new responsibilities.

Chapter 17

(Central Manchester, 29 October 1904)

Florence and Mary, complete with home-made banners and flags, followed the assembly of women from the central Piccadilly Bus Station. The volume of the procession increased as they moved towards Albert Square, the venue for speakers and their supporters to meet.

'So many people, Florence. I've never seen such large crowds in my life.'

Florence smiled and held Mary tightly by her arm. She too was nervous and more than a little frightened by the numbers, and the now increasing shouts and chants in support of the movement.

'We're amongst friends, girl. Stay close to me. Let's see if we can get closer to the stage to see and better hear Mrs Pankhurst.'

They attempted to move forward but the sheer numbers prevented much progress without the risk of being crushed.

'Let's move to the side Mary, we'll still get a view from over there.'

Within minutes of their arrival the speeches commenced. A number of the early voices repeated the objective of the body and clearly were intent on preparing the crowded square for the main event.

As they stretched to see over the crowd, Emmeline Pankhurst climbed to the stage. Much smaller and less of a physical presence than they had expected.

Despite this, her passionate words and energy enthused the audience and they shouted and applauded her every phrase. She presented a strong set of principles and actions to drive the push for franchise. Her agenda called for direct action – much removed from the earlier more measured attempts to quietly influence the ruling powers. She demanded that the supporters take steps to more forcefully send their message home to their Members of Parliament and the influencers across the country, demanded that the members of the WSPU 'make their mark' in a manner which left no misunderstanding of the passion of their mission.

'Is she proposing we indulge in violent acts, Florence? That we risk arrest and imprisonment?

'She is saying just that, Mary. Do you not support her call? Women have sought the vote by gentler means and have been dismissed and ignored. We have faced laughter and disdain. I agree with Mrs Pankhurst. We have to make ourselves more forceful if we are to achieve our end.'

Mary nodded but was clearly uncomfortable with the shift in the tactics.

The speakers concluded their presentations and the crowd seemed imbued with a passion and hostility as they left the area. A large police presence had assembled at the edge of the venue and, appeared initially to be intent on guiding the participants away from the area.

As Florence and Mary joined the exiting procession, there was a series of outbursts at their head and it appeared some of their number had indulged in a confrontation with the officers. There was an air of panic and, as the crowd broke into disarray, Mary lost contact with her friend and was caught in the push towards the conflict.

As the crowd separated, she was thrown to the front and landed heavily against a policeman, who despite his bulk, was bowled over against the pavement. He caught Mary as he fell dragging her to the ground with him.

Florence fought her way towards her friend and pulled her to her feet, pushing the officer as she did so. She turned to draw Mary away from the incident and felt a blow to her head and fell to the ground.

The officer stood above her, Mary clutched around her throat and Florence dragged to her feet.

'You're being arrested for assault, woman. Both of you.'

Chapter 18

(Brawmarsh, 30 October 1904)

Jack woke early on the Sunday morning. As he reflected on the previous day, he felt elated. He felt the need to run and breathe some fresh air. He dressed quickly in a rough shirt and a pair of old trousers and ran from the house along the surrounding country lanes.

As he turned back towards his home, he thought about the last few weeks. The successes and the difficulties.

There was no doubt that his relationships within the local Labour Party would, in future, be strained but he stood by his principles and beliefs. Within the Union, he believed he would have created enemies and, perhaps an affinity with others. Regardless, he knew he would revel in the opportunity to drive his compensation agenda and was looking forward to a new challenge away from his routine duties.

And Florence? Jack puzzled. Had they moved on and settled their differences or could there be more? He found himself imagining a new future for them, but was reluctant to build any expectation given past experience. Nothing had changed in their circumstances….

His sister Mary had accepted Thomas' proposal to the delight of family and friends. He was pleased that they had found each other and seemed a good match.

He returned home, washed and dressed and, given the lack of company, decided to wander to the Club. Perhaps Thomas or Seamus might have dropped by?

As he entered the Club, he was met by the Chairman, Frankie Bullivant who stood red-faced and breathless.

'Bloody hell, Jack. I was just about to send someone round to your house. I've had a phone call from Manchester police, lad. They've arrested your sister and Florence Davies for assault.'

'Assault! What the bloody hells happened?'

'Wouldn't tell me. Insisted they needed to speak to you. I've scribbled their number down. Here.'

Without waiting for the standard permission, Jack rushed through to the office and dialled the number.

As the phone was answered Jack interrupted the formalities.

'I'm Jack Prendergast. I'm told you have my sister and her friend in custody. Mary Prendergast and Florence Davies.'

He was asked to hold and the voice confirmed that he was correct.

'Yes sir. They are both held at the Central Manchester Station. They'll be up in front of the magistrate tomorrow on a charge of assault of a police officer.'

Jack swept his brow.

'What happened, officer/'

The voice responded in a weary and distant manner.

'I don't have the detail in front of me. You'll need to attend the station if you wish to see them. Thank you'

The phone went dead.

'Bastard!' shouted Jack as he slammed down the receiver.

He found Bullivant in the corridor.

'Frankie, I need to get to Manchester today. Where will I get a bus?'

'A bus on a Sunday to Manchester. No chance lad. I don't think as there'll be a train service either.'

Jack banged his hands against the wall in frustration. *What the hell could he do?*

'Is there a taxi I could call, Frankie?'

'A taxi, lad! You must have money to burn. Cost you a fortune but to be honest you'll not get any locals to do that run on a Sunday.'

74

Jack wracked his brain and then fell on one option.

'Is there a bicycle I can borrow?'

'A bike! It's nigh on forty miles...'

'No. Just a local run to where I might get some help'

One of the regulars volunteered a loan of a rickety model and Jack pushed out towards the Manor, throwing the cycle to one side as he arrived and knocking forcefully on the door. Following the usual extended wait, and his repeated thumps to the heavy frame, Blewitt, in his usual laconic manner and air of condescension, greeted the visitor.

'I need to see Lord Rotherham...urgently!'

The butler looked down his nose and, without further comment, closed the door leaving Jack unsure of whether he would convey the message or not.

'Bugger this.' He thought, as he moved to the side of the house, finding a small gate.

He saw a figure through the library window clearly dozing, in an armchair set against a dwindling log fire.

'Lord Rotherham...Bill!'

Rotherham stirred and then rose abruptly.

'Who the bloody hell...!'

He rubbed his weary eyes and peered towards his visitor.

'Jack Prendergast...frightened me to death lad, creeping up on me.'

He opened the external access door and sat Jack down, listening as he was told the reason for the disturbance of his afternoon nap.

'Mmm. So, you need a bloody chauffeur again, Prendergast. Getting to be a bit of a habit. Right young man, give me five minutes.'

Chapter 19

They arrived and, brazenly Rotherham parked immediately in front of the station in an area marked 'Officials only.'

'Some benefits for the aristocracy, young man.' he laughed.

They were greeted by an officious Duty Sergeant who took Jack's details and disappeared to a room behind the counter. On return, he led him through to a small closeted room, followed by Rotherham who brusquely waved the man away when he sought to refuse his entry.

Mary and Florence were escorted into the room where the former fell on her brother in tears. Florence, whilst more restrained, was clearly upset and looked pale and distressed. They explained the occurrences of the day before pleading their innocence. Rotherham intervened occasionally to confirm and clarify some of their explanations.

A junior police officer had been installed in the meeting and disinterestedly gazed at the wall.

Rotherham stood and approached him.

'Please go and ask your senior officer to join us.'

The young man looked bewildered at this proposal and open and closed his mouth unable to respond.

'Do I need to repeat myself? Please extend my gratitude and advise him that William Harcourt, the Lord Rotherham, would appreciate him joining us. There's a fella.'

The officer, still uncertain, nodded and quickly scurried to find assistance.

Rotherham turned to Jack.

'Right, listen to me. Dismissive as you are of the likes of me and my ilk, this is not the time for your aggression or tirades. Shut up, sit back and let me deal with the issue. Understand?'

Jack felt to argue but then nodded and held his hands in submission.

Within minutes they were joined by a tall, heavily built and grey-haired figure who carried the bearing of authority.

Rotherham stood as the man started to speak.

'And you are, officer?'

'Inspector George Anderson.'

That would be Inspector George Anderson, My Lord, would it not?'

He looked aghast at the abruptness of Rotherham and stuttered his reply.

'Apologies, My Lord. Not used to dealing with ....well, the peerage as it were.'

'Clearly.'

Jack had to prevent himself from laughing aloud.

Rotherham turned to the wall, his back to the inspector and continued.

'Now, I would welcome a synopsis of your case against these two young ladies. I believe they were part of a meeting which, as I recall is still entirely legal, and a feature of the democracy which is acceptable in this country. Am I correct?'

Anderson produced a notebook and proceeded to hesitantly summarise the commentary. He was frequently asked to repeat elements and, evidently un-nerved by the interruptions, repeated himself and lost track of the detail.

His interrogator studied him for a good thirty seconds before turning and waving his hand in a gesture of contempt.

'I am advised that one of the women was pushed by the crowd into the officer. Does your evidence refer to that in any way? I'm further advised by Miss Davies that your officer struck a blow to her head. Again, I ask do you have any record of that element?'

The inspector looked at the notes and shook his head.

'No, My Lord. No reference to those incidents, but the two women are to be presented to the magistrates later this morning and they will assess the evidence.'

Rotherham looked directly at him and raised his finger.

'And I will attend Inspector. I will raise the issue of assault by your officer. It seems, that it is one word against another and your evidence is thin, to say the least. Bear in mind, that you are seeking to gain a guilty decision against one of my trusted employees. That will not reflect well on her and me. I suggest you consider that I will be obliged to bring my best efforts to defend both her and my name in this case. I have no doubt that I could call upon the magistrates to adjourn this trial and seek to source attendees to provide evidence in support of their case. I am sure you will acknowledge that they will be only too happy to provide this?'

He threw an arm of release to the officer who stood for a moment, both confused and disarmed, before he left the room.

'My God Bill. That was some performance!'

'Ah well Jack, I was quite the amateur dramatist at my school. That, and my eminence comes in handy, when required. Now I suggest we give it thirty minutes or so. By my estimation, the arresting officer will be having his whatnots kicked and we should then be on our way. If they are looking for me, I will be enjoying a cigar outside'

Unsurprisingly, the four of them were in Rotherham's car on their return to Yorkshire within the hour. Florence and Mary, exhausted by their ordeal slept in the small back seats.

'My thanks Bill. You were correct. I would have let my temper get the better of me. I don't know any way I can repay you – other than funding your fuel and time.'

Rotherham glanced briefly towards Jack.

'Two things I want to say to you, young man. Number one, perhaps you'll take a little less of a negative view of the upper echelons of the country in future. We have our uses.'

'Number two. Sometimes wit beats shit, if you'll exclude my crude language. I've found you to have a good capacity. Please don't let your passion defeat your intellect. I suspect I'm not the first to say that to you.'

'Oh, and a third point, whilst I reflect. Get yourself another bloody chauffeur. I don't want your money, but neither do I need to run you around the north of England every time you and your family get in a mess!'

He turned to Jack and, after assuming a hard glare, he smiled.

'My third point is said in jest. Always happy to assist someone I hope I can call a friend, despite our backgrounds?'

Jack reached across to grasp the man's shoulder, seeking not to distract his driving across the winding Pennine roads.

'Aye Bill. Friends. For God's sake, don't tell my socialist colleagues!'

Rotherham and he engaged in discussion for the duration of the journey.

'So, you now have yourself lumbered with this compensation drive, Jack. How will you tackle that?'

Jack outlined his elementary plans and, candidly admitted that he had yet to enter into any detailed promotion of his proposals.

'I've two problems, Bill. Both the same really. Getting my members to contribute and getting the employers on board.'

They drove in silence for some time before Rotherham spoke.

'I have no influence- or frankly the capability - to influence the employees, Jack. Perhaps I may be able to assist with the employers but no commitment. Leave it with me.'

They pulled to the roadside in Brawmarsh, awakening Mary and Florence.

As Jack leaned into the car to extend his thanks, Rotherham held up his hand.

'I was happy to help. Two final points. Remind Mary I expect to see her at work prompt tomorrow. And finally, make sure you get the bloody wreck of a bike off my land as soon as possible or I'll have it thrown in the quarry!'

Chapter 20

Jack had collected Florence from the end of her street, not wishing to prompt any speculation from Emma and Thomas. They walked the half mile to the Queens Arms, engaging in light conversation and both carefully avoiding any reference to their previous relationship.

They sat with their drinks and gradually, their discussion eased as they considered family issues - particularly Thomas and Mary's future life together.

'When do we think the wedding will be?'

Florence opened her arms wide.

'Thomas is keen as hell to set a date next Spring but Mary is insisting that they need a nice place to live. She's not keen on the flat above the workshop but 'needs must' as they say. Early days in Thomas's business and it seems like a good option given he's already bought the place. I suspect he's got a plan to do up the place with the help of Seamus.'

They remained quiet for a few minutes.

'And what about your commitment to the women's movement, Florence? I assume you'll take more care in future after your brush with the law?'

Florence laid her hands to the table and scowled.

'Listen to me. I am absolutely convinced of the need to take whatever steps are needed. I will continue to support Mrs Pankhurst in her convictions.... totally and without reserve! We will not win by simpering and pleading.'

Jack looked perplexed.

'Florence, the WPSU are extremists. They are condoning – no encouraging – violence. You know I support your cause but inevitably, you and your associates will face increasing sanctions. They will fine and imprison. They will not stand for disregard for the law.'

'Then so be it, Jack. So be it.'

He pointed his finger towards her

'Well, my sister won't be involved in this nonsense...'

Florence raised her hand

'Your sister will not be your responsibility soonest, Jack Prendergast. That decision will between her and Thomas. None of your business!'

They both fell into silence, conscious that their earlier cordial exchanges had, once again, moved to disagreement.

'Why do we constantly end up in a fight, Florence?'

She thumped her hand angrily to the table.

'I'll tell you why, shall I? It's because, despite your socialist views and your patronising words of encouragement you are, like most men, a bigot. You still believe that a woman is to be subject to your control and direction. You can feign your support, but you are as much of the problem as the politicians who stand in the way of women's rights.'

Once again, despite their best intent, they had quarrelled and both now avoided the others gaze.

Jack reached out to touch her shoulder.

'Florence, I understand what you are saying but I simply don't want to see the two women who are important in my life facing those sanctions and damaging their lives.'

He stopped realising what he had said. Florence looked back to him in disbelief.

'Important in your life, Jack. I used to be.'

'You will always be the only lady for me, girl. Maybe I'm speaking out of turn given our past issues but that will never change...never.'

Florence held his gaze, stunned by his statement. She held her hands to her face and then spoke hesitantly.

'I have something to tell you Jack.'

She paused for seconds and Jack anticipated that she was about to tell him that there was someone else in her life. He closed his eyes waiting for the blow to his heart.

'Jack, I am leaving the hospital. I have been offered a position with a lady who we have nursed for some weeks. She is wealthy enough to employ a nurse during the day. Her daughter now manages her late father's clothing business and cannot attend during the daytime. The hours are regular and I would only be required to work on occasional weekends. She will match my wages and I would no longer be required to work shifts. Occasional hours when the daughter takes short holidays but otherwise not.'

Jack sat nonplussed by her declaration.

'But you will lose your career, Florence. You have dedicated the last few years to nursing and you will be sacrificing any chance of progress. Eventually the lady will die and your job will end.'

She nodded and smiled.

'I know that Jack. I have fretted over my decision for a week or so. However, I've realised that I have to wait in line for any promotion and that will frustrate me and cause me to become more disillusioned. As to the future, well I will take that as it is.'

She sat, clearly reflecting on her decision, before waving her hands in dismissal of the issue.

'And you, Jack. I was surprised at your connection with Lord Rotherham. How can a man of your convictions be a friend of the aristocracy?'

Jack had dwelled on this contradiction over the time since he had met Rotherham and now felt comfortable in explaining his position.

'Let me start by saying that Bill Harcourt is not the same as his peers. He has an understanding of the working class and that's displayed in the way he deals with his mine workers. Yes, he's upper class and yes, he enjoys his status and its benefits, but he has a broader mind than men at his station. He appreciates that his employees will deliver more if he displays compassion and has their interests at heart. I'm not stupid. I know he makes money from his pits and that will always be a priority for him to live the life he enjoys.'

He paused and took a drink, watching Florence's still questioning eyes.

'He's a good man, Florence. I can't say we'll always agree but he's helped me out a couple of times and I'll always be able to justify my friendship with him.'

She nodded and understood.

Chapter 21

(Welfare Club, Brawmarsh, Mid December 1904)

Christmas was approaching. The weather had turned and left a deep covering of snow, but it was crisp and still warm for the time of year. The town had made an effort to decorate the streets and many houses were bedecked with streamers and glowing candles as Jack wandered down the lane towards the Club.

As he entered, he met Thomas.

'Bloody hell lad. Our Mary's let you out of her clutches, has she?'

Thomas laughed and smacked lightly him around his head.

'Listen Prendergast, I've been down the bloody workshop all morning finishing the flat. You'll love it fella. All re-plastered and painted up. It looks a picture. Seriously, I'm taking your Mary down there later to see it finished. Seamus has been a bloody hero. We've a main room, two bedrooms and an inside bathroom. Not many of them in Brawmarsh, is there?'

They entered the Club, despairing of the efforts to invite the festive spirit to the place. A number of bedraggled banners and garlands, rescued from their dusty residence in the loft, had re-appeared and had been draped without any finesse across the nicotine coated bar.

Jack shouted across to the Chairman,

'Bloody hell, Norman you've thrown the boat out this year, fella. Must have spent a fortune on this set up. You'll be raising the subs next year then?'

Frank Bullivant took umbrage at the comment and mouthed a foul-mouthed response across the room.

'And a Merry Christmas to you Frankie! Miserable old bastard.'

They laughed and clinked glasses as they settled in a corner table.

'I believe you've been seeing my sister then, Jack Prendergast?'

Jack, caught in mid-drink, spilt his beer in surprise. He presumed their meeting had been held in confidence.

'Small town fella. You'll get away with nowt around here.'

Jack rolled his eyes and laughed.

'We met for a drink. A catch up, Thomas. Don't start any hares running, do ya hear? Nothing more.'

Thomas looked sceptically at his friend.

'So, she'll have told you about her new job then?'

'She did mention it, Thomas. Seems like a rash move to me. Sacrificing her career, isn't she?'

Thomas reached over and gave Jack a gentle slap to his head.

'And you're a bright fella, so mebbe you've grasped the upshot of her decision...'

Jack looked at him blankly and shook his head in bewilderment.

'She'll not be subject to the restrictions that the nursing authorities demand, Jack.'

'She can marry...?'

'Aye, lad. If only she could find the right bloke eh?'

Chapter 22

(Emma's House, Brawmarsh, Christmas Day 1904)
Emma had insisted that Jack and Mary join them for the day. She had also invited Joseph but he had declined, insisting he had already made plans to join other staff at the Manor for the festivities.

Joseph was an infrequent visitor to his brother's home these days. Mary saw him almost daily and had indicated that he appeared to be enjoying his work. She understood, from their brief exchanges, that he was socialising with a group of friends and was happy with his life.

Emma, Thomas and Florence had erected a Christmas tree and heavily decorated the home, to the extent that there was little space to move in the small main room. Everyone had contributed to the day – Jack had found a goose from a 'contact' – he said that they should ask no questions. Mary had brought vegetables 'donated' from the big house. From somewhere, Thomas had found a source of home-brewed ale. Emma had cooked an enormous plum pudding, so they were well sufficed for their feast.

Seamus had also been invited. This, on the basis that his nephew was occupied elsewhere…

The three ladies, cramped within the scullery, performed their miracles with the food whilst the men sat – having already enjoyed two or three beers at the Club – laughing and telling their now garbled stories.

Florence turned to the three men.

'Any chance of you lot getting off your backsides? Mebbe help set the table and pour us some drinks? Or are you planning to be waited on hand and foot? Remember you're dealing with women who will have a vote shortly and then we'll run the country as well as the house!'

Thomas turned to his colleagues and pushed his fingers to his ears, raising his eyebrows in mock shock.

'Aye, lass. We're listening and waiting for you to take over the world, sister.'

Florence, hands on hips, scowled at him.

'Get ready, lad. Our time is coming.'

Thomas fell back in his chair and effected to throw his hands in surrender. He was struck by a metal spoon on his forehead, projected accurately by Florence.

'Bloody hell, Flo! That was unnecessary. Only having a laugh.'

She dismissed him with a wave of her hand.

'You'll learn, Thomas. You'll learn, lad'

Emma shushed her and they returned to the preparation, whilst Seamus volunteered to organise the table settings and Jack poured drinks for them all.

They ate their meal in a better atmosphere, influenced by the alcohol. Florence had created make-shift crackers, which they shared with some enthusiasm and fun.

Seamus fell back to the settee.

'My God, Emma that was grand. If you were a younger lass, I'd marry you. I only need my food to keep me happy.'

'Aye Seamus, save your bloody Irish blarney for the younger lasses and behave, you silly bugger!'

The whole table laughed at Emma's remarks and moved with their drinks to join Seamus on the chairs and seating.

Jack fell into the settee next to Seamus who stood and stretched.

'I'm outside for a cigarette. Here, Florence, take a seat.'

He winked at Jack as he stood and walked away.

Jack turned towards her, the drink increasing his confidence spoke quietly.

'So, lass. Thomas tells me you're now free to marry me?'

Florence sat upright and turned abruptly towards him.

'And why would I want that, Jack Prendergast? I've grown up a lot since we were last betrothed. You still wish to rule any woman's life. Why would I accept your proposal – if that's what it is?'

Jack returned her stare.

'Because, Florence Davies, there's no silly bugger would take you on with your views and your new-found independence. We still are in love with each other and we always will be. Bluntly I'm your best option...'

She sat open-mouthed at his assertive behaviour.

'You've had too much to drink, Prendergast. Your offer is not the way a lady needs addressing....'

'Does that mean no or yes then?'

With that he took her by the hand and, to the amazement of the room, led her to the garden.

'Florence Davies, I am now formally asking you to be my wife. I know we'll have some disagreements, and I know that you are no longer the young and naïve lass I met some years ago. I understand that you will pursue your passion for your vote. I recognise that I will not control your life, but I hope that we can, at least discuss and agree how we can both advance your allegiances. Will you accept my proposal now?'

He then reached into his waistcoat pocket and withdrew a ring.

Florence looked aghast.

'Is that my ring?'

Jack nodded and placed it on her finger.

'This ring has never left my pocket since we broke our engagement. I kept it here in the hope that, one day, it would be returned to your hand, Florence. Please don't deny me this time'

Florence allowed him to push the ring fully on her finger.

'That will never leave your hand again, girl. Never.'

Chapter 23

(Rotherham Manor, Brawmarsh, April 1905)

Their engagement was greeted with joy, but no great surprise. Family and friends simply commented that this outcome had always been inevitable.

Emma however was over-joyed.

'Two weddings. I shall need a new hat!'

She saw herself as the matriarch and, over the following weeks, proceeded to propose arrangements and plans for the forthcoming nuptials until she was dissuaded by the respective brides.

Florence, particularly, was robust in declining her suggestions.

'For God's sake Auntie Emma. Jack and I have yet to even consider when, let alone the detail.'

Regardless, she ploughed on and appeared to eventually have more influence on Thomas and Mary. It became clear that – in Emma's view – a grand church wedding would be required.

It was no surprise, that consequently, he found himself escorting his sister to the altar at the Church of Saint Mary in March of the year. He was uncomfortable with the ceremony and could not help gazing at the adornments and vestments of the priest, the ornate wall decorations, ceremonial vessels and paintings. The congregation of this and other churches lived in poverty but were constantly harangued to contribute to the upkeep of the well-fed clergy and their religion. He could not countenance this within his socialist principles, but was obliged to subvert his views for the benefit of his sister.

Seamus had acted with unexpected finesses as Thomas's best man and, at the subsequent wedding breakfast, had made a carefully crafted speech, albeit with some bawdy references to the impending nuptials, causing red faces amongst the older ladies in attendance.

'Thomas is known to be occasionally clumsy in his work. I hope he performs more adequately with his tools tonight....'

The party was raucous but well-mannered and Mary and Thomas were sent on their way to their new abode with the standard best wishes and some off-colour shouts from the more inebriated members of the well-wishers.

Jack and Florence had yet to agree their own wedding arrangements and neither had felt the need for urgency, much to Emma's frustration.

They had continued their courtship quietly and met to walk and discuss the future Florence had not attended any further emancipation events but, as she stressed to Jack, not because of loss of commitment. She had simply been more occupied in her new role, caring for the demanding Mrs Glossop.

Jack had raised the wedding arrangements, requesting that they look at alternatives to the formal religious procedure. To his surprise, Florence had acknowledged that, under the circumstances and, given his views, it would be hypocrisy to undertake any ceremony of that type and suggested they simply follow a civil ceremony when they decided to marry.

Emma was indignant.

'That's the route of bigamists and the ignorant!' she proclaimed.....

***

His drive for a compensation fund had been only moderately well received. Jack had established two alternatives for the Union members. A 2 pence per week contribution for a basic death cover and a further option of 5 pence per week which provided both a death provision and some income for four weeks for the family. Inevitably the majority of the workers had baulked at the cost and fewer than one hundred had agreed to participate. The Union – with the manipulation of Norman Braithwaite – had marginally reduced their political contribution and had supplemented the compensation pot.

However, the fund was still substantially insufficient. Should there be another disaster, they would not be able to meet their obligations.

Consequently, the meeting which Jack was to attend today was significant. Bill Rotherham, good to his word, had contacted him to invite him to be present at an afternoon gathering of his contacts – a number of owners of the foundries throughout the south of Yorkshire.

Rotherham had been candid. Many of the businessmen had declined. Others had agreed to attend but, he was told, more with the expectation of good wine and food at the event.

It was therefore, with some lack of expectation, that Jack trudged along the drive towards the Manor. He had made some effort to be presentable, shaved and clothed in his Sunday best. He had prepared some brief comments – a scribble no more – to seek their support.

As usual, Blewitt greeted him as if he had stepped in some unpleasant substance en-route and escorted him to the extensive Dining Room. There were some fifteen men already present, engaged in deep conversation and following brief glances, he was ignored and moved uncomfortably to a corner of the room carrying the glass impressed on him disdainfully by the butler.

Bill Rotherham broke away from his group and moved to join Jack.

'Listen lad, you've a tough audience here but doubtless not unexpected? You have a couple who are sympathetic and want to hear more. Probably half a dozen who are up to be convinced. The rest are here to enjoy my benevolence and will be hard to convince. Tight as a duck's arse, in the main.'

He moved to the centre of the room and clapped his hands.

'Gentlemen, as you are aware, I have a motivation for inviting you here today. This gentleman....' he waved towards Jack. '...is seeking to build a provision for the compensation of your employees in the event of their injury or death whilst in your employ. If you wish to enjoy my hospitality in due course, I ask that you allow him to outline his proposal'

He turned to Jack and gestured to him to step forward.

Bloody hell thought Jack. He'd expected fewer numbers and, perhaps informal and separate discussions with the attendees – not to give a formal speech.

He stepped gingerly to the front and dry-mouthed addressed the group.

Whilst initially reticent, he soon found that his passion and previous speaking experience increased his confident delivery.

He spoke for some ten minutes with conviction and clarity. As he presented his case, he sought out the expressions of his audience and noted that the majority listened intently.

He closed and Rotherham stepped forward.

'Well stated, Mr Prendergast. Any questions or comments, gentlemen?'

A large, ruddy faced and well-dressed man stepped forward.

'I am Arthur Atkinson, owner of three foundries in Sheffield. Why would I give you funds when an Act of Parliament has already placed an obligation upon me to provide compensation for any of my employees injured or losing their lives?'

Jack smiled quietly expecting this question.

'Good afternoon, Mr Atkinson. Can I state that I appreciate yours and the attendance of all the gentlemen here? You are correct. The Workmen's Compensation Act places an obligation upon you and other owners to fund a payment to any workers and their families who suffer as a consequence of an accident at work. However, what this law does not cover is a number of things.'

'One, where another workers contribution causes the issue you escape any liability.'

'Two, where the incident is deemed to be you not to be at fault, you are not obliged to pay – your employees lack the funds to challenge this but be clear that, in the not-too-distant future, trade unions will grow and have sufficient income to take up these legal issues and support their members. You will lose a number of these and you will incur costs for the presentation of your cases at court. The Union will expect their legal costs to be returned as part of any claim.'

'Three, currently the law does not cover the effect of disability and death caused by industrial disease.

He stopped as another man called from the rear.

'No evidence, young man. Our workers know the risk when they take their jobs!'

Jack held up his hand to hold the comment and then waved his hand towards his audience.

'Every man who enters your employ within our industry is subject to metal fibres and dust, skin disorders due to the constant exposure to the chemicals used in processing the materials. Many have lost their sight due to the same elements. You may seek to deny this but rest assured the coincidence of these medical problems is undeniable. Again, in short time as diagnosis improves, you will be found at fault and the costs will be significantly higher than the costs of occasional accidents, believe me! Our trade union has already commenced an analysis of these complaints and we will act against any employer who chooses to disregard the impact of your failure to correct these deficiencies.'

The room fell silent as Jack continued.

'I am not here to threaten, gentlemen. I'm here to offer you the opportunity to both support your workers and to - potentially – reduce your liability by contributing to the compensation fund. I'm asking you simply to match your individual worker's weekly payment.'

He reached across and raised a bottle of wine from the table.

'It will cost you less than you'd pay for this on a weekly basis...'

He closed by thanking them politely for their attention and returned to sit in the corner, watching as a fevered debate broke out across the businessmen.

After some five minutes, and preparing to leave in disillusionment, Rotherham and Atkinson approached him.

Atkinson held out his hand.

'You presented your case exceptionally well, Jack. I am prepared to support your cause. I will advise my accounts people to match your payments from this month. A number of others here will also do so but frankly are reluctant to advise you openly. They will...'

Jack extended his thanks and was left somewhat awkward as Rotherham moved away.

Atkinson leaned forward to continue.

'I'm impressed with you Mr Prendergast. You speak well and with conviction. Have you considered standing for local election? I am very influential within the local Liberal group and believe that you would make a strong candidate for our Party.'

Jack looked at the man and looked him in the eye.

'Mr Atkinson. I am a member of the growing Labour Party. There is no way my views and principles would allow me to move from that body. If I am to be honest, I believe your party will lose the support of the working class over the next few years. My movement will represent the workers and, in due course, will be the government of this country. Thank you but no.'

Atkinson nodded and smiled moving back towards his peers.

Jack felt he had done all he could and, more to the point, uneasy in the social setting moved to leave.

As he arrived at the main door, he saw Rotherham in conversation with a man at the entrance.

As he moved closer to the exit, he recognised the uniform of a senior police officer and caught the end of the conversation.

'...and consequently, your son has been arrested and held'

Rotherham, pale-faced, called to Blewitt and was provided with a heavy overcoat. He observed Jack edging to leave and placed his hand on his chest to arrest his departure.

'Jack, wait. You need to come with me. My son has been accused, along with others of indecent behaviour. Your brother is one of those detained...'

Chapter 24

(Sheffield Police Station, April 1905)

It became clear on their arrival, that Rotherham's status would carry little weight under these circumstances. They were asked to seat themselves in a cold and bare waiting area along with others awaiting the opportunity to meet their friends and family members.

One woman, roughly clothed and toothless, tried to engage them in conversation.

'So, what's your team in for then? I'm here to collect him again. Total bloody waster. Here just about every weekend I am. They chuck him out eventually. It'll be either take him home or – if he's been scrapping – another bloody fine! No wonder me kids have no decent clothes or regular food. He's a total pillock. Spends his wages every bloody time, he does.'

Rotherham and Jack smiled thinly at the woman who soon turned her abuse to the duty officer.

'Lord Rotherham? Perhaps you would come through?'

Both he and Jack stood. Though apparently uninvited, Jack determinedly followed and they were led into a large interview room. The inspector invited them to sit.

'Right, let me outline the position. Your son, George Harcourt is in our custody along with a number of other young men. We were advised that the assembly were believed to be meeting and participating in indecent activities in breach of the Criminal Law Amendment Act 1885. That is to say engaging in buggery or believed to have indulged in such.'

Rotherham dropped his head to his hands whilst Jack listened in total bewilderment.

'Our evidence is clear. We have interviewed a number of those arrested who claim to have been observers. They have provided statements confirming our basis for arrest and....'

Jack interrupted.

'And Joseph Prendergast?'

The officer gave a cursory glance in his direction.

'And you are?'

'His brother, Jack Prendergast.'

'Then you should be aware that your brother was...how shall I say...named to be a participant in the indecent act performed before others.'

He turned away clearly offended by the need to provide any detail.

'My Lord, I will allow you to see your son. Follow me.'

Jack stood and in exasperation shouted to the man.

'And me. Am I allowed to see my brother?'

He was completely ignored as he saw the door closed firmly before him.

Chapter 25

It was some three weeks later that the court case was to be heard at the Rotherham Magistrates Court. Whilst there had been some rumours and title tattle in the community, no facts had reached the public domain.

Mary had proposed that she attend in support of her brother but, given this would be a simple hearing before referral to the senior court, she accepted Jack's suggestion and agreed that he should be present at the initial hearing.

Jack had eventually been allowed to see Joseph and had sought to comfort and re-assure him. He had listened to his brother's version of events – that basically he had been instructed by George Harcourt who had insisted on his attendance at the party – and felt confident that his defence would result in him either facing a caution or acquittal of any charges.

The courtroom was typical of its time. A wooden cladded and forbidding setting pervaded by the odour of sweat with austere and rudimentary seating. The bench on which the legal officer would reside stood above the general area with a small dock set closely to one side. Benches for the clerical retinue and representatives were stationed immediately below to allow reference and private discourse when required.

The magistrate entered as the court was called to order. A severe elderly man, he nodded to the attendees to be seated. Jack noted, with some discomfort, that he appeared to smile and acknowledge the presence of Lord Rotherham and other parents of the more well-heeled defendants. He leaned forward and glared at the men in the dock with an air of both condescension and disgust before addressing the court.

'This case presents some complexity in how the courts should deal with the defendants. I have, with the respective police officer, considered the circumstances of the arrests and the somewhat confused and vague statements presented by the parties.'

'Normally, this case would have a preliminary hearing before referral to a higher court, given the original charges. Having reviewed this, and consulted with the court officials, I have reached a series of decisions with the agreement of all parties.'

'The evidence supporting the original charges do not provide a sufficient prosecution case for gross indecency and the allegations of buggery. Consequently, the charges will be reduced to those of indecent behaviour.'

Jack privately clenched his fist – a lesser charge. He caught Joseph's eye and nodded positively.

'Under these circumstances I am advised that I have the discretion to deal with these cases under offences against the local by-laws and therefore the case will be dealt with today with any penalties at my discretion.'

Jack now ceased his quiet celebration and looked to the man with growing concern.

'Additionally, I have decided that it is inappropriate for this case to be placed in the public domain and therefore will be held 'in camera'. Consequently, I am requiring all but the defendants, their representatives, the court officers and immediate family to leave the court immediately. I have also decided to place a court order that no reporting of the case will be allowed. Any breach will result in a charge for contempt of court'

There were shouts of incredulity from the small number of local journalists who had seen the opportunity to present a good and turgid story to their readers.

'This is a ruling against freedom of speech.' shouted one scribe as he was escorted from the room.

Jack was now increasingly perturbed by the manner in which the case was being managed. He stood and raised his hand to the bench.

'Sir, your decisions are unreasonable. The lack of a jury trial and the penalties being determined by yourself are an affront to our legal system...'

The magistrate rose to his feet and thrust a finger aggressively towards him.

'You will desist from any interruptions. This is my court. You will be ejected and held in contempt if you disturb these proceedings again!'

He turned to the six accused and invited their pleas. All declared themselves 'not guilty'

Harcourt and his friends had clearly sought to avoid the proximity of Joseph and the other young defendant, and talked freely amongst themselves, smirking and waving to their families across the room.

To Jack's dismay, the trial appeared to be conducted with undue haste.

Following the evidence from a police officer, they were one by one, escorted to the dock to give their account under questioning.

Jack sat in disbelief as he watched the defence of the wealthy young men delivered by a very proficient and distinguished solicitor, obviously known to the magistrate. Each denied participating in the indecent acts, claiming that they had merely expected to attend a party celebrating a birthday. Each gave well-rehearsed statements implicating Joseph and the other young stable-lad as the guilty parties.

Joseph was the last to be called and was supported by a court appointed, young representative who, clearly inexperienced, proved to be inept in his questioning and allowed Joseph to respond nervously and without conviction.

The court was in session for less than two hours before the magistrate ended the contributions and stated that he would take some time to deliberate. All attendees were prohibited from leaving the court to prevent any leak of the proceedings to the press.

Jack gazed around the chamber and noted the confident and relaxed attitude of Rotherham and his associates. He felt despondent and knew, in his heart, that this had been a co-ordinated and pre-determined procedure likely not to bode well for his brother.

Within thirty minutes, the court was re-assembled and the magistrate addressed the defendants one by one.

George Harcourt was fined £30 for attending an event 'likely to offend public decency.' It was deemed that he was an innocent party who had attended the event without any prior awareness of its nature.

Another three of the accused, from 'good families' and equally supported by quality representatives, received equivalent penalties.

Two of the accused – Joseph Prendergast and a young stable boy from the estate – were deemed to be the instigators of the incident. Both were sentenced to six months imprisonment for public indecency.

As was led from the court, Joseph smiled weakly and hung his head in tears. Jack again shouted to the court but was ignored as the officials exited.

As he left, he saw Bill Rotherham engaged in conversation with his solicitor and stormed to confront him.

'So, money speaks again! My brother was amongst the youngest of the accused but is accused of being the instigator. Bloody lies, Rotherham and you know it.!'

Rotherham reached to place his hand on Jack's shoulder which was abruptly shrugged away.

'Jack, I am sorry. I have done all I could, as a father, to help my son. I didn't expect this outcome for your Joseph.'

Jack laughed in his face.

Of course, you expected this, you bastard! You and your cohorts and the corrupt and fawning justice. All bloody planned.'

He spat at the ground and turned to leave.

'I trusted you. I believed you were a man of honour. I was wrong!'

Chapter 26

(Brawmarsh, June 1905)
The month had proved to be amongst the worst times in his life.

He and Mary had requested permission to visit their brother but this had been declined. Not because the authorities had objected. Joseph had refused their application.

They were told that he had become very despondent and had faced both physical and verbal abuse from a number of other prisoners. They were further told that he made no attempt to mix as a consequence, and spent the majority of his time sitting alone, having to be ejected from his cell to exercise.

They were finally told that he had written a letter to them and shortly afterwards had taken his own life, hanging himself by a leather belt which he had secretly obtained from, it was claimed, an unknown source.

They sat together in tears reading his short and poorly constructed note.

'*Broter and Sistr,*
I did no rong. It was the rest as made me do it.
Sory'

Jack had exploded into a fury, punching the wall until his fist bled.

'This lad was innocent. Drawn into their depraved bloody games and now dead…'

Mary hugged him but he wrested away.

'I will have some revenge for my brother. Trust me I will!'

She placed her hand on his shoulder.

'Come Jack. We should leave now or we'll be late.'

He threw his hands in submission and collected his best jacket from the chair. They set off and walked to the church and joined Emma's family and friends as they filed inside.

Only a few months earlier they had celebrated her sixtieth birthday where she had laughed and danced. One week ago, Florence had found her, laid still by her armchair. A heart attack, they said.

The church filled to capacity. Her coffin was carried to the altar by her nephew, Jack, Seamus and other pall bearers. They sang her favourite hymns, heard Florence and Thomas speak briefly, but with passion and affection for both Emma and her late husband and how they had helped them recover their young lives. They watched her lowered to join Arthur Davies and scattered earth with their respective farewells. They walked sombrely away from the churchyard, each deep in thought and reflection.

As the procession moved towards the gate, Thomas caught up with Jack.

'Listen, fella. I'm so sorry about Joseph. He didn't deserve his end.'

Jack turned and held his brother-in-law and, despite himself broke into sobs.

'I let him down Thomas. I could have done more for him.'

He was stopped by a hand to his face as Florence brought him towards her.

'You have never let anyone down, Jack Prendergast. I believe he lived his life – short though it was – as he wished. I feel that Joseph was too gentle and innocent to survive in this world.'

She kissed him gently on his cheek, took him by the hand and wiped his tears.

'Time to move on Jack…time to move on…'

***

As Emma would have wished they drank to her health at the wake.

Jack stood privately reflecting on the loss of two people who he had lost – a brother who had barely known, a woman who had welcomed him into her family when he had first arrived in the area. He had indulged in drink, for him heavily, and was becoming maudlin in his thoughts when he was embraced by an inebriated and emotional Seamus.

'Now, feckin get a grip, Prendergast. You've been a great support for Emma over the years. You made her happy with you and Florence re-uniting. She saw Thomas settled. Her last year has been happy. For Christ's sake, she even got me dancing!'

Jack broke into a smile – his first for days. Seamus was always good for cheering up and saying it as it was.

'Thanks fella. You're always direct.'

He stopped, breaking free from the grip and realised that he had held no conversation with Seamus for some weeks.

'Anyway lad, enough of me. How's things with yerself?'

Seamus gave a wry smile.

'Frankly Jack, I've had the odd issue meself the last few weeks.'

He stepped to one side and – for the first time in Jack's experience – pushed his hands to his face, seeking to hide his emotion. He wiped his face and waved his hand in embarrassment.

'I've had to kick my nephew out of the house and off the job, lad. Michael is mixing with some bad sorts down Sheffield. You'll know of his strong views. It got to the point where we couldn't go anywhere, without he took too much drink and spouted his fecking mouth about our friends in the old country. God knows how many times over the last few months I've had to haul him away from confrontations and scraps, abusing the English. Took a few blows along the way meself. I promised my sister he'd be ok but he's a crazy bugger.'

He paused and shook his head.

'I'm telling you something I probably shouldn't, Jack but I trust ya. I know you have some sympathy with our cause?'

He stopped and waited for some acknowledgment of acceptance.

Jack grimaced.

'Seamus, I understand your drive to be independent. If I was a native Irishman, I believe I would fight along your side…but from what I've read and heard you are about to start a bloody war in your country. You'll be badly beaten Seamus, so take care what you do.'

Seamus nodded and sucked against his teeth, clearly hesitant to continue.

Jack chose to interrupt.

'Listen. I don't know what you know. I suspect you have heard more than you're prepared to tell me and to be frank, I don't believe it's in my interest for you to tell me more. All I will say is that if you are aware of any threats, you should do all you can to both stop them and remove Michael before he faces major trouble.'

Seamus wrapped his hands to his face and slapped his hand to the table, causing a number of the attendees to break their conversations and glance towards them.

'Calm fella, for Christ's sake.' whispered Jack.

'How the feckin hell do I sort this, man! I'm aware of a plan. If I inform the authorities, they'll arrest the bloody lot, including the lad.'

Jack sat despairing of a way in which he could help Seamus. He eventually leaned into his friend.

'Here's what I think you could do. Get Thomas to come to meet you over here under any pretence. Once you've got him here take him out on the drink – somewhere where he can make himself known…'

'What you want him to attract attention to himself, create trouble?'

Jack nodded.

'That's right Seamus. In fact, if he can get arrested that'd be grand.'

The Irishman looked bewildered and threw his hands upwards with a shout.

'For God's sake, I'm trying to keep him out of trouble!'

Jack looked around the tables, nodded and waved gently to a number of the mourners to suggest he was in control of an emotional friend.

'Listen Seamus. get your voice down…you're being noticed. Last thing you need! You get Michael to yours. If you give me some information as to names and addresses, I'll contact the authorities. If your nephew's in the local cells he won't be involved fella, will he?'

Seamus grasped his arm.

'You'll do that for me, Jack?'

'I will. It means you've done nothing wrong, neither have I. Michael - despite being a total shit – is taken out of the scene and you fuck him off to Ireland the fastest way you can. Understand?'

The Irishman reached across and clutched his face.

'You're a bloody friend, you are. I'm in your debt if we do this…'

Jack took a deep breath.

'Give me a name and address…'

Chapter 27

(Brawmarsh, 20 June 1905)
Michael had reluctantly agreed to join his uncle for a meet and drink. By the time they met at the Royal, he was already ill-tempered and berated Seamus for the loss of his income and home.

'Michael lad, you're a bloody problem. You're abusive and aggressive. You need out of the area before you got yourself into real trouble. I think it's time you got yerself back home.'

Michael glared at him prodding his chest.

'Ah, you've no need to worry about that. I'm on my way back after I've sorted one or two issues.'

Seamus took a long draw on his beer before pushing Michael's hand away.

'And what will they be then, fella?'

'Nothing you need to know about, Uncle. You'll find out when we're done.'

Seamus grasped him by the collar and drew him towards him.

'Listen to me. I know you're passionate about our mission, but you'll be no good to us in prison or worse! You're young and bloody naïve, lad. Go back and keep your head down. Our time will come.'

Michael laughed in his face and pushed his hands away.

'That's the trouble with your type, Seamus. All bloody talk. We need action. We need to send a message or two to the English Government. They treat us like feckin peasants. They offer no hope of our independence. It's time to take up a fight, to stop the polite chat and make a mark. To make them listen.'

He turned, his temper rising and looked away, draining the last dregs of his second pint.

All working to plan thought Seamus. *Now's the time...*

He pulled Michael's glass from his hand and returned to the bar, ensuring he stood close to two thick set men who he had observed drinking heavily since their arrival.

As he collected the two beers, he deliberately caught the shoulder of one, spilling the ale over his shirt front.

Seamus ensured his enraged shout carried throughout the pub.

'Ah, ya clumsy bastard! Feckin idiot!'

The man wiped his front and pushed Seamus away.

Now was the time for some theatrics.

'What did ya say, fella? I'm a feckin ignorant Irish bastard, am I?'

The man – having not spoken looked bewildered – and was caught by surprise as Seamus threw a fist to his face.

Much as he expected, Michael jumped to his feet and entered the fray, throwing a blow at the other man and then grasping him around his neck pulling him from his stool. As the four men rolled across the floor knocking tables and glasses to the floor, the landlord ran to the rear and dialled the number for the local police station.

Jack had positioned himself on a bench across from the Royal, hidden in the shadows. He had watched Seamus and Michael through the grimy window and smiled to himself as he saw Michael jump to his feet and charge to the bar. He waited some ten minutes until two officers ran to the door, truncheons raised, and then sauntered slowly to the Club.

Obtaining permission to use the telephone for a 'family emergency', he dialled the number for Sheffield Police Station. He silenced the policeman who answered.

'Don't ask any questions. You need to raid a house in Parkley St – residence of a fella called Doyle. Don't wait. It's a bomb plot.'

The officer had stuttered and demanded his details.

Jack had simply repeated 'Don't wait' and replaced the receiver.

***

As expected, Seamus and Michael had been detained overnight and hauled to the courts two days later.

Both were charged with and found guilty of drunkenness and breach of public order. The sentences were declared as seven days hard labour or a fine of 12 shillings and 6 pence.

Seamus smiled to himself as he paid his fine and was released. Knowing Michael did not have the required funds he chose to leave his nephew to suffer his jail sentence – both to prevent him from seeking his friends in Sheffield and to teach him a lesson.

He was to find that his scheme had worked better than he could imagine. Not only was Michael mortified by his week of imprisonment, but he had additionally been advised that the local police would now be keeping a close eye on him. Any future infringement would result in a substantially heavier sentence and, in all likelihood, his rapid ejection to his homeland

Given the substantial reports in the local press – the arrest of three Irish men and the discovery of explosive materials and plans related to a major railway connection – Michael determined that he had only one option and, within days, gratefully accepted his Uncle's funding of the ticket back to Ireland.

After seeing his nephew to the train, Seamus joined Jack and Thomas at the Club.

He raised and clinked his glass against Jack's.

'You'll be relieved that chapter of your life is over fella then'

Seamus shook his head.

'For now, lad. For now. Trust me he'll be back and that won't be good news for any of us...'

PART TWO – COMMITMENT

"A change is brought about because ordinary people do extraordinary things."– Barack Obama

Chapter 28

(Brawmarsh, March 1908)
Florence stood hands on hips facing Jack.

She had – as he'd asked – withdrawn from attending any emancipation event over the last three years. She had continued to exercise her support by correspondence to the local press and letters to national newspapers – none had been published. She had insisted that she continue to contribute one shilling per week to the cause.

'Jack, I will not stand back anymore. I've done what you've asked and avoided the processions and protests. Our views continue to be ignored.'

Her husband of two years stood in confrontation.

'No, Florence. They are crazy women. The Pankhurst's are determined to cause violence and bloodshed by their stupid orations. I've always been a supporter, but I believe their extremism will only build up the hostility against you. Times are changing. A Labour government is coming, Florence.'

She turned and laughed.

'29 bloody seats, man! You got 29 seats in Parliament and only those because the Liberals didn't stand against you in most of those constituencies. The Liberals won by a massive majority, Jack. It will be years and years before there's socialists in power. Made a longer wait by the lack of votes, unless more men and all women have the right. My women's group have dismissed the connection with any political party. None are capable of delivering our vote.'

She turned to walk away and swung around.

'…and changing the party's name won't carry any effect either …pitiful!'

She stormed from the room and Jack slumped into his chair, once more at a loss to calm her.

They had eventually married in March two years earlier and, almost inevitably, their relationship, both before and after the wedding, had been turbulent. The decision to hold the ceremony quietly in the Rotherham Registry Office was easily reached. No Emma to push the formalities, no large group of friends. Held simply with Mary and Thomas as witnesses and a couple of drinks followed by a celebratory fish and chip supper.

Their life since had been haunted by the lack of a child. Thomas and Mary had produced a daughter, Margaret – known lovingly as Peggy who was now eighteen months old.

Florence remained convinced that her previous aborted pregnancy was the cause and Jack often found her in tears after her 'monthlies' had once more shattered their expectations. He caught her regularly gazing at Peggy and she committed her strong affections to the child in the absence of her own.

Jack's working life had been more positive. His push for a compensation scheme had gained momentum amongst the membership – sadly driven by other losses of life and injuries within the local industry. The Union had supported his efforts and, in his role as Compensation Officer, he had the mixed emotion of comforting the families and allocating financial support – a surprise to many of the wives and widows, many unaware of their spouse's payments.

The contribution from foundry owners remained negligible – his issues with Lord Rotherham appeared to have, unsurprisingly, reduced their enthusiasm. Arthur Atkinson had been good to his word and supplied matching donations from his businesses. Only a few others had offered any assistance or support.

He reflected on his failed relationship with Bill Rotherham. He was saddened that their friendship had ended and missed the debate and discussion from another political perspective. His anger at his brother's prosecution and subsequent death had subdued, recognising that Joseph – whilst misled by others – had been subject to his natural urges and lifestyle. He, in the cool light of day, acknowledged that, had he been in Rotherham's position, he too would have done all he could to protect his son. Still some bitterness, but now more accepting.

The new Liberal Government – driven by the small number of Labour members – had introduced new laws on compensation, covering both injuries and industrial diseases. Jack, whilst welcoming any positive change, suspected that the more uncompassionate employers would still continue to seek loopholes to avoid any liability.

Much as he hated to admit it, Florence was correct in her reference to the Labour Party performance at the election. The seats won had been fundamentally gifted to them where the Liberals had agreed not to stand. The bulk of the socialist MP's had been successful in the Manchester area.

The performance of his party had been poor in Yorkshire with none elected in the industrial south – some in the west of the county – but not the momentum they had hoped to achieve.

His relationships in the local branch of the party had improved since the Chairman, Charlie Hall had stood down on 'health grounds'. Those in the know had quietly recognised that his drinking habits had worsened, and were relieved that his increasingly erratic and irrational behaviour was no longer restricting the debate at group meetings.

His successor, Cliff Roberts, was a significantly more measured character, and he and Jack had established a mutual respect for the other over the last twelve months.

His thoughts returned to Florence and her determination to move actively to the women's vote mission.

The WSPU had become far more forceful in delivering their message. They had adopted specific colours – purple, white and green – representing loyalty, purity and hope. They had been named the Suffragettes by a journalist as an insult, but had adopted the term with pride. Their slogan 'Deeds Not Words' described their new approach of civil disobedience, acting to disrupt political meetings and encourage violence amongst their followers.

Florence's regenerated enthusiasm left him deeply concerned. His sister, Mary, who had previously accompanied her on their past protests was now otherwise occupied by her daughter and had been a moderating influence in the past.

How was he to reason with his wife and discourage her participation?

Chapter 29

(Brawmarsh, April 1908)

The cemetery was, despite the Spring late morning warmth, a sad and desolate place. The very edge of the place, where 'sinners' were allowed to be deposited, was rough and uncared for.

His brother lay here. Dismissed by his religion for his sins – his homosexuality seemed to be secondary to his suicide in the eyes of the church.

As he reflected on the simple and dismissive service for Joseph, he recalled his blunt exchange with Father Reilly at the graveside.

'Despite his mortal sins we send our son....'

At the conclusion of the burial, he had approached the priest.

'So, you understand, my brother was led astray by others.'

He declined to refer to the man by any title.

''He took his own life, son and therefore can never be accepted in the house of our Lord.'

Jack laughed as he had held the priest's gaze.

'Frankly, I doubt he'd enjoy the heaven you have in mind, fella!'

Reilly gave a contemptuous and dismissive glance of his hand.

'He chose his lifestyle.'

Jack barely held his temper as he confronted him.

'He did not choose his lifestyle, you ignorant bastard. His lifestyle chose him!

He spat at the ground.

'Your religion, and that of other churches, are despicable. I want you to return to your church and gaze at your treasures – your gold, jewels and decorations. If you

sold those and stopped taking money from your impoverished parishioners, their lives would be considerably improved. Their lives have been continually damaged over time by wars over religion, whilst the poor have suffered as a consequence.'

'You – as a representative of your so-called caring faith – should be bloody ashamed. You bury my brother in a desolate corner for fear he contaminates your brethren. I doubt there is a God, but should I be wrong, I hope he holds you in contempt for your treatment of a gentle young man.'

Jack had stormed through the few mourners and walked away........

He now wandered from the graveyard, still feeling the resentment of that day.

'Bloody hell fella, you must be desperate if you're seeking help from our creed.'

He looked up to see Seamus holding out his hand.

'You're in need of a drink, Jack.'

He wrapped his large arms around his friend's shoulders and guided him towards the Kings Head, a quiet public house on the edge of the town.

The landlord had only just opened his doors and looked in disbelief at the prospect of customers at this time. He tidied himself – tucked his shirt and hitched his trousers – seeking a more presentable image.

'I suppose you've been abusing the bloody Church again, Prendergast.'

Jack nodded and shrugged his shoulders.

'Ah, you've heard my views many times, Seamus.'

Seamus took a long drink and placed his glass gently to the table.

'I've listened to ya views for a good while, lad. So, let me tell you something, will ya? I'm not a strong believer in all this religious palaver. However, I understand those who feel the need to have a faith, to hope for something beyond

118

their miserable bloody lives as it is. If that makes them happy and more content, who are you and I to dismiss their beliefs and hopes?'

Jack went to speak and was silenced by a large hand to his face.

'You'll let me finish. Frankly I don't give a shit whether a man or woman chooses to give their well-earned money to the clergy. If they feel that they get some sort of comfort from it, so be it. I believe they think of it as a down payment to a better afterlife.'

He laughed out loud at his own observation.

'So, what drags you out of your pit at this time of day, Seamus?'

The Irishman waved his finger in the air.

'You'll find that I'll be a changed man in the future, Jack. My heavy drinking and lazy life are about to be brought to a close.'

Jack started at him and shook his head.

'You're joining the priesthood then, fella. That's the only way you'd make those sacrifices!'

Seamus sat back, determined to continue the mystery.

Well lad. Here's the shocker for you then. I'm getting meself wed.'

Jack looked over in amazement.

'What the bloody hell! You...getting married? Does the woman know?'

'She not only knows, fella. She's accepted my proposal.'

Jack sat dumbstruck and open-mouthed at the revelation. He raised his pint and the two tapped their glasses.

'Bloody shocked, Seamus. You've kept that quiet. Who the hell is this unfortunate woman? Is she blind as well as stupid?'

Seamus was enjoying the mischief his announcement had caused and seemed determined to draw out the guessing game.

'I'll put you out of your misery, fella. She's neither blind or stupid. She's accepted she's a lucky lass to capture such a grand fella in the prime of his life. Her name is Teresa. She's a lass from the other side of Rotherham so you'll not know her. Irish descent so that's grand as well.'

Jack was still astonished by the revelation.

'You've never mentioned any lady in your life, Seamus. How long have you known her? Are you rushing at this?'

Seamus raised his glass and drained his beer.

'You'll be wanting to buy me a celebratory beer then and I'll tell you more.'

Seamus settled back to disclose his story.

'I've been frequenting an Irish Club in the town. Meeting with some of the lads from the old country to catch up. Any way one evening one of the boys brings along his sister. Well, cut a long story short, we got along like a house on fire, lad.'

He drew on his beer, clearly determined to keep his audience in thrall.

'That was about six months ago and I've been seeing her on and off since then, finally without her bloody chaperone brother! She's a grand looking girl, Jack. A few years younger than meself but not too much of an age gap, ya understand?'

Jack could not stop himself interrupting.

'You're mid- thirties. How old is your lady?'

Seamus smiled and clapped his hands.

'Teresa is twenty-one, lad. I believe she was taken by my maturity.'

They both burst into laughter.

'Or your bloody money, fella. So, when are you planning the wedding?'

'Three weeks' time, fella. And if you'd accept, you'll be my best man.'

Jack was stunned by both the proposal and the short notice. Seamus undaunted continued.

'I knew you'd be fine. Catholic Church in Rotherham. All bells and whistles. Then the Irish Club for the party.'

Jack indicated his agreement and reached to grasp his friend.

'Congratulations, Seamus. Really happy for ya, fella. Of course, I accept – be a privilege. Will you stay in the area or move?'

Seamus again adopted his bemused face.

'Well, there's another thing. I'm lodging so not practical. She's at her parents so that's not happening. So, I sat and thought a while. Since Emma passed Thomas and Mary have taken up her property and Florence has obviously moved to your house. That left the flat above Thomas workshop vacant. So, I sorted with yer man and that'll be our matrimonial home. Works all round fella!'

Jack acknowledged this was a good option and started to speak.

Seamus held up his hand to silence him.

'One final thing Jack. My family will be coming over for the wedding...including Michael.'

He responded with no enthusiasm at this remark.

'Oh shit, Seamus. Not good. Not good at all'

.

Chapter 30

(Leeds, May 1908)

There was no doubt that the mood had changed. The procession was subdued and serious.

The women proceeded in an orderly group towards the centre of the city. With the company of a police escort and facing constant abuse from bystanders – mainly men but some women - along the way. They sought to disregard the comments and, heads held high, arrived at the central square.

Florence held her banner aloft as she walked in the midst of the women's march. Disappointed that Mary had declined to accompany her but understanding of her circumstances, she joined a boisterous group towards the front.

As the protest reached their destination, they were confronted by a line of policeman, each of them equipped with truncheons and compressed together to prevent access. Florence found herself in the front of the line and sought to retreat as she saw the anger and resentmentin the patrolling officials.

The women pushed forward in response to the barricade and she was thrown before two of the defenders, falling forward and colliding with them.

'Strike the fucking bitches'

She heard the call and sought to turn away from their violent assault. She was struck twice around her shoulders and fell to the floor under the drive of her associates, trampled and kicked by the rampaging footfall of both groups.

Florence was hauled away. She had been dragged to the side of the street by some of the women. In a haze, she sat up and looked with horror as she saw the police, both on foot and mounted on horses, drive towards the procession throwing clubs and fists. Numbers fell by the roadside, many bloodied and battered. The group had been thrown back and dispersed under the brutal onslaught. They fled in terror as the horses rode into their midst, kicking out and causing more to fall on the rough cobbles.

She recalled little of the next hour. Ultimately, she was grasped and half-carried to the train station by her sisters. By good fortune, one woman from Rotherham accompanied her to the town station and then insisted she escorted Florence on the bus journey to Brawmarsh and her home.

Jack was not home. She blessed the woman who left quickly without leaving any details, then crawled in pain to her bed.

***

Jack spent the evening at the Club with Seamus discussing the arrangements for his wedding.

The latter seemed more focused on his stag night rather than his matrimonial duties.

'Ah, it'll be right, fella. Teresa has told me to bugger off out of it so I'm doing what I'm told. I just need to turn up washed and polished with a ring!'

Jack shook his head in disbelief. His friend had clearly abandoned any element of the organisation and appeared totally relaxed at the proposition.

'Now then Jack, my stag night. Night before the wedding we'll do a bit of wandering around the pubs in the village and enjoy the craic. We'll ourselves get scuttered, bit of singing and arsing around. Then I'll go home, sleep well and get married. Simple.'

He drained his beer and looked bewildered at his friend's reaction.

Jack studied him for a moment.

'No Seamus. There's no bloody way I'm taking you out the night before the wedding. You'd never get your arse out

123

of bed to turn up in time. So, it'll be on a Thursday. We'll have the craic fella – only a day early. Understand?'

Seamus nodded and then mumbled quietly to himself.

'We'll do the Friday without you then. you miserable bastard…'

Chapter 31

(Rotherham Hospital, May 1908)

It was austere and cold in the waiting area. Relatives and friends sat – and frequently stood - pacing the floor in fear and apprehension. The medical staff entered and many jumped up hoping it was their turn for good news or worse. They were passed by as people were drawn from the room and taken quietly to a more private place to be given the good or bad.

One man, who could clearly not accept the expectation and stress, threw his hands in the air, swore loudly and then, in tears, fled the room.

Jack sat in a corner, caught up in his own thoughts. He had returned from the Club to find Florence in bed and, clearly in severe pain. She was sweating heavily and unable to speak with any clarity, simply moaning in agony.

He had called on a neighbour to run for the doctor, who had quickly contacted a local man with cart and horse to transport Florence to Rotherham. She had been subdued by some basic anaesthetics – thank God the doctor was a man of modern views and practices.

Nevertheless, the journey of nearly three miles along the rough streets was uncomfortable and difficult at the late time of night. He had held her hand and tried to speak reassuringly to her throughout the journey but to no effect.

Eventually it was his turn to be called.

'Mr Prendergast. Can you come with me please?'

The nurse was tired and abrupt at this hour. Jack stopped himself from any comment and followed her meekly into a small room.

'Your wife has been very poorly Mr Prendergast…very poorly. She is now hopefully recovering…but sadly I'm afraid she has lost her child.'

'Her… our child. I didn't know. Oh my God!'
He fell to a nearby seat and wept.

Chapter 32

(Brawmarsh, Late May 1908)

They sat together – her in the bed, he at her side. She was pale and withdrawn, blaming herself for the loss of their child. He could not address her pain, nor could he say anything to take away her guilt. Florence was dismissive of his affection and he felt both bereft and empty.

'Florence. Talk with me please? I don't hold you responsible my love. It's the bastards who beat you.'

She raised a feeble hand and turned to look towards him.

'My fault Jack. Entirely mine. I didn't know I was expecting or I would not have gone to the parade. I'm sorry...so sorry.'

As he left her to sleep, his sister walked into the house and wrapped her arms around him.

'It will happen, Jack. They'll be another time.'

Jack turned away and fell into tears.

'You don't understand, sister. Florence has suffered badly in the past and...'

Mary raised her finger to his lips.

'Jack, I know far more than you are aware of. Florence and I have become very close friends. She speaks to me in confidence as I do her. We are now more like real sisters. She has told me about her experience in her first home and the consequences...I know what happened, brother. Trust me, she will have a child or more...she will.'

She reached out and gathered him into her arms.

'So, this Thursday, Jack you will accompany Seamus and his friends on his bachelor night. Florence insists. You have a responsibility and an obligation to be with your friend and keep any eye on him.'

He shook his head fiercely

'I'll not leave her until she's well.'

'Jack, bluntly you're not helping her by your maudlin and miserable approach. For God's sake, man she doesn't need your sympathy. She wants to talk about things and you can't help her with your despair. Bugger off and let a woman deal with her will you!'

Chapter 33

They had visited three public houses over the last two hours. Invited to leave two so far.

The group comprised Jack, Thomas, Seamus and a variety of Irish brothers and cousins, all of whom were becoming increasingly more intoxicated and louder by the minute. Two had already stumbled into the gutter and fallen face down only to be re-erected and carried to the next watering hole.

Michael, whilst in attendance, had been noticeably subdued and stayed at the rear of the group. He had exchanged brief and cursory handshakes with Jack and Thomas.

'Your nephew's unusually quiet tonight, Seamus.'

Seamus, after consuming several pints already, moved close to Jack wagging his finger and slurred a whispered response.

'Ya see the big fella up front of the group. Black hair, looks like a feckin gorilla?'

They looked towards the man, who was supporting two others on their staggering journey.

Seamus tapped his nose conspiratorially.

'That's Conor, his da. My sister's husband. Even-tempered sort of fella most the time, but he's a feckin animal when he's roused. Seen him lay out three men at once when they go awkward in a bar back home. I had a word when they arrived. He's told Michael that any shit from him this week and he'll be knocked from Cork to Dublin.'

He smiled and winked, wrapping his arm around Jack's shoulder.

'Seems he understands ...'

They weaved uncertainly towards Lower Sparkgate to the Anchor. A hostel Jack would generally avoid, given its reputation and questionable regulars. The entry of the first number prompted an immediate hush and hostile looks from a number of the locals.

Immediately afterwards the door was thrown open. Conor Rafferty stood, arms on his hips, virtually filling the entrance. He scanned the room and shook his head.

'Now gentlemen, is that a way to welcome your friends from across the sea? Seems to me we can sort this one of two-ways. Either we all settle down and share a few beers in good humour and respect, or you can put up your hardest bastard and he and I will hold a short and swift exchange.'

He removed his coat, handing it to one of the group, rolled up his shirtsleeves and bare-armed, moved confidently to the bar. There was only silence from the regulars.

'Ah that's grand. Who'll have a drink with me then?'

Over the next hour the atmosphere moved from unwelcoming to convivial as the Irishmen and locals consumed the alcohol provided by their visitors. At the end of the night, with the Landlord seeking to close, the entire pub had joined in the singing of the songs of the rebellion before being steered to the exit.

Seamus unsteadily wrapped his arms around Jack and Thomas.

'Been a grand night, fellas.'

Jack put both hands to Seamus' face.

'Now listen, you soft bastard. No heavy drinking tomorrow …understand?'

His friend laughed and slapped him gently around the head.

'Have ya seen this group lad? Can you imagine them staying home with a cup of tea tomorrow….?'

With a wave of his hand, he stumbled to follow his friends.

God help us thought Jack.

Chapter 34

Despite his concerns, Seamus had arrived at the church, with his entourage, on time and well-dressed. A closer look at his eyes suggested that he had not followed Jack's advice and appeared to have indulged on the previous evening. He composed himself to undertake the lengthy ceremony without any significant issues – other than briefly forgetting his bride's name, but recovering without too much embarrassment.

His wedding party – both men and women having evidently partied on the Friday – conducted themselves dutifully and with appropriate respect for occasion.

The bride, Teresa, was a stunningly attractive young woman. Jack and Thomas glanced at each other, clearly thinking that Seamus had found himself a partner beyond his – and their – expectations. Looking to the side at her mother, Jack believed her reservations were much, more clear…

Reluctantly, he had left Florence in the care of Mary, and their apologies had been tendered to the groom. She appeared to be recovering and, although still looking pale and tired, had insisted that he must undertake his best man responsibilities.

The Irish wedding party had travelled by two well-decorated horse carts and these were organised to return the group to Brawmarsh at the end of proceedings.

Jack was still puzzled on the accommodation arrangements for the large body of visitors.

'Lad, they sleep where they fall at our place. Not a problem.'

Inevitably the celebrations were enthusiastic and unrestricted. By the time to leave, the guests had been subjected to a variety of solo and group refrains. These became bawdier and more robust as the night concluded and continued on the journey home.

Almost inevitably, Michael had become disruptive later in the evening and, apparently had sought to draw one of the bride's young relatives into a compromising position. Thomas and Jack had only become aware of the fracas after Conor had quietly wandered across to the pair and, drawing his son to one side and without fuss, delivered him a rough open-handed slap to his face. Michael was hauled to a corner chair where he remained incapacitated for the rest of the celebration. He was now thrown on the rear of the carriage, clearly oblivious and disregarded by the group.

As agreed, Thomas and Jack left the carriage close to the former's house where the wives had demanded they spend the night to avoid disturbing them.

'It was a good day' said Thomas.

'It went better than expected brother-in-law. Pity young Rafferty had to leave the night so early....'

Chapter 35

(Brawmarsh, June 1909)

It was mid-summer as Jack and Florence walked through the park. The last year had flown by and now, as he stopped himself from again resting his hand on her growing stomach, he could not recall a time when he had been happier.

So much had happened. Another child for Thomas and Mary – a son named William – his grandfather's name as promised.

Seamus had wasted no time either and Teresa was expecting their first child within weeks.

Their family and friend's life were looking so good after all their issues.

As they strolled, he dwelt on other aspects of his life.

His role as Compensation Officer had significantly developed – overtaking his other role as an officer of the Union. He was coping with both but felt committed to driving the protection of the members in either.

His presence within the Steelworkers Union had grown and he was a very well- respected contributor at both local, and now, national level as the membership had combined to include the Welsh and North-Eastern and North-Western groups of employees.

And his political interests.

He was proud to be part of the Labour Party who, through Parliament, had helped to deliver the first British old age pensions for men and women over the age of seventy. He remained frustrated and angry that these remained at the whim of local administrators, who were allowed to decide who – 'those of good character' - should receive what was a small payment of only five shillings per week to the single person. Around a quarter of the income of most. Further restrictions based on their residency in the country and capability to work limited the payments. Better than nothing and a start.

Henderson had been elected as Labour leader. He was not to the taste of Jack. A moderate unable to connect the party and the trade unions. Not yet the radical organisation he aspired to be involved in. There was time.

The most recent blow – a court case – had determined that the trade unions could no longer deduct political contributions from their members fees.

Jack privately shook his head when he had heard of this decision. Once again the men with money could contribute to the government of their choice – not so the working man.

His thoughts returned inevitably to Florence. She had suffered emotionally for several months after her miscarriage but had gradually accepted that the fault was not hers. Her pregnancy had been a total surprise.

As they sat she turned to him.

'Jack, I need to tell you something. I think I'm expecting….'

He opened his arms and fell on her in tears.

'Are you sure Florence?'

She held his head and kissed him.

'All being well Jack. I've missed three monthlies now, so I think I am.'

He started to hurriedly speak and she held her hand to quieten him.

'Now listen. I do not want you to coddle me. I don't need you to protect me, Jack. Let things take their course. What will be will be. Please just let things run their course.'

Jack had started to protest but she again reached out to him.

'Jack. What will be will be. Let's just enjoy the time and live in hope, shall we?'

He nodded and embraced her once more.

Chapter 36

(Steelworkers Trade Union Office, Rotherham, August 1909)

He felt 'on top of the world'. He looked out of his window watching the people of Rotherham undertaking their daily shopping in the summer heat. Several old boys sat on the benches in the street below, exchanging opinions, laughing and gesticulating.

Florence was blossoming in her pregnancy and, following a recent doctor's visit, it had been confirmed that all was well this time. He crossed his fingers and wondered whether he should pray, despite his atheist views. No, probably pushing too far.

To add to his pleasure, Seamus and Teresa had produced a baby boy, inevitably a heavyweight at birth. He had been named Patrick.

'Ah, the least we could do for the mad bastard.' said Seamus, with his usual finesse and bluntness.

Jack continued to work on his speech to the next Labour Party meeting in a few weeks' time. His main agenda was the continual push for the party, both locally and nationally, to offer better cover for both industrial compensation and now, a new proposal – that the older and poorer people should receive some form of pensionable payment. This was yet to be a Labour policy but he hoped that he – and others of a similar mind – could influence the support of this within the organisation.

The telephone rang disturbing his thoughts. Irritated at the disruption he answered tersely.

'Prendergast, Steelworkers Union.'

The voice at the other end of the conversation was calm and controlled.

'Good morning Mr Prendergast. I am calling on behalf of Lord Rotherham.'

Jack recognised the voice of the butler. Blewitt.

'And Mr Blewitt, why should I take this call? Bill Rotherham and I have ended our friendship some time ago, as I'm sure you are aware?'

He heard the man sigh with an air of contempt and condescension.

'Shall I continue Mr Prendergast…'

Jack chose not to respond awaiting any further comment.

'I assume I should continue then. I am to advise you that my Lord would like to meet with you, and asks if you could attend at the Manor at a time of your convenience. I should add, though not instructed to do so, that if you wish to meet you should perhaps do so sooner rather than later.'

'What are you telling me, Blewitt?'

'I am suggesting, sir that Lord Rotherham is very ill. To be frank, he has weakened considerably over the last week.'

Jack found himself confused and saddened. Despite their animosity, he had appreciated Bill Rotherham's support over the years.

'If the Lord is available, I will call at the Manor tomorrow in the afternoon.'

In his inimitable style Blewitt replied.

'I am sure that would be acceptable. Thank you'

The call was ended abruptly.

Sanctimonious old bastard thought Jack and then he mused.

Why the hell would Rotherham want to see him?

Chapter 37

For some obscure reason, he had dressed again in his best suit. As he approached the vestibule, he stood for a moment and recalled that the last time he had visited was to borrow more books.

Rotherham had not been at home and Blewitt had opened the door and reluctantly, it seemed, had escorted him to the library, and then had stood sentry like, monitoring his every move.

Jack had selected two books – one on the development of the Liberal and Whig Party over the preceding century and a second book – a novel, *Sybil* written by Benjamin Disraeli describing poverty in British families in the mid 1880's.

He had read the first in a bid to understand their political views. The second, he intended to browse and dismiss as the ramblings of a Conservative politician. However, he had found Disraeli to be observant and, surprisingly. a supporter of wider voting for men and action to reduce the suffering of the working classes.

He had made a point of returning any books by asking his sister to leave them in the library in the course of her housemaid duties at the Manor.

He rang the ornate doorbell and, as usual, awaited the delayed response from Blewitt. He was not disappointed and, after being subject to some minutes wait, the door was opened and he was asked to 'follow me' in the standard cursory and disdainful manner.

He was led to a small drawing room towards the rear of the property, where he found Bill Rotherham seated in a large armchair looking towards the garden and the acres beyond.

Rotherham didn't look up and continued to gaze over the view.

'Thank you for accepting my invitation. Please sit.'

He waved a thin hand towards a seat to his side.

He eventually lifted his head and turned to face his visitor.

Jack was stunned and upset at the deterioration in the man. He had lost almost half of his weight and was lined and haggard. His eyes were misted and his previous stature and presence had substantially diminished. His once well-tailored and neat presentation had been lost as he now sat in a stained and creased dressing gown.

He spoke quietly, stopping to take deep breaths. Barely audible.

'Let me speak. I understand, given all that has gone before, that your visit to me has not been without difficulty and some substantial reservations. I understand, Jack.'

He sat up and rested his hand on Jack's arm.

'I was sorry to hear that your brother took his own life. I am sure you have held me responsible for his death – at least in part. I was seeking to protect my son. In retrospect I wish I had not done so. He has proved to be a self-possessed wastrel, Jack.'

Jack went to speak but was silenced by Rotherham's upraised hand.

'Allow me to finish. I allowed my perceived father's obligations to completely cloud my judgement. For that I wish to profoundly apologise. I wish I could turn back the clock.'

Jack grasped the old man's hand – he felt the skin stretched thinly across the bones.

'Bill. I too have reflected on my brother's death. He was not without fault, although he was not the instigator and was badly treated by the court. I wish I could have done more to help him, but I have recognised that – were I in your position – I too would have done anything to help my child.'

He watched tears appear in the old man's eyes and reached to brush them gently from his cheeks. Rotherham nodded his understanding.

'You will observe that I am far from well. I'm advised by my doctor that my condition is uncurable and my life is moving to its close. I have few regrets other than those I have just stated. I will be re-united with my beautiful wife, Susanna. My great sadness is that George Harcourt will inherit my title.'

He shuffled uncomfortably, clearly in some pain and continued.

'Frankly, Jack Prendergast, you are the son I would have wished for. A man of principle, of passion for his beliefs. I have welcomed our too short friendship. You have led me to understand more about the working people of this country than I ever could have imagined.'

'And you, Bill. Your kindness and help when I've asked for it has always been forthcoming. Giving me access to your books and your wisdom has allowed me to take a more balanced view of our society. I doubt we will ever agree on the best way forward for the people, but there always needs to be a balance for all the parties. As they say 'all arguments have two sides but some have no ends.'

Rotherham patted Jack gently on his arm.

'Thank you for your kind words, young man. Now, I am tiring so, regrettably I will need to conclude our discussion.'

He reached to a small table at his side.

'This, Jack, is the first edition of 'Das Kapital' which you borrowed some time ago. It will be wasted on my son. So, my gift to you as a thank you and with my respect.'

Jack looked at the man with astonishment.

'Bill…I can't accept this…it is too much…'

Rotherham waved his hand once more in dismissal and fell silently into a deep slumber.

***

It took less than a week for Lord Rotherham's life to end. The funeral service was held in the chapel of the Manor, as was the tradition.

Jack joined the mourners quietly to the rear and listened without enthusiasm to the high church service. He was there because of his respect for the man, not the sanctimonious blessings of the clergy and their prayers for the new Lordship. He left as soon as he could, his own memories more important than those delivered by the cleric

Chapter 38

(Labour Party meeting, Rotherham September 1909)
'What's your decision then, Jack?'

He stood with the Chairman, Cliff Roberts.

His speech on workers compensation and pensions had been very well supported by the Committee and a vote had confirmed that the local party would actively campaign for this, both at any future election and at National level.

The group had turned to address the forthcoming local council by-election, called as a result of the sudden death of the current Liberal holder of the role.

Roberts had spoken candidly to the members.

'The Liberals have nominated a strong candidate, Bill Hassall. Very popular local man. Owns the green-grocers in Sparkgate. The Tories have no bloody chance. Some man from outside the area just chancing his arm. No hoper.'

He turned to the Committee.

'We had hoped that Joe Arthur might stand for us but he's now approaching sixty and has said he's had enough. We need a good candidate, gents. Having listened to Jack Prendergast tonight I'm asking him if he would represent our party in October. What's your view, Jack?'

There was an approval of his suggestion around the table.

He sat back and stunned by the proposal.

'Gentlemen, much as I appreciate the confidence you have exercised, I have to think very seriously before I am committed. Three points. One, I am still a young man and the electorate have always preferred a more mature candidate.'

'Two, I have a child on the way and would need to discuss the demands placed on my time with my wife. My current commitments to my job and the broader trade union

141

and socialist movements already demand much of my time.'

'Finally, you are asking me to place myself against a popular Liberal candidate. I have not considered standing for public office but, should I do so, I have to ask myself whether as a younger man with impending family and little chance of success is the best option at this time. I will go away and think about this, with your agreement?'

Roberts stood with Jack at the end of the meeting.

'You're our best option, Jack. Please think hard about this. This will not be your last chance. You are a great proposition for our party, but sometimes you need to stick your head above the parapet, lad. Get yourself known even if you don't win this time.***

Jack was surprised by the response from Florence.

'Of course, you should stand. Of course, you should! You may lose, but take the chance, Jack. Roberts is correct. It may not be your time, but soon it will be. You are made to be a politician.'

'Florence, if I'm elected, I'm taking more time from our life together and our child…and hopefully a larger family.'

She pushed him to the chair and stood firmly above him.

'And if you don't? You will regret it Jack. You have my blessing to fight for the things we believe in. For the people in this community. You are doing nothing different to your day job. You must stand and, if you fall, go back again and again. You are a good man. Go out and sell yourself Jack.'

142

Chapter 39

(Steelworkers Union Office, Rotherham Early October 1909)

Inevitably, Jack's workload had risen given his increasing other commitments.

Two men had been dismissed for fighting at one site. He had read a short report and visited to speak to the owners and, subsequently, the accused employees. Having listened to both parties and other witnesses, he had reluctantly accepted the decision. It appeared that the men had been indulging in some secreted drinking, and had fallen out over who had taken the last drops from the bottle.

The second case involved – in his view – a clear failing by the factory owners. Heavy material had been piled defectively on the instructions of the manager in his urge to move production more speedily. The mass had collapsed and three men had – stupidly in Jack's opinion – sought to stand and prevent the fall. Two broken legs and a broken arm. There was no admittance of guilt by the manager or Company. He was continuing to collect evidence statements on this incident.

He now sat preparing his final speech to be presented at the Town Square in Brawmarsh on Monday. Three days before the election date. He had a good draft prepared and he felt that his contact with the voters had been very positive so far.

The Labour Party was still struggling to make a major impact with the working class. Despite his own attitude, some of his colleagues had sought to sell extreme views – this remained uncomfortable with people who remained servile and uncomfortable with any disruption of the status quo … 'better the devil you know.'

There was a hard knock at the main door. Jack rose reluctantly hoping this was not another issue at this time.

'You are Jack Prendergast?'

He looked the well-suited man up and down.

'And who are you?'

The letter was pushed into his hand with undue speed and the agent walked quickly away.

Jack, puzzled, opened the envelope and only read the main elements of the correspondence.

You are required to attend the Rotherham Civil Court on 9 November 1909.

You will be asked to respond to a claim for damages relating to your removal of documents and/or books The Manor, Rotherham in or about August 1909.

Please confirm your attendance at this time.

There was substantial legalise around the rest of the letter which was incomprehensible.

What the hell was this about?

Chapter 40

He had found the last few weeks an exceptionally hard time.

The news of his case had been leaked to the town and – given his already difficult contest – he had lost by a substantial majority in the local election. Despite the concept of 'innocent until found guilty' the people had found him liable.

Even his union colleagues had distanced themselves – he had been suspended from his duties pending the decision of the court

He knew that he faced a difficult situation. The claim – raised by the new Lord Rotherham, George Harcourt, - indicated that he had borrowed and not returned a first edition of 'Das Kapital'. This had been declared as a volume of significant value by the prosecuting legal advisors to the new lord.

He was bewildered as to why they had chosen a civil route.

His colleague and union Chairman had attempted to clarify.

'It's very simple, Jack. Proof of theft means intention to permanently deprive. Hard to prove, lad. You were in the habit of borrowing books and returning them. However, the civil case serves two purposes.'

'If they win, they will take money from you – recompense of some form'.

'And, secondly, they will damage your reputation. You clearly have upset someone, Jack – some person with a bit of authority or status.'

Jack shook his head.

'I don't know of anyone who'd wish me so bloody ill.'

Florence wished to accompany him to the court, despite her condition. Jack had persuaded her otherwise.

He had decided that he would seek to carry out his own defence, albeit he suspected that the other side would be armed with highly qualified and well-paid legal representatives.

Harcourt – the new Lord Rotherham – stood with his team and gave a dismissive glance towards Jack as arrived. Jack could still not understand the enmity from the man. They had never met or spoken.

The civil court was less ornate and fussy than his previous experience of legal proceedings. The judge – still adorned in wig and robes – opened the case by inviting Rotherham's solicitors to present their case.

The evidence was produced. Great emphasis was placed on Jack as a 'user'. They claimed he had, for some years, taken advantage of an elderly and progressively senile gentleman.

He had demanded the late Lord use his vehicle to freely transport him as required. He had influenced him to assist in raising funds and had received monies from Rotherham to further his own political and union aspirations.

They stated that 'Prendergast had made free with the Lord's library, removing books, returning them at his leisure, often damaged and torn.' They declared that that it appeared other books 'borrowed' by him appeared to be missing and that the court should make their own assumptions in this regard.

Jack sat completely stunned by this fictional account shaking his head.

Harcourt's solicitors advised that they had only a single witness to support their claim.

The judge called Blewitt to the stand.

At this point Jack fell into despair. He had thought to call his sister, Mary to the stand to confirm that she had religiously returned the borrowed books in good condition, but had determined she would not cope with the situation and attention.

However, the appearance of Blewitt would be the nail in his coffin. The man hadnothing but contempt for him. He slumped back and waited for the damning evidence.

'You are Reginald Blewitt, until recently the butler and manservant for the late Lord Rotherham' stated the solicitor.

'I was, until his death, the butler for Lord Rotherham. I did not regard myself as a manservant, sir.'

Jack had to smile quietly at the continuing pretentiousness of the man.

'Well, Blewitt, regardless of your perceived station, I have two simple questions for you. Did you observe the book 'Das Kapital' on the side table before Lord Rotherham's meeting with Prendergast?'

'I did. I placed it there myself at the Lord's request.'

'And Blewitt, did you observe that the same book had been removed after this meeting?'

Blewitt was clearly becoming visibly irritated by the dismissive and arrogant nature of the questioning.

'I would welcome you addressing me as Mr Blewitt, sir. I am not your servant! But yes, I can confirm that the book was no longer on the side table after Mr Prendergast's departure'

He seemed to lay great stress on the 'Mr' when referring to Jack.

The solicitor appeared flustered at the unexpected rebuke by someone he regarded as a mere retainer who would respond as required.

'Mm well yes, yes. But to continue the document in question had not been replaced on the library shelf to your knowledge?'

Blewitt smirked and was clearly enjoying dealing with the man's discomfort.

'Sorry sir, I understood you had two questions. However, to respond to your third, the book was not replaced on the library shelf to my knowledge.'

The solicitor had clearly made his case and, smugly clutching his fingers behind his braces, he advised the court that his questioning was completed.

As the judge waved to Blewitt to allow him to stand down, Jack raised his hand.

'I have some questions for Mr Blewitt, sir if you please.'

The justice gazed across at Jack with a look of disbelief.

'You wish to ask questions to the major and only witness for the plaintiff? Well, if you wish…'

'Correct sir.'

Jack stood and approached the witness stand.

'Good morning Mr Blewitt. Can I confirm that you stood as a butler for Lord Rotherham and before that his father?'

Blewitt confirmed.

'So, you will have been familiar with the library content held during both times?

'The second Lord was far more of an accumulator of books and other literature, Mr Prendergast. One of my responsibilities was to record and maintain a full bibliography of the collection.'

Jack hesitated. He felt that Blewitt was toying with the court and possibly that he may offer more in his defence.

'You were aware that Lord Rotherham and I had built an unlikely but good friendship over the last few years?'

Blewitt nodded.

'His Lordship spoke well of you Mr Prendergast. He indicated to me that you were welcome to visit him and that he enjoyed your company.'

Harcourt's solicitor jumped to his feet.

'M'lud, this is surely irrelevant. Our case accepts there was a relationship between Prendergast and Lord Rotherham, but that it was strongly driven by the former's regrettable influence on the Lord….'

The judge threw his gavel heavily to the bench.

'Shut up and sit down! I wish to understand the relationship as I believe it is fundamental and pertinent to this case.'

Jack took this as an opportunity to continue with his questions without disruption.

'Tell me, Mr Blewitt, did you understand that I had the liberty to take books on loan?'

'That was my understanding.'

'Did you monitor the removal and return of these books and the condition on their return?'

Blewitt mused and appeared to consider the question for a moment.

'I can confirm that one of my responsibilities was the management of his Lordship's library. In that context I maintained a record of the contents and their condition.'

'And, to your knowledge are there any books missing from his library?'

Blewitt reached into his inner jacket pocket and withdrew a thick notebook. He made great play on scrolling through the pages before returning his attention to his questioner.

'The only book that my records show as not being present is a first edition of 'Das Kapital' written by one Karl Marx.'

Jack noted that the plaintiff's lawyer sat forward at this point as their claim was reinforced. He hesitated and was considering his next question carefully when the butler continued.

'I should add that each of the books borrowed by Mr Prendergast was recorded and returned without any noticeable damage.'

'Mr Blewitt, you indicated that the book in question was placed by yourself on the side table. Can I ask when and why this was done?'

There was a short delay in his reply as he pursed his fingers and leaned forward towards Jack.

'The document was placed by myself at the specific request of Lord Rotherham. He instructed me to do so immediately prior to the arrival of yourself, Mr Prendergast.'

'And did he state for what purpose?

Blewitt nodded and seemed to enjoy the moment of suspense before responding.

'He stated clearly to me that it was his intention to present this to you as a gift as a token of your friendship. He further added that he regarded you as having the qualities he would look for as a son.'

There was uproar in the court at these comments. George Harcourt took to his feet and bawled furiously at the judge.

'You can't believe this statement from a bloody servant. How can we trust what he says? A bloody liar!'

The justice once again brought his gavel heavily and repeatedly to the bench.

'You will desist from your uncouth shouting in my court, Lord Rotherham or I'll hold you in contempt and have you ejected! This gentleman was offered as your main and only witness and has presented his evidence, in my view in a truthful and respectful manner.'

He stood and held his hand to silence any further comment.

'Having heard the evidence, it is clear that the book was a gift to Mr Prendergast – pre-determined by the late Lord and given without any duress or coercion. I find the case against Jack Prendergast to be totally unproven and my judgement is in favour of the respondent. You are free to leave this court with your reputation unstained, Mr Prendergast.'

He paused and pointed to Harcourt and his legal group.

'I additionally find that your case is frivolous, vindictive and has wasted the time of this court. I therefore award damages of ten pounds to the respondent, payable within the next two days or this will be doubled.'

With that he stood and walked from the court.

George Harcourt was hauled away by his representatives as he continued to call abuse towards Blewitt.

'You are bloody dismissed, Blewitt. I'll make sure you can find no employment. I'll see you in poverty, you treacherous bastard!'

Reginald Blewitt stepped down from the witness box and walked directly to the man with a broad smile breaking across his face.

'You are a contemptuous little shit. Your father thought you were an ignorant, ungrateful and unprepossessing individual lacking any class or redeeming features. With regard to my dismissal, when you return to the Manor you will find my letter of immediate resignation waiting for you.'

He paused, turned to walk away and then once more addressed Harcourt.

'And for clarity, I will not require further employment as your father allocated a generous pension to me prior to his death. Do not seek to challenge that – I have correspondence outlining his generosity, specifically drafted at my request in the expectation that I would not wish to continue in your employ. As a final point, you will require a new cook-housekeeper, as the lady currently in your employ has accepted my proposal of marriage and will be joining me in a restful retirement. I sincerely hope you rot in hell. Good day.'

He stepped directly to face Jack, leaving Harcourt open-mouthed and speechless.

'Mr Prendergast, despite you believing that I was offhand and dismissive of you, I wish you to understand that I had a great regard for your person. You brought great pleasure to the late Lord with your friendship. I was obliged to fulfil my duties in a particular style and manner.'

He stopped, laughed and in a broad Yorkshire accent said.

'Thank God, I can stop putting on the bloody airs and graces, Jack. Tek care lad and my best wishes for you and yours.'

With that, he laughed, nodded and walked towards the door.

Chapter 41

His name cleared, Jack returned to both union and party roles.

The local newspapers had communicated the decision of the court in great detail and had made no secret of the attitude and arrogance of the new Lord Rotherham.

He had received a scribbled cheque for the £10 damages awarded by the court. He had – he felt appropriately – contributed this to the Union Compensation Fund. He believed Bill Rotherham would have welcomed his decision.

There had been the inevitable backlash. Mary had been dismissed from her position at the Manor. She had been initially distraught at the loss of income, but Thomas was comforting and his view was that their income was sufficient from his growing business.

Additionally, she could now devote herself to the care of their children and this resulted in a reduced cost for the payments to a local child-minder.

Seamus had also lost work at the Manor through his association with Jack. He too had been sanguine and accepting.

'Listen fella, I wouldn't have wanted to carry on working for the new man. He was seeking to cut my money and treated me and my lads like feckin domestic helps. I told his man to tell the Lord to stick his job where the sun don't shine. From talking to other lads in the trade I doubt there'll be many willing to take up the slack. His reputation is poison.'

'My workload had already started to run down, Jack. Me and Teresa have talked for a while about the future. Likely as not we'll be moving back to the old country. I feel like I need to support some of the lads over there in the fight for independence. Your government continues to ignore our views and I believe that we are moving towards a civil war in Ireland. I need to be there…'

He and Teresa had left with their family in the last week, promising to keep in touch. Jack would miss his friend but understood his need to leave.

Florence was coming to the end of her term and so far, all appeared to be well. Her work nursing the old lady had continued until the last month, when at Jack's insistence, she had accepted that the frequent demands to lift and transport her could cause issues at this time. The old lady had reluctantly accepted Florence's decision and had insisted that she would find temporary nursing cover awaiting the possibility she could return.

He was reluctant to leave Florence at this stage in her pregnancy. However, she had insisted that he needed a break – as did she - from his constant attention.

Leaving his wife in the care of his sister, he and Thomas had agreed to partake of a couple of pints at the Club. They now sat together over the first of these.

'Well, fella make the best of this. Once you've a child, your drinking days ull be well cut back!'

Jack tapped glasses and laughed.

'It seems like you're still able to get away, Thomas!'

'Aye, only because your Mary wants me to bugger off and give her some peace.'

'That'll be because you're bloody harassing her for another bairn. You've two – leave her alone for a while, you mucky old sod!'

They sat in silence for a few minutes, watching the raucous snooker matches and domino games, the participants abusing and insulting each other's capabilities. In another corner, a group of card players broke into a loud discussion about the rules of the game.

Bloody cheating, that is.

Don't call me a cheat lad.

Or what…. what are you gonna do?

As the men stood to confront each other, their companions pulled them apart and a Committee member scurried across waving his hands.

'You can bloody knock that off! Either calm down or you'll be leaving…'

They returned to their seats, initially glaring at each other until one of their group laughed.

'Hope you two are better at scrapping than carding…. are we playing or not?'

The whole group burst into laughter.

There was then a brief discussion of the rules, agreement that it had been a misunderstanding and a shake of hands. The game then continued, no less energetically or with less insults but now apparently returning to some level of agreement and calm.

Thomas and Jack shook their heads at the fracas.

'Never a bloody lack of entertainment in here is there.'

They were disrupted by a shout from the door.

'Jack Prendergast? Lad at the door for you.'

Jack found a breathless young boy in the entrance.

'Mr Prendergast. Mary Davies has sent me. You're to get home soonest…there's a baby coming they said.'

Jack returned to grab his coat and joined by Thomas they ran to the door. The boy stood in their way.

'They said I might get a penny or so for coming, Mr Prendergast?'

He and Thomas dove in their pockets and threw a few pennies at the lad who jumped aside and scrabbled along the floor, revelling in his reward.

They arrived gasping at Jack's home to be met by Mary, carrying hot water and towels.

'Right, the pair of you sit down. All under control. Midwife's here. Keep out of the way.'

155

Jack could hear his wife crying out in the room above and paced around the room. Thomas reached out and grabbed his arm.

'Sit down for Christ's sake. This is women's work. Just keep out of the bloody way, fella.'

He reluctantly sat back down and then, within seconds, was back on his feet.

'How long does this go on Thomas?'

'As long as it takes, lad. You did the hard work at the start…..'

Jack laughed at the remark and sat and stood again for the next two hours. Mary returned to boil more water and Jack rose expectantly.

'On the way, brother. She's fine. Always takes a while with the first.'

It was another two hours before he heard the cry.

'My God Thomas. That's a baby.'

Thomas smiled.

'What were you expecting Jack? A bloody donkey or summat?'

Jack grabbed him as they laughed together.

'It's a child My child. Florence's child. Oh God we thought it might never happen.'

He broke into tears overcome by the moment as Mary threw the door open.

'You're a father, Jack. I'm so happy for you brother!'

He hesitated before embracing her forcefully.

'Are they fine, Mary? Are they both alright?'

With a broad smile, she nodded.

'Both grand, Jack. Florence obviously sore and tired but the bairn is good and healthy.'

'And a boy or a girl, sister?'

'You'd better go up and find out, lad.'

Jack took the stairs two at a time and threw open the bedroom door as the cossetted baby was passed gently to Florence.

He threw has arms around his wife.

'Gentle, young man!' shouted the midwife. 'She'll be tender for a few days yet.'

He released his firm grip and crouched by the bed.

'Meet your daughter, Jack. Your beautiful little daughter.'

He cuddled Florence and wept.

She lifted his head and laughed.

'For a tough man, you let your emotions out sometimes, so you do. We need a name, Jack Prendergast?'

He looked in her eyes and they both nodded.

'Welcome to the world, Emma Prendergast.'

Chapter 42

(Brawmarsh, May 1910)
'The King is dead' Florence wept openly and looked to Jack for support.

He openly sighed and raised his head with a lack of enthusiasm.

'Florence, I frankly am totally disinterested in the change in our monarchy. Another man who uses our resources for their own self-interest. Edward was an extravagant arsehole who was unfaithful and profligate. How can you expect me to have any sympathy? His successor will continue to regard the working class as bloody peasants. No change over centuries. When will you open your eyes, woman!'

She scowled and dismissed his comments with a wave.

'I love the Royals. They are the heart of our country. I will always be loyal to our King.'

Jack laughed out loud.

'Here's a woman who wants a vote. Do you think the bloody royals want you to have that? The last King had total disregard for women. He took mistresses as he could. He was unfair to his wife. What makes you believe that the next one will do anything different?'

Chapter 43

(Labour Party Meeting, June 1910)
Jack listened to the opening speech of the Chairman, Cliff Roberts and sought to control his temper. He focused on his notes and glanced around the room at the other ten attendees. They sat, nodding in agreement as Roberts outlined the progress of the Labour Party over the last year or so. He had already spoken for five minutes and appeared to be enjoying his opportunity to deliver his discourse

'And so, gentlemen, we should congratulate ourselves and the party nationally. We have 40 seats in our parliament and have commitments from the Liberals to move our agenda forward. It has been a bloody good year for the Labour movement.'

Jack held his hand up to intervene. Roberts, annoyed by the disruption, waved him away and continued.

'Our movement is progressing, brothers. We are a growing influence locally and nationally and…'

Jack raised himself from his chair and interrupted him.

'Mr Chairman. I have listened intently to your triumphal speech. I have to state that I entirely disagree with your view of the impact of the Labour Party both locally and countrywide.'

The Chairman held up his hand in an attempt to take back control.

'No Cliff. You have had your ten minutes. Let someone else speak…'

The room was silenced with Roberts, arms folded, clearly angry by the disruption of his speech.

'Gentlemen, as I said I do not recognise this claim of success for our party. Across the country we won 40 seats. We have less influence than the Irish MP's who won more. The Labour Party won two – let me say that again… two seats in South Yorkshire! Most of the socialist successes were in Manchester, Scotland and London. We achieved bugger all in our area.'

The group shuffled uneasily at the comments.

'We won very few seats in our local elections. We are failing miserably on two counts, brothers. We still don't have enough voters from the working-class community. I've asked for a push to sign them up but it doesn't seem to be happening.'

'Second. We're seen as scrambling around the Liberals – a small pressure group, no more, hoping they'll prioritise our issues. Not a bloody chance! The Irish are more important to them and with their push for home rule, we'll always be at the back of the pack.'

A voice from the end of the table interrupted.

'Listen, Jack if you're going on for a bit can we get a beer. It'll get bloody dry…'

The meeting laughed at the intervention and Jack threw his hands up.

'Aye I've a bit more to say!'

As they re-settled with their drinks, Jack stood again.

'Bear with me while I make a couple more points. We've had lots of promises from the Liberal Government, but I don't believe they will deliver these. And even if they do so, it's not enough. The average wage for a working-class family is eighteen shillings a week….'

He paused to refer to some scribbled notes.

'Twelve shillings on food, three shillings on heating and lighting, three shillings on rent. What's left? Nowt. Bugger all for clothes, shoes, any pleasure. We know that some of these families see their husbands spend money on drink. That comes from food or heating. It means they can't pay their rent. If any child is ill, they have to depend on charity for treatment and medicine. How can we declare that the Labour Party has progressed the lives of these people?'

George Frankley – a recognised moderate – raised his hand to intervene.

'Jack, we all know their plight, lad. But we have to bide our time. Our movement will succeed in time. Patience is needed.'

Jack, now red-faced, showed his impatience by throwing his notes to the table.

'And the poor keep suffering and dying, George!'

Roberts stood to silence the meeting.

'So, what's your answer then, Jack Prendergast? It's fine telling us summat we already know. What do you think we need to do different then?'

His comments prompted voices of support around the room.

'We need to do several things. Make our case with proposals that our voters need. Unemployment benefit, health cover for all, a drive to increase wages – bluntly gentlemen we need class warfare. Let our potential supporters hear our voice more strongly.'

'Second, you, me, our families and our members need to get off our arses and visit in the community. Help them apply for their vote.'

He paused and slapped his hand hard to the table.

'And finally, gentlemen.' He pointed directly to Harry Harris, the known misogynist in the Committee. 'All of us, including you Harry, need to support the campaign for women's suffrage. They are half of the population. They experience most of the misery and deprivation. They are our supporters if we go out and claim them.'

Harris bridled at the suggestion.

'No bloody way are women ready for the vote, lad. They don't understand. Never happen. Waste of time.'

Jack walked and stood above him.

'Then, it's time whether you decided that your bloody old-fashioned views are in line with the future of this party,

Harry. Frankly you don't represent the attitude that we need to progress!'

He stood to confront Jack.

'A bloody johnny come lately you are! I've been a member for twenty years. You tried to get elected with your sodding extreme views and they rejected ya! So, clever bugger, if you believe your views about women and the rest are correct, stand again, lad. The men ull laugh you out of court, trust me lad.'

Jack bent to meet the man face to face.

'The next local elections are in October, Harry. I'll stand again with my views, not your bloody 'bent over backwards' support for an easy option. And if I win, you'll leave the Committee and take your outdated opinions into retirement, brother! Agreed?'

'Aye. And when ya lose, you'll stand down and we'll be better for it...!'

Chapter 44

(The Club Trip to Scarborough, July 1910)
Both Florence and Mary had been adamant that the two families should join the Welfare Club annual trip to the coast.

The men had avoided this in past years *'Kid's trip – no fun for us.'*

Now both family men, they could not excuse themselves and at 7.30 am, on the Saturday morning, found themselves with around a hundred men, women and an age range of children clambering aboard the steam train to the coast. The males were happy having been given time from work – without pay....

The Committee men wandered through the carriages allocating sweets and fruit to the young ones. They also received three pennies each to spend on entertainment and ice creams. Jack noted with sadness, that a number had been relieved of the money by their fathers.

Inevitably, within the following hour, two of the children, having greedily consumed all their treats had been violently sick. As their mothers fussed around, cleaning as best they could, another two or three joined them in a vomit party. The carriages were consumed by the smell and windows were thrown open in despair.

Jack and Thomas hung their heads from the train.

'You'd think we'd be used to the smells by now, fella?'

Jack laughed at Thomas remark.

'Aye lad but it doesn't get any more pleasant does it?'

They were interrupted by a Committee man sidling alongside.

'Ayup gents. If you move to the front carriage where us Committee men sit, you'll find it a bit more comfortable like.'

He winked and the two of them followed him, entering the carriage at the head of the train.

Sure enough, as they proceeded, they found a peaceful area free of children and, at one end a large barrel of beer.

'Committee meeting, lads. No entry to the general public. You're invited as some of our regulars.'

As they scanned around the room, they saw a group of around thirty men, undisturbed by the bedlam within the rest of the train.

Thomas stared in disbelief and breathed a sigh of pleasure.

'Bloody hell Jack. Where's your politics of equality for women now, lad?'

Jack walked forward and drew a long draught of beer into a pint glass.

'Sometimes they need a day off Thomas. A day off...'

The station was overwhelmed with families tumbling from the train. Women trying to grasp their children who were now ecstatic at the thought of the day ahead. Some of the men tried to help, shouting loudly to control their brood. Others, having consumed a volume of alcohol, simply watched and laughed at the frenzy.

The mothers pulled their groups to order. Several of the offspring stood in tears having received a hefty smack to their legs for their disobedience and a stern warning about being 'put back on the train' whilst the rest of the family enjoyed their day.

Jack and Thomas had – in their view – behaved themselves, having only partaken of a couple of beers.

They returned to their wives and – despite their protests - had received 'a Scarborough warning' as to their behaviour for the rest of the day.

Florence had been particularly offended.

'Is this how you intend to behave, Jack Prendergast? People are watching you! Remember that you are seeking to represent them in the Council. For God's sake, behave man.'

'Am I not allowed to relax then, Florence? I'm out having fun at the seaside, lass.'

'No, Jack. You're out with your wife and daughter at the seaside. You can't have a go at the men spending their wages on beer and then wander around with my bloody stupid brother worse for wear.'

He watched Thomas being addressed in a similar manner by his sister and joined him at the rear of the group leaving the station.

'So, that's us told, Jack. Shall be buy them a stick of rock apiece?'

'Aye and I know where it would end up... '

***

They had been led to the beach, where the women set out blankets and prepared their children for an experience of the still cold North Yorkshire sea.

On instruction. they walked to a small stand to request some large pots of tea and ice creams for each of the children.

'Look Thomas. There's spades and buckets. Shall we buy a couple of sets for the children?'

Listen, brother-in-law, you've always been rash with your money. Mebbe we buy one set and let them share?'

'You are right bloody tight arse, Thomas.'

'Aye but I fancy fish and chips from that place over there. Mebbe we get them for the lasses and us to share...buy us a few good marks after earlier?'

Between them they paid for the toys and two large portions of the meals. They trudged back to the beach.

'Here you go girls, should be enough for all of us and some for the bairns.'

Both Mary and Florence shook their heads.

'Well maybe Peggy will have a few chips but how old do you think William and Emma are, you silly buggers?

165

We've food for them anyway. Put the tea down, give the babies their ice creams and then you can help build some sandcastles.'

Florence winked at Mary. They both knew the men were seeking to 'do their bit' with their family but were looking to join some of their male friends for a beer.

Jack sought to introduce the subject.

'Are the bairns enjoying themselves then? Are you two having a good time?'

'Aye Jack, Peggy is down the beach chasing around with some others. The babies are ready for a sleep now. Mebbe Mary and myself ull have a walk and leave you with them for a spell.'

They both watched and stopped themselves from laughing out loud as Thomas and Jack both gave thin smiles.

'If you like lass…'

Mary was the first to collapse in giggles.

'Oh, for Christ's sake, go and have an hour with your mates! Back here by 3 o'clock though. Understand? We want an outing on Peasholm Park lake before we go home.'

They needed no more prompting, and both kissed their partners a quick thank you as they scurried back to the promenade and on to the Bay Horse public house where, as previously discussed, they knew their fellow men would collect.

***

They left their colleagues and, as promised returned – marginally late – having had another quick beer at last orders.

'Jesus, Jack there's a few lads in a bit of a mess in there. We could be missing a few on the return trip.'

'Good luck to them then. The train won't wait and I suspect their women won't either!'

Florence and Mary frowned as they returned.

'You're late.'

166

'Aye, we got lost in the town, lasses but we bought you these.'

They presented each woman with a fruit flavoured stick of candy rock.

The gifts were not well received.

'Thomas, if you come near me with that, you'll struggle to walk back to the train!'

Jack leaned quietly over to Thomas.

'What did I tell ya earlier, fella?'

The party packed their children, blankets and various bags and passed them silently to their husbands.

'Peasholm Park, now!'

Thomas and Jack, given their intake, could not stop smiling at the women's mood.

'Oh, I do like to be the seaside…' Thomas sang loudly before quickly ceasing with a thin smile as Mary shot him a harsh glare.

The mood had marginally improved as they, and the babies, settled into a dinghy and the men took the oars and rowed gently around the lake.

It was almost certain, given the volume of alcohol some men had taken, that at least one would fall from their boat. Sure enough, one young father, deciding to show off to his friends, rowed his dinghy towards them. Following the collision, he was hauled spluttering from the water and, soaked to the skin, was laid, broadly unaware of his state, on the lakeside for later collection

Many of the older children indulged in a water fight and, despite their mother's reprimands, were also drenched and experienced a swift clip around their heads as they were pulled from the vessels.

The whole party formed a crocodile back to the train station, amidst further rebukes and tongue-lashings – both men and their broods.

167

They clambered aboard the home train at around six o'clock. Many of the younger children were carried ready for sleep following the excitement of the day.

The Committee men counted the passengers to the train.

'We're missing two of the men, George Thomson and Arthur Hall. Anybody know where they are?'

A voice from the last carriage erupted loudly.

'Aye, they're probably still in the bloody pub or laid out somewhere. Leave em and let them find their own way back.'

'Thank you, Mrs Thomson. Are we sure?'

'Too bloody right I'm sure, fella!'

They shook their heads, climbed onto the carriage and waved the guard.

'Every bloody year we lose at least one or two.'

'Aye, and they always come home in one shape or form.'

The train pulled away. The majority of the train was subdued carrying the sleeping bairns. Some of the other youngsters ran around before calming down within the hour and joining their siblings at rest.

Jack wrapped his arm around his brother-in-law.

'Bloody hell, Thomas. Remind me not to do this next year!'

They wound their way to the Committee carriage in the hope of further refreshment, but found themselves disappointed. They met one man at the door.

'All done on the way out, lads. Greedy bastards have done all the beer.'

He looked at the two of them and winked. 'Mind look here.'

He drew out a small bottle of whisky from under a seat. 'Tell no buggers lads'

Chapter 45

As Jack wandered downstairs from his bed on the Sunday morning he was met by the banging of pots and pans. The baby Emma smiled as she saw him. It was to be the only welcome he received that morning.

'Morning, Florence.'

She turned with a curl of her lip and returned to her deliberately loud activity.

'Not in the good books then....'

He was cut off as she stormed across the room and confronted him.

'You and my brother were totally out of control yesterday! You left Mary and me with the babies and came back stinking of whisky. Here's a man that claims to support the women of this country, a man who believes he has the capability to represent this community. You are bloody pathetic, Jack!'

She spun around and dealt with the baby.

He held his head, still feeling the effects of yesterday's drinking, and then grabbed his coat.

'I'm going out for a walk, Florence. I'll talk to you again when you've calmed down.'

As he slammed the outside door, he stormed away towards the park.

He initially stormed in a rage through the trees and grassland and eventually sat on a bench in the warm morning sun reflecting on his behaviour.

Mebbe she was right. He and Thomas had treated the day as a boy's trip, perhaps the opportunity to let their hair down. Neither had really had a young man's life had they? But now he had to recognise his responsibilities...

He stood and determined that he could not yet go home. Let Florence cool down a tad. He found himself at Thomas and Mary's house.

As he knocked and entered, he found Thomas laid on the sofa.

He jumped to his feet.

'Bugger, I Thought it was Mary coming back.'

Jack and Thomas stared at each other.

'My God lad, you look like shit!'

'Aye Jack, that's what Mary said. Only she said it with a bit more venom before she took the children out for a spell!'

He settled alongside his brother-in-law.

'Wasn't a great performance by us yesterday, was it?'

'No lad, I think we messed up a bit. But one good thing though...'

Jack turned and shook his head. Thomas hushed him and continued.

'Can you remember me talking to a couple of younger lads in the pub in Scarborough?'

'I can hardly remember talking to you, Thomas, so no...'

Thomas waved him to a stop.

'They were a couple of fellas on another trip. Keith from Brawmarsh and his cousin Eddie from Sheffield. Well, it turns out they're both trades lads – a carpenter and bricklayer.'

'Lad, I've bit of a headache so is this a long story or what?'

No listen, Jack. I've a chance to start some new house building in Lower Brawmarsh. Factory houses – basic but a chance for some to move to more updated homes. I need some lads with skills. These two could be right.'

Jack puzzled for a few moments.

'And do you know these lads and their work? Do you know anyone who's worked with em?'

Thomas waved away Jack's comments.

'They told me where they'd worked, fella and I'll ask around. But here's another bit of benefit. The Brawmarsh lad lives with his parents so that's handy. The lad from Sheffield would need to move over here so I've a plan. He can lodge with us! So, I save money on his wages for his cost. Bloody marvellous!'

Jack screwed up his face in disbelief.

'So, let me understand your plan. You're taking on two lads ya know bugger all about. And then you're inviting one of em to move in with ya and my sister and your family?'

'Aye lad. It'll be fine.'

Jack shook his head and stared hard at Thomas.

'I've two questions. Where will he stay in yours given you've only two bedrooms, and does Mary know about this bloody daft idea?'

Regardless of the comments, his brother-in-law continued enthusiastically.

'Aye, well here's another bit of my plan. We'll add a bit of modern plumbing work in the loft and he'll have his own washing facilities. I'm thinking of putting one in our bedroom so that'll make my wife happy too....'

Jack held up his hand.

'Have you talked to Mary about the new lodger and your proposition?'

He waited for the inevitable subdued response.

'Well, I will do – once she's a bit calmer like – after yesterday...'

'She'll cut your balls off, lad. Trust me.'

***

He wandered back to his home hoping that Florence had let off steam since he'd left.

Despite the summer heat, the atmosphere, as he entered, was as cold as ice.

'Are we going to carry on like this for a while Florence or will you accept my apologies.'

Florence turned and he dodged a cup thrown at his head.

'So, probably not then….'

She marched across to him.

'I've put Emma to bed and you and I need to talk, Jack Prendergast. When I married you, I saw a man who cared about my beliefs. A man who supported the right for the women in this country to have a say – not to be treated like they had been twenty or thirty years ago! Your behaviour yesterday told me you're just like every man in this community. You think you can do as you like and treat me like a bloody chattel. Well, learn again, fella I'm not going to be a downtrodden female accepting your behaviour. Are you hearing me?'

Jack opened his mouth to speak and was immediately cut off.

'No, you'll listen to me. Your bloody Labour Party, your bloody Union. Neither of them appreciates or support the women's position, do they? Your Union has no women members. None! Because they still don't understand. Well, I'm telling you, Jack I'm back with the suffrage movement from now on. I'll be going to their meetings. I'll do what I need to do until we can get you, your bloody socialist friends and the Government to listen!'

She turned and moved in tears to the scullery. Jack, totally taken aback by her tirade, stood for a moment and then slumped into a chair.

'Listen Florence, you are absolutely right. I misbehaved, but sometimes I need a break, lass. My job, my commitment to our beliefs – odd times I need a bit of a chance to enjoy meself.'

He stood and moved to embrace her.

'Please listen to me now. Mrs Pankhurst and her followers are becoming increasingly radical and dangerous. They have attempted to attack some senior politicians, they've hurled stones at meetings, they have broken windows. They are extremists, Florence.'

She shrugged him aside.

'Of course they are, man. No one listens. The Tories will only propose to give women with property the vote. The Liberals won't support that as it will increase the Tory vote. The Liberals will give all women the vote but that would increase their vote so the Tories will not agree. Your precious bloody party dances around the edges. Women need to force the issue until men listen.'

She prodded him hard in the chest.

'And your bloody union movement does nothing! They won't allow us to join as that will – in their view – increase the numbers of 'cheap labour'. If an organisation supporting the working class doesn't give us any credence, why should the monied folk?'

At that moment, Jack had an idea forming in his head.

'Bear with me Flo. I've a thought on how we can put these views across to union members. Listen....'

Chapter 46

(Thomas and Mary's house, Brawmarsh, July 1910)
Mary had returned with the children sometime after Jack's departure and seemed to be in a better frame of mind. Thomas took the opportunity to apologise and helped to bathe Peggy and William before bed.

Sitting with their cups of tea, Mary appeared to have put the issues of the previous day behind her, and spoke enthusiastically about her few hours away from the house.

'We bumped into Jenny Spencer on our walk. She's got a little girl of Peggy's age. They played so nicely in the park, Thomas. I need to get our little girl out and about more to make more friends.'

Thomas, given her improved mood, decided to raise the issue of the prospective lodger.

'Mary, you'll know I've a good bit of work coming my way with these houses. Well, I met a couple of fellas yesterday who I could employ to help me. So, I'm thinking of taking them on but there's a bit of an issue with one of them'

Mary listened intently, expecting some comment around their skills or character.

'Well, see it's like this. Eddie currently lives in Sheffield but need the work and is fine moving to Brawmarsh but he'd need some accommodation....'

She studied him and interrupted.

'Well Thomas, what about the rooms above your workshop?'

Aye, well ya see, I've let them out to a fella who's up from the middle of the country doing some business in Rotherham for six months or so. Good money, love and I can't go back on my word now, can I?'

She looked puzzled.

'Where's the other fella live then?'

'He's a Brawmarsh lad – they're cousins, but no room at his parent's home. Anyway, I thought that we could mebbe put the lad up here…only short term. Saves me money on wages as well….'

Mary was silent for a minute or so.

'But Thomas we've a lovely set up here – you, me and the bairns. It would be uncomfortable having a stranger stopping in my house. Where would he stay?'

He took the chance to lay out his plans for the loft and improving their washing facilities.

'We'd have privacy, Mary and it would only be for a spell. Once the other fella leaves, I'll look at the workshop rooms for Eddie.'

She was clearly unhappy with the proposition but Thomas continued to sell his idea to her.

'Mebbe I'll ask him to drop around and, if you're still not happy, I'll think of summat else?'

She nodded uncertainly.

***

In the following week, Mary had met both Keith and Eddie at her home. Despite some reservations, she had to acknowledge that both appeared to be pleasant and well-behaved characters.

Keith was a short fellow, carrying a tad too much weight for his early twenties and clearly, a lad who enjoyed both his food and drink. Eddie could not have been more different. He was taller and slim, had a more confident air about him without being arrogant or cocky.

Both had a strong sense of humour and, within an hour of meeting them Mary felt relaxed in their company.

Eddie had eventually raised the possibility of lodging at their house.

'Listen Mary, I understand you would not want any intrusion into your family life. I would not wish to cause any inconvenience to yourself and Thomas. If you'll allow me to rent your room, I will not disturb you.'

Mary studied him and eventually responded.

'Look Eddie, I'll admit that I am happy with just Thomas, myself and the children living here. But if things work out, I'm fine with you staying here for a while.'

They agreed arrangements for rent, meals and any other issues during the evening and confirmed that Eddie would move in within the following week.

Chapter 47

(Brawmarsh, October 2010)

The summer had passed by without any noteworthy issues.

Florence had accepted that any direct involvement in the extremist WPSU was not currently sensible, given her family commitments. She insisted that she continue to submit letters of support and continued to follow the movement passionately.

The old lady whom she had been nursing at home had died. She had left a bequest of £20 to Florence with her thanks for her care. This, and Jack's reasonable income, meant that she could focus on looking after Emma. They had hoped for a further child to be on the way by now. but to no avail.

Whilst his working life remained relatively peaceful, Jack had also had some success in addressing the incident of twelve months earlier, where men in his union had suffered broken limbs at work. Ultimately, evidence had proved that the employer's manager had been at fault and a small level of compensation – mainly covering wages – had been paid reluctantly to the injured three men. The manager had been dismissed. Jack felt no sympathy for him.

He was now preparing for two significant events. First the local Council elections on the coming Thursday. This would be followed by the annual Union Conference on the Saturday. It would be an exceptionally busy time over the next couple of weeks.

The current Liberal councillor, Bill Hassall was standing for re-election and on the odd occasion he and Jack had crossed paths, he was bluntly dismissive of his opponent. Jack found him to be an arrogant shit and tried to avoid him.

As he and Florence had been visiting properties in Lower Sparkgate, he had bumped into Hassall.

'You keep trying, fella. Some day – when I'm done, you and your socialists might have a chance but probably not. I'll win by a bloody big margin this time, lad. Your Labour Party will never have the support here!'

He laughingly nudged his colleague supporters as he waved a flippant hand towards Jack.

'God Florence, I'd love to beat that smug bastard. He's done absolutely bugger all since he was elected. Led by the bloody nose by his party friends. Happy to take the benefits but sit on his arse and do nowt.'

She stroked his arm and then held his face.

'He doesn't appreciate the work we've put in, Jack. The visits to the houses, the pubs and clubs. The efforts to get men to register to vote. It's all going to work in your favour. Hassall has sat back on the party label. Trust me, you will win!'

She was correct in terms of their endeavours. They had worked every house in the area seeking to gain support, to encourage registration and to sell their view of the future. They had fought against apathy and negativity at many doorsteps. They, along with Thomas, Mary and a few loyal supporters had placed their foots in doors to make people listen. They had literally worn themselves out, but had no idea whether they had done enough.

The day of the election was no less frantic. The Labour group – organised by Florence – had knocked on the door of every potential supporter. They had stopped every man at the entry to the voting station and repeated their proposition. They had done all they could.

Florence had – through whatever route – identified that there were 752 registered electors in the ward. She had also discovered that some forty of these had registered in the last few months. Whether these were supporters of Jack they did not know. At the last election, Jack had lost by over 100 votes and therefore there would need to be a substantial shift in the elector's affections to deliver any change.

178

Jack and Florence attended the election count, having deposited Emma at her brother's house for the night. As they entered the village hall, they encountered George Frankley who, as usual, was looking anxious and tense.

'I've seen the boxes come in, lad. They are all in now. Looks like a good vote altogether.'

Jack turned to his wife.

'What a bloody waste of time he is! Doesn't tell me owt!'

'Calm Jack. He can't know anything, can he?'

They stood, holding hands as they watched the count. Bill Hassall strolled around the room meeting and greeting his colleagues with a confident air.

'He looks happy, Flo. If I lose, I won't try again....'

She grabbed him hard by his shoulders and pulled him towards her.

'Jack, they're still counting. Stop being so bloody defeatist or I'll kick your arse!'

He was used to his wife expressing herself strongly by now, but her outburst shook him out of his despondent mood. She turned away from him and he watched her murmur the count numbers as she watched.

'Look at the stacks Jack. Watch the stacks...they're about the same....'

They watched as the official joined the tellers and engaged in a long and worrying discussion. He eventually strode to the podium.

'I have to advise the candidates that we are requiring a re-count so the ballot papers will be tallied once more. Thank you.'

He was clearly harassed by the situation and Jack watched as Hassall hurried to the edge of the counting group.

'He's worried Jack. It's close.'

179

Eventually the official walked to the stage holding a piece of paper recording a scribbled version of the votes tally. He coughed and shuffled uncomfortably.

'Right. We've counted the votes three times now and I can now announce the result.'

'William Hassall – Liberal Candidate 262 votes.'

'Jack Prendergast – Labour Candidate 264 votes.'

'I therefore declare that Jack Prendergast is elected to serve as the councillor for this ward'

The room fell into uproar – Hassall's supporters demanding another count, Labour associates celebrating the appointment of the first socialist councillor in the area.

Florence threw herself around his neck.

'Jack, you've done it! Now make it count, fella.'

Chapter 48

(Welfare Club, Brawmarsh, October 2010)
Jack – with the blessing of Florence – joined Thomas on the following evening for a celebratory beer. He had made it clear that, given he had to attend the Union Conference on the following day, that he would not over indulge.

Thomas was accompanied by his new workmates and following congratulations, Keith and Eddie moved to play snooker.

'So, we've a politician in the family now. You'll still talk to us, lad?'

'No Thomas. I shall expect you to bow and bloody scrape like the peasant you are.'

They clinked glasses and Jack turned his attention to the lads playing snooker.

'How's it going with these two then?

Thomas smiled and smacked hi on the shoulder.

'Bloody grand, fella. They're both good craftsmen and fine company when we're working. As long as I keep Keith well-fed he's happy! Eddie is a character. A bit of a ladies man, or so he thinks, but a good laugh.'

'And how's the lodging working?'

'It's working out very well, fella. Eddie keeps himself to himself. Joins us for meals at an evening and he's a hunter and fisherman so we do well from the stuff he brings back.'

They dropped into a quiet mode until they were interrupted by a large man approaching Jack, clearly having consumed enough beer.

'So, you're the new councillor then?'

Jack looked up and studied the intruder.

'I am. Jack Prendergast. What can I help you with…?'

The man prodded Jack in the chest and waved his hand to his face, before belching and leaning over him.

'I'm waiting for some sorting of my money, lad. I'm due some employment money but they won't give me owt.'

Thomas moved to intervene but Jack held his hand to stop his involvement.

'Listen, I was elected yesterday. I'm the only Labour councillor so I'll try and help you once I've got my feet under the table. Mebbe come see me again in a week or two's time and I'll look at your case.'

He moved back as the antagonist swayed towards him.

'Same as the other shits, you are. Get elected and then ignore us, don't ya!'

He grabbed for Jack's throat and pushed his face forward, his stinking breath erupting across the table. At that point Thomas rose from the table and dragged the fella back by his shirt collar.

'Listen, arsehole. Mr Prendergast is constrained by his position. I'm not! So, if you lay your hands on him again, I will sort your employment problems. I will drag you by the balls to the door and I'll guarantee you won't be able to work for a few weeks. I reckon you are an idle bastard who spends the family money in here. So, I'm recommending that you bugger off now and leave me and my friend to enjoy our evening. Understand?'

By now the Club had fallen into silence. Thomas pulled the man to the exit, placed his boot up his backside and ejected him onto the pavement.

'Now then Jack, were where we....'

'Appreciate your help fella but I suspect that's another vote I've lost next time around...'

Chapter 49

(Trade Union Conference, Sheffield, October 2010)
As usual, the assembly contained groups of middle aged and older men reconvening for many years. They shook hands, grasped each other firmly in gestures of long-standing friendship and settled in their seats to listen to the standard speeches and orations.

Support the growing Labour Party. Increase the membership. Fight against the oppressive employers.

The majority of the delegates had heard the speeches time and time again and, bluntly were present to meet their old friends and colleagues, to exchange gossip and vocalise their opinions about the companies they worked for and how poorly their members were treated.

Jack would be asked to speak as usual to summarise his contribution. However, this year he had decided that he would not follow the standard agenda, the party line. This year he wanted to shock the conference. He had decided to offend their expectations. To 'stir the pot' and upset the status quo of this moderate and conventional organisation. This year would be different....

He listened to the routine contributions. Nothing dramatic, nothing perceptive, nothing that could be viewed as taking the body forward. He was called as the last of the officials and watched as the delegates talked amongst themselves and examined their timepieces, pending the opportunity for the next break and the odd beer.

'Gentlemen. Thank you for your continued attention.'

He laughed inwardly as the members ignored his sarcasm.

'My speech will be extremely short today.'

Voices from the floor

Thank God. Get on with it!

He stopped to raise his hand and waited for the murmur to subdue.

'Aye, the reason I will be short is that I'm not going to deliver my report. This year I have nothing to add other than what I've said in previous years. You didn't listen last year or the year before. So, this year I'm not attempting to sell my ideas.'

Good to hear! Open the bloody bar fella.

He paused for effect and moved to the side of the podium.

'Gentlemen, this year I have invited an alternative speaker to address you.'

He waved his hand towards the stage side.

'Members, please give attention to Mrs Florence Prendergast'

Initially there was silence which soon erupted into a number of protests from the audience.

Mr Chairman..out of order!

Not a member ...shouldn't be allowed!

Several of the delegates stood, and subsequently waved their arms in protest before leaving the room. Others exchanged voices of dissent between themselves.

At that point the Chairman, Norman Braithwaite moved to the podium and waved for silence. He sought to hide his smile.

'I was unaware of the next speaker, members. As usual, Mr Prendergast has caught us on our back foot by his intervention. However, given the fact that I have attended some twenty conferences and have – in the main – been bored shitless by the mundane presentations, I am intrigued by the option of allowing a different perspective.'

He waved his finger across the auditorium.

'I have allowed this speech. If you have no mind to listen, then feel free to bugger off and demonstrate your ignorance. Mrs Prendergast. Come forward, lass and say your piece.'

184

Florence moved to the rostrum, conscious of the continuing negative mumbling amongst the delegates. Some had left the room – she suspected that it was a good excuse to retreat to the bar for a few beers.

She looked down at her notes and realised that they were sparse and not well thought through. She looked up at her audience and paused nervously. Jack moved alongside.

'Flo. From the heart love. Just speak ...'

She nodded and commenced with some uncertainty.

'The more observant of you will see that I'm a woman.'

This prompted a few ribald comments which were quickly silenced by a pointed finger from the Chairman.

'Yes, a woman. You may think I'm mad to stand before you. Some may think I should mebbe be locked up.'

She paused as some voiced their agreement. Others looked puzzled by her comment.

'If so, I would be a lunatic or a prisoner. And then I would have something in common with them because, as a woman I'm grouped with the incapable and the illegal. None of us have the right to vote.'

'I stand here representing your mothers, wives, daughters. Around one half of the numbers living in this country. The women who have borne you, fed you, clothed you, carried your children and hold your hopes for their future. Do you remember them all?'

The room fell into silence as many of the men reflected, particularly on their early lives – mothers now no longer with them.

'I know a number of you will laugh when I speak about leaving your wives...'

Many of the men shouted agreement.

Aye I'd be better off.

Best thing you've said, lass..

She paused and held their attention for a few seconds.

'If you leave your wife, she has no rights to see her children...none. She has no right to share your property.

185

She can be thrown out, despite looking after you and your children for however many years. It doesn't happen to men.'

'Here's another thought. Many working-class women have turned to prostitution to support their families. The only way they can feed and clothe their bairns. And then do you know something? Some twenty years ago they were the guilty ones. Women were forced to be examined for any signs of venereal disease and could be locked away for months...sometimes for a year.'

She laughed with cynicism in her voice.

'Haven't we moved on gentlemen? Poor women can now be prostitutes without fear!!'

She held their gaze for the conclusion of her speech.

'So, we can be 'harlots' but we still are not accepted as your equals with voting rights. We still are perceived by your unions as 'cheap labour' and not accepted as members. Someday, this country will need women's labour. Men – as always – will go to war. Who will run the industries when they go to fight?'

She threw her hand across the congregation.

'All women want is to be recognised as having the right to influence the direction of the country, with you for their families, their children and – gentlemen – for you. Please support our mission.'

The members one by one stood and applauded. As she left the stage Jack embraced his wife.

'My God Florence, you bloody well delivered your message. Wonderful girl...bloody wonderful!'

He drew her away from the lectern and led her to the side, as Norman Braithwaite moved to replace her.

'Now then, there's a pitch, gentlemen! You'll either agree or disagree. For me I completely hear what the lady has said. I will propose that our Union does two things'.

'One. we will from now on accept female members to our body.

'And two, we will vote to support and encourage the push for votes for women'

Some of the members threw abuse at the proposal and voiced their views from the rear of the auditorium.

No bloody way!

Not a chance. We are a man's group!

From the edge of the body a large and imperious presence stood and turned to them.

'I'm Geordie Johnson. I've been a long-time member of this Union and attended a lot of these meetings. I'll say my bit now and expect you to listen.

Geordie was a quiet but sensible man and well respected by his colleagues. He only spoke when he felt it appropriate. However, his physical bearing and equally substantial voice stopped the protests.

'I've been at many of these conferences and I've dropped to sleep in most of them. Here's a lady that's caused me to think and reflect. It seems to me that we've to think about what's happening in our industry.'

The meeting fell into order and now listened attentively.

'You'll all know that foreign countries – America and Germany in particular – are producing steel cheaper than we can in this country, and at increasing volume. Our employers are pushing change. They have bought machines that replace a lot of the old craft skills and we've tried to fight it. We have to accept that we'll lose this fight, gentlemen.'

There were some quietly voiced disagreements. Johnson held up his hand.

'Open your bloody eyes, for Christs sake! We had lock outs twenty years or so ago on this issue. It will happen like it or not. So, there will be more unskilled workers in our industry – and women will become increasingly employed as the work is not as heavy.'

'Seems we have a choice here as I see it. Embrace the women and other low skilled workers in our Union. If we don't then they'll be unrepresented and all our wages will fall. If we bring them in, we can have some influence. If not, we'll have bugger all of a voice.'

He paused and waved his hand around the room.

'The lady asked us to support votes for our women. Like many here, I've not agreed with giving them the vote in the past. I've changed my mind. It seems to me that if we want a Labour Government in future years, if we want to look after the poorer members of our community, we won't do it by the limited number who'll vote for us now. We need to get our working-class women on board. So, I'm supporting the proposals.'

He moved to sit and then stood again.

'Aye, one more thing. Given we're now limited on contributing to the Labour Party from members fees, there must be some funds available. Use them to push this women's vote idea until we can win back our right to contribute – comes at it from another approach, fellas? Any way that's my view'

The Chairman moved to address a subdued room.

'Look gents. I agree with Geordie and welcome his contribution. I know some of you will be reluctant to go with these propositions, so here's a compromise. We contribute to the women's movement providing half of what would have been our monies to the Labour Party. I'm proposing that Mrs Florence Prendergast is accepted as an honorary member of our Union - our first female member. '

There was no negative reaction from the audience.

'Good, gentlemen. I'm glad you agree as on that basis, I am asking her to help with the drive to attract female membership.'

He held up his hand to quieten the membership.

'To calm some of our delegates who find this uncomfortable, I'm additionally proposing that we establish a separate Women's Union Group.'

Immediately there were calls from the floor.

If you give em a full vote I'm done!

The men need to run this bloody Union!

There was a supportive protest from a small minority. Braithwaite waved to silence them.

'OK gents. I accept that, at this time, the women will have to wait for full voting rights and so they'll pay half the men's weekly dues.'

The men appeared to quieten on this suggestion, despite a few disgruntled comments.

Braithwaite continued.

'And, given Geordie's suggestion about funding, I'm asking the conference to agree to the allocation of half our withheld political funds to support a campaign to promote votes for women.'

He saw some of the members rise to protest.

'Let me finish! As Brother Johnson has said, we have the funds. They were planned for political purposes. If we get the women's vote, that's benefitting the Labour movement so I'm happy to allocate that. Again – in conjunction with our Treasurer- I'm asking Mrs Prendergast to assist in this exercise.'

Florence stood at the side of the stage and turned to her husband in disbelief.

'Jack, I only wanted their support. I'm being asked to take on responsibilities I never planned to assume?'

'Aye lass. But it'll keep you occupied and out of trouble for a spell...'

She watched in apprehension as the Conference by a majority agreed to the propositions.

Chapter 50

(Thomas and Mary's house, November 2010)
'She's so off-colour, Thomas. Hot and not eating well. I'm worried ...really worried.'

Peggy was laid in her small bed, her nose runny and continually coughing. She was clearly running a high temperature. Mary mopped her face and body in cold cloths in seeking to cool her.

'She's no go in her either. She was fine on Wednesday when I took her to the park. She and her friend Lindy Spencer were running around and playing fine.'

Thomas stroked his daughters sweating brow.

'Look Mary, it'll be a bit of a child's illness. A touch of a cold. They catch everything when they mix. Let's see how she goes on eh?'

Mary nodded without conviction.

'How's our William.'

He moved over to his son's cot.

'He seems fine, Mary.'

She smiled and nodded.

'I'll sit with her a while, Thomas. You get off to bed.'

Thomas yawned and moved towards their bedroom.

'She'll be alright lass. Give me a shout if you need me for owt.'

With that, he kissed his daughter and wandered to his bed.

***

When he awoke on the next morning his wife was not at his side. He washed quickly before knocking to wake Eddie for their work and then looked into the children's bedroom. Mary stirred and immediately placed her hand on her daughter's brow.

'She's still very hot, Thomas'

He sat alongside them and embraced them both.

'Look, if she's no better later we should ask the doctor to call. Do you want me to drop by his house on the way to work?'

She nodded.

'I don't want to bother him if it's just a cold, but if he could pop by just to check her that would give me some comfort.'

'Mebbe I'll move William's cot to our room. Do you want me to feed him before I go?'

She again nodded quietly and Thomas picked up his son's small bed and carried it to their bedroom.

After he and Eddie had left for work, Mary left her daughter to attend to their baby. She could hear Peggy snuffling and coughing and prepared more cold cloths to seek to cool her.

The doctor arrived within the hour.

'I had a call along the road so thought it convenient to call, Mrs Davies. Let me see the child.'

He carried out a brief examination and then stood back with a frown.

'Has Peggy had contact with other people? And yourself and your husband?'

'Myself and Peggy have only had contact with our baby William and we met with Jenny Spencer and her little girl in the park a couple of days ago. What's the matter with Peggy? Is it just a cold?'

The doctor continued.

'And your husband?'

'Well, with our lodger Eddie and his other workmates. I don't know who they'd be.'

She looked at him worriedly.

'She's going to be alright though, isn't she?'

He placed his hand gently on her shoulder.

'I hope I'm wrong Mrs Davies, but it may be that Peggy has the early symptoms of measles. I will need to check all the people you've had contact with as soon as possible.'

'Measles…but that's serious doctor isn't it? Oh God will she be alright….?'

He pursed his lips and considered his response carefully. This was the third child he had seen in the last two days with similar issues. If this was measles, and an epidemic in the town, then the consequences were dire.

'Measles is a very serious illness, Mrs Davies. If she has the disease, Peggy will become very ill. The next signs will be spots in her mouth and a body rash. All I can ask you to do is to keep her cool and try and get her to feed as much as possible. I'll need to check the baby.'

He left Mary alone as she brought her child to her arms in tears.

'Oh live, darling. Fight it for me Peggy.'

Chapter 51

(Brawmarsh Council Meeting, November 2010)
Jack decided that he should approach the meeting confidently and not allow the established members to deflect or browbeat him. Easier said than done. He was the only Labour member elected.

He entered the ornately decorated Council chamber and found the rest of the councillors already present and gathered in their respective political groups.

The longstanding members of the majority Liberal group had been comfortably re-elected and many deliberately ignored him, he having displaced their colleague.

The small Tory group evidently dismissed him as a temporary intruder into the cosy environment. He found himself placed in a seat at the very end of the large ornate table and clearly expected to remain a secondary consideration at the session. There was no agenda placed before him.

The Chairman, Arnold Hill, opened the meeting and quickly rattled through the formalities of acceptance of the previous minutes. He welcomed the appointed Council members and, clearly, with a gesture of dismissal, commented that the meeting was joined by 'comrade' Prendergast, causing a tirade of laughs and series of dismissive waves of their hands by the attendees.

As he moved on to the first agenda item, Jack stood and placed his hands firmly on the oak table.

'Good evening gentlemen…and I use the term loosely, for none of you have the manners to welcome and accept a new member who has upset your little party.'

Hill stood and banged his hand to the table.

'We have a protocol here, Prendergast. You ask the Chairman before you speak. Do you understand?'

Jack moved around the table and stood above Hill. He glanced around the members, who sat astonished by his breach of the formalities.

'Now listen to me. I may be one member of my party. I may be – in your view – an inappropriate choice as a councillor. However, the majority of the electorate in my ward believe I am the right person to represent them. I intend to do that to the best of my capability. I will therefore expect you to treat me with respect – you've clearly failed to do so today. In future, my name is either Jack or Mr Prendergast. That's to all of you, including the Chairman.

He paused as the councillors expressed their quiet hostility to his comments.

'So, for absolute clarity, I will ignore your bloody protocols. I will speak when I have a point to make. I will represent my constituents. I am not part of your cosy bloody arrangements and cordial co-operation. I don't care a toss whether you accept this or not. Now Mr Chairman. Do you understand...!'

He resumed his seat and smiled broadly to the assembly.

'Please feel free to continue.... Arnold..'

***

He returned home at ten o'clock, pleased with his attitude towards his opponents.

Florence met him at the door visibly in a stressed state and pulled him towards her.

'Jack, I've has a message from your sister. Peggy is very, very unwell. They think she has measles. It's suspected that the town has an epidemic coming.'

He pulled her close and pushed his head to her.

'My God Florence that's terrible news, lass. What have they said?'

'The doctor has told her that there's no treatment. She just has to sit and wait. Oh Jack, the poor lass. The poor bairn...'

Jack turned to the door.

194

'Husband, what are you doing?'

'I'll go see if I can help, Florence.'

She pulled him back and grabbed his arm.

'No, Jack. We could catch the disease if you have any contact. Worse still, Emma could pick it up. There is no way I will allow you to go to their home. If you go, I will lock you out of our home. You have to stay clear.'

He slumped into his chair and threw his hands to his face.

'Bloody helpless, Florence. I've always been there for my sister and Thomas.'

She moved across and held him.

'Well, this time, Jack Prendergast all you can do is hope. I'd ask you to pray but there's no chance of that.'

He gazed up at her.

'Do you know Florence, if it made a difference, I'd pray lass…I'd drop to my bloody knees and pray.'

Chapter 52

They had been restricted to contacting Mary and Thomas by scribbled notes, none of which provided much information. Jack had visited their home, knocking on the window and seeking to understand more of their condition from Thomas at a distance.

'Have you picked up any more, Jack? How is Peggy? And little William?'

Jack shook his head and turned away from her, struggling to hold back his emotions.

'Florence, all of them have the disease. Thomas and Mary seem to be least affected, although they are unwell. William seems to have the rash, but his temperature has calmed from what they've said. Eddie had no real contact with them but he's moved to his cousin's for a while'

'And Peggy, Jack?'

He turned to face her.

'She is worse, lass. Her fever is still very high. From Thomas' brief comment, she is very ill. She has the rash across her body and her breathing has worsened. She's taking very little food. The doctor has visited regularly but can do nothing.'

'But she'll be fine, Jack?'

He did not know how to answer her question. Whilst walking through the town, he had learned that the Spencer girl had died overnight. He chose not to tell Florence.

As she turned away in tears, Jack left her for a while and then sought to distract her by any other means available.

'Have you thought about how you might push women's membership in our union, Flo?

She remained anxious, but eventually gathered her thoughts.

'You have really put me on the spot! How can I, as a woman supporting votes for my sex, sell membership to women members who will not have a vote in the union proceedings? Bluntly I'm trying to sell something I don't believe in, Jack'

'But you volunteered to do this, Florence. Why didn't you object at the time...?'

She interrupted him and fell into her full flow.

'Because, husband I listened to your members and had very little say! They barely voted for women members. There was a substantial minority who still do not support women's franchise. They are supposed to be the socialists – supporting 'all are equal'. I can stand before you now and laugh, man. So, explain to me why I, as a woman member, would pay fees and have no say, no vote in your bloody organisation. Tell me?'

She turned away from him.

'How is this important when my little niece is so ill. Frankly, Jack your bloody priorities – as usual – are wrong. I don't give a shit about anything other than that little girl. Do you not appreciate that?'

She threw her hands high in the air and stormed to their bedroom.

***

It was the following day that they found out that Peggy had died.

A beating on their door at ten o'clock that morning. Thomas on his knees at the step.

'We've lost her. My lovely lass...we've lost her.'

He and Florence gathered him from their doorstep and brought him into their home.

Thomas was uncontrollable, striking his own face and wailing hysterically. They collected him to their arms and did all they could do to show him their love and that they shared his loss.

He broke away and cursing furiously, pointed at Jack.

197

'My lovely girl is dead. It's your bloody sister has caused this. Mixing with that other child. That's why my little Peggy has gone!'

Jack moved to seek to hold and console him, but was pushed away.

'No fella. Your Mary has killed my daughter by her actions. Bitch! I'm done with her!'

He turned and, still sobbing threw open the door and left the house.

'Go after him, Jack.'

'No, lass. Let him calm. I'll talk to him later.'

Chapter 53

(Brawmarsh, January 1911)

It had been a terrible winter. Heavy snow and cold frosts had created a desolate and miserable mood across the town. The measles epidemic had now dispelled, but in its trail had left seven households grieving the loss of a child. Two women and one elderly man had also been victims.

To add to the melancholy, the steel works had suffered reduced orders due to cheaper imports from the United States and parts of Europe. As a consequence, some thirty had lost their jobs – predominantly craftsmen replaced by unskilled labourers, as the business turned to increased automation of their processes.

Inevitably the resulting poverty amongst the population had led to near starvation, violence to the women as the men, frustrated by their perceived impotence, took their anger where they could. Their drinking increased, falling into debt with the local landlords, as they chalked up a 'tab'. This vicious circle resulted in the further lack of income and further abuse and deprivation.

Jack faced a series of pressures. His full-time employment, election to the Council, attendance at the Labour group meetings and trade union meetings. He had a full diary over the next few months and, bluntly his frustration with all these groups was growing.

And then, the not minimal impacts on his family life….

Florence had been an angel. She had supported Mary through her bereavement and sought to deal with the aftermath of Thomas' rejection of his wife.

Inevitably Peggy's funeral had been traumatic – she had been required to stop Mary throwing herself into the grave. Thomas, clearly – even at the late morning had taken a drink - and stood away from the family group as he wept.

199

Jack had searched the local hostelries to speak to him but was unable to find him . It appeared he was walking to other villages to drink. Whilst still staying in the house he – as he understood from Florence – was sleeping in the downstairs, and only speaking to his wife brusquely when needed. They had no idea where he was taking his meals but clearly – according to Mary – he was not eating well and had lost much of his weight.

Worse still, his work commitment was suffering badly. Both Keith and Eddie had continued to work with him, but the latter, having now moved back to the lodgings at their home, had confided to Mary that he was contributing little and leaving the job at early afternoon on most days. The contractor for the building work had attended the site and commented with irritation at his absence and the consequent delay in completion.

Jack was now, this evening, attending another Council meeting. Not much had changed in the attitude of the other members, other than they had ceased from any direct negative remarks towards him. He had no doubt that these continued out of his hearing but had decided to ignore them.

He listened to the usual routine – at least he now had been given an agenda to scribble on as his frustration grew.

'And how will we deal with the unemployed in our community'

The members looked at him with bewilderment.

Chairman Hill looked at him with disdain.

'Once again our socialist member disturbs the meeting. We, 'Mr Prendergast', have already set in place support for the people who are disinclined to find work.'

Jack rose and glared at the man.

'Disinclined! It's your bloody supporters who have decided to dismiss these men.'

Hill sought to wave him away.

'Because they are too expensive to employ. The employers are a business...they need to find economies when our trade is suffering. We have offered assistance through various routes'

Jack bridled and remained on his feet.

'That'll be the workhouses for those thrown out of their properties, will it? Your 'Friendly Societies' seeking to draw men away from contributing to the compensation option. You look at me as if I don't realise your motives. Oh! join our friendly society groups – stop paying to the schemes under the Compensation Act. Stop paying to your trade unions. We will look after you. Your bloody schemes stop members claiming for any injuries or illness. You get them to opt out of their legal rights! You make me bloody sick!'

He screwed up the agenda and threw it across the table as he left the meeting.

Chapter 54

(Thomas and Mary's house, Brawmarsh, January 1911)
Still no sign of Thomas. Another day and another night without his company, his embrace, his support.

Every night she had cooked for him but to no avail. She had turned to her bed every evening and listened as he stumbled in to the house late in the night.

She had poured her heart out to Florence.

'I still have my little William, but my God I feel the loss of my little girl. She was just coming to her life. Just growing...just growing up...'

Florence was lost for words but sought to help her as best she could. There would never be anything she could say to ease her pain.

'And Thomas? Where is he?'

'Drinking, Florence. Doing little work and grieving. He's lost his mind, sister. I can't speak to him. He still holds me responsible .... I didn't know...how could I?'

After holding and seeking to comfort her, Florence left despairing of what else she could do. She determined to speak again to Jack to go out and find her brother, and attempt to bring some sense to his mind.

Mary laid back on her bed. She had brought William's cot into the room in the last few weeks to both keep any eye on him and to give her some close comfort.

She heard the house door open and close. She sat up. It was still early and perhaps Thomas had come back to talk to her and present some hope of re-building their relationship.

She listened to the footfall on the stairs. A voice called to her.

'Are you OK, Mary?'

It was Eddie, not Thomas. She broke into sobs as she struggled to hide her disappointment.

'I'm alright Eddie...I'll be OK thanks.'

He pushed open the door and looked at her shaking his head.

'You're far from alright lass.'

He sat with her on the edge of the bed and wiped her tears with his hand.

'I feel so alone, Eddie.....'

He drew her into his arms and pulled her to his chest. Mary, initially seeking to resist, eventually was drawn into his embrace.

She watched as he removed his shirt and then lifted the hem of her nightdress drawing the garment over her hips and then gently beyond her breasts, casting it to one side. She sought to cover her nakedness with her hands but did not resist as Eddie pulled them away and pushed her back to the bed. She watched him remove the rest of his clothing and offered little struggle as he laid upon her body.

Chapter 55

Late January. Yet another meeting. The local Labour Group.

After his exit from the council meeting, Florence had cautioned Jack that he needed to control his temper. He was conscious of her comments and maintained his humour throughout the meeting. This was assisted by the absence of Harry Harris who, in fairness to his earlier commitment, had resigned. Two new and younger members had been elected to the body.

Willy Arthur was a man in his early thirties, a local miner who appeared to contribute in a measured manner. He supported the odd comment Jack had raised and appeared to be a potential ally with a similar attitude towards his politics.

The second man, Joe Malton, was a different type. He had said very little during the session. Jack took time to occasionally watch his behaviour, and had a feeling of unease about him. Nothing he could put his finger on....

As the meeting closed, Cliff Roberts pulled him to one side.

'Jack, we need a quiet word. I understand you stormed out of a council meeting the other day.'

'That's true Chairman I did.'

'Listen fella, I know we've had our disagreements in the past, but your behaviour doesn't help our cause. One, we need to have you there for the full meeting to challenge anything we can't support. And second, your conduct impacts on the reputation of the overall party. What the voters hear about is a man who can't control his temper. Your hot-bloodedness may be acceptable in our sessions, but not in public meetings. You – and as a consequence our movement – will be seen as incapable of conducting ourselves in a rational manner. Our appeal to the community will be affected. Do you grasp that?'

Jack raised his hand in submission.

'Aye Cliff. I understand your comment. It's bloody frustrating being one against the rest, but I've been told similar by my wife, Florence. I'll calm in future - as best I'm able!'

Cliff grasped him by his shoulder.

'You have so much capability but you need to stop being the angry young man now, Jack. We want more councillors for the Labour Party. Your performance will determine whether that happens over the next year or so.'

He raised his hand and they shook as Jack nodded his acceptance of the comments.

Chapter 56

(Brawmarsh and District, February 1911)

'Florence, I have so many demands on my time, lass. You want me to search for your bloody idiot brother through the local pubs and clubs. I did that many years ago. What makes you think I can sort him out this time?'

She took him by the hand and looked deeply in his eyes.

'Because it's now become more important than ever.'

He studied her for a moment curiously.

'He's a bloody drunk, Florence. He's walked away from his wife and child. He's in danger of losing his business. His employees are sick of the need to cover his arse with the contractors. Mebbe it's time to give up on him. Take care of my sister, and let him live his sad life as he will.'

She held his face and spoke quietly.

'Because Jack, we have a very sensitive situation. He and Mary are still grieving over Peggy and....'

He waved her away.

'And they will be forever. Why is it so important that I chase him down?'

She pulled him close again.

'Because, Jack Prendergast, we are about to have another child...'

He looked at her stunned by her announcement and spun her around.

'Gentle, you silly bugger! I'm due in July if my numbers are right. Sadly, that is around the date that their Peggy would have celebrated her 5th birthday. God knows how Mary will react. She needs Thomas back with her. Go and find him, fella ..please?'

As Jack collected his coat, she sat back with apprehension. He must never know of the secret which Mary had tearfully disclosed to her some days earlier.

The conversation had been stilted and difficult.

Mary had been clearly upset and subdued before she broke down and revealed the truth of her infidelity.

'Florence I'm so ashamed, but I was lonely and needed some comfort. I've betrayed your brother. I'm sorry.'

Florence studied her and then gathered her to her arms.

'My brother let you down, lass. You were bloody stupid and he took advantage of your situation. I have two questions. Is this the only time you have succumbed? Second, did you have any protection, girl?'

Mary turned away from her.

'He had me once more, sister. And no. I didn't have protection.'

***

He left the house with a mixture of elation and trepidation. He had no clue where he would find his brother-in-law nor what he could do to encourage his return to the family. His starting point was the public houses in the rough area of Sparkgate.

His search was proving aimless. Those who knew him had no idea where he would be. Those who knew where he would be declined to give any information. He eventually arrived at the Dog and Duck – the lowest pub in the area. He reluctantly entered and scanned around the bar. Thomas sat in a dark corner.

'So, you've come to this, have you? The roughest shithole in the town. No doubt they love your custom.'

Thomas, having indulged for the majority of the day, looked at him through glazed eyes.

'Oh, it's you is it? The brother of my bitch wife. The woman who killed my child. The bloody cow … '

Jack could stand no more. He stepped towards Thomas and threw a punch to his face knocking him to the floor. He dropped on to his chest and clutched his throat.

'Now you'll listen to me, Thomas Davies and then you'll either go back to your wife or piss off out of her home and her life! You are a sad excuse of a man. Your wife sits at home with your child looking for your support since you lost your girl. To be honest, I don't give a shit whether you go home or leave.'

He tightened his hand around the man's throat.

'But – and you'll listen to me well – my sister is a good woman. I will not allow you to wander around this town abusing her name! I'll kick your arse out of the area if you do that again. Understand Thomas?'

He threw him to the floor as the publican dashed across threatening the police.

'Landlord, feel free to fetch the law. I'm done with this bastard...'

Chapter 57

(Welfare Club, Brawmarsh , February 1911)
It was some days later when Jack, sitting alone in a corner next encountered his brother-in-law.

Thomas approached him unexpectedly and reached out his hand.

'Jack, I've been an arsehole. I want to try and start again with Mary, but I don't know how to approach her after all I've done?'

Jack was unprepared to address this sudden intrusion and waited for a while before replying.

'Thomas, you are wasting your time talking to me. You need to speak to your wife and soon. I am prepared to forgive anything if you and Mary can resolve your issues. But I won't forget, lad. I might forgive you anything if she will...but I won't forget. You've made her life a bloody misery for months. If you're serious, don't sit here with me. Go home and sort out your issues.'

He reached out and took Thomas beer and poured it to the floor.

'Now piss off and go home! Tell her that you've understood. Tell her that you are still her man. Now go and we'll talk when I believe you've become a better man'

He turned back to his pint and – with a wave of his hand – dismissed him.

He sat back and sought to calm himself.

Were the demands on his life becoming too much now? What could he give up, given his second child was on the way?

Deep in thought, he did not hear the man approach and was slapped gently around his head. He looked up quickly and raised his hands to defend any attack.

'Aw, put your hands down you silly English bastard. I'd have torn your feckin head off by now!'

'Seamus, where the bloody hell have you come from!'

The Irishman burst into laughter as he joined Jack at the table.

'Well, short story fella. Teresa's old fella hasn't been well and she's nagged me to death to come over and see him. If it'd been her mother I'd still be in Ireland – stuck up bloody bitch she is…'

'Are you here for a while?'

'Open ended, lad. Done well for meself over the last year. I've set up a building business back home and had more work than I can handle. I've four fellas working for me so I've left them to keep things ticking over. No panic. And how's things with yerself and the lovely Florence. You'll have a child now?'

They spent some half hour updating each other on family and other general issues. Seamus and Teresa had another child.

'Aye lad, born twelve months after the first. A grand little girl named Caitlin – after my mother. Doing well.'

Jack divulged that he and Florence were now expecting another child to congratulations and another beer.

'And how's Thomas and your sister?'

Seamus noted the hesitation in Jack's reply.

'And what's the silly bastard been up to now?'

Jack, reluctantly told Seamus the story, feeling comfortable that he would hold this in his confidence.

'Well, my sympathies. I hope they sort themselves, lad. Your Mary should kick his arse out if he can't behave.'

Jack sought to change the subject.

'And how are things back in Ireland, Seamus.'

He pursed his lips and shook his head before responding.

'Not good, lad and getting worse. Your bloody Government have made promises on our independence but the bloody aristocracy in your Lords are the obstacle. Even

210

then, the proposition for my country is not going to be accepted. The English to decide our foreign policy, our customs duties. Not the independence we're looking for. It'll end up in tears fella, trust me.'

He took a long draw on his beer before continuing.

'I'm classed as a moderate but I'm getting bloody frustrated so you can imagine how the extremists are reacting. There's private armies being formed – both Ulster and the south. I can tell you privately that there's some foreign interference as well. Monies and arms coming to the cause from abroad – mainly the Germans. They're after stirring the pot lad, so I can see some serious problems on the horizon.'

'You think they'll be a war, Seamus?'

'I wouldn't bet against it Jack. The Kaiser has his mind set on expanding his empire in my view. He's already interfering in the Balkans as you'll have heard.'

Jack nodded. He was acquainted through the national newspapers with the manipulations of Germany.

'But you'll find if there's no war in Europe, Jack you'll see one in Ireland.'

'And your family – will they get involved?'

Seamus smiled thinly.

'They already are, lad. As you'd expect, Michael is in at the deep end. He's joined the Republican force. Still as crazy as hell. More concerning, he's drawn his younger brother into the group. Ronan is only seventeen, but he's committed. A real concern for my sister, fella. It will get violent unless your Government sorts it soonest.'

He took a further draw on his beer.

'Trust me, Jack. There's trouble coming!'

***

Thomas had followed Jack's advice and returned to his home. He entered the house quietly and slowly moved to their bedroom.

As he pushed open the door, he gazed at his sleeping wife and child.

'Mary.'

'She awoke with a start.

'Mary. I'm so sorry lass. I've been an idiot, a fool. Can you forgive me? I want us to start again…'

She did not speak but drew him to her arms and pulled him to the bed.

Chapter 58

(Jack and Florence's house, Brawmarsh, April 1911)
Your sister and Thomas seem to be fine, Jack.'

He nodded and continued to read his newspaper.

'Are you listening at all?'

He folded the paper, clearly not being allowed to ignore her comments.

'Good Florence. I'm pleased they are back together but if you want me to be happy about it, I'm not! Your brother is a bloody waste of time. I've already told him how I feel.'

She moved across and threw his newspaper to one side.

'Look, you and I need to accept him again for Christ's sake'

She hesitated before speaking again

'There's another problem, Jack...'.

He looked up and studied the worry on her face.

'Another bloody problem! Florence, I can't deal with many more of these with this couple. What now?'

'She's pregnant. Mary is expecting.'

He looked at her totally perplexed.

'Well, that's a surprise lass. Show's they're getting on. Why is it a problem?'

Florence paused. Should she reveal Mary's infidelity to him? He had returned to his newspaper. She decided this would be one secret she needed to withhold from her husband...

'Well, I just thought it was a bit soon after all their issues, that's all...'

He looked up and shook his head.

'They'll be fine. Means you and Mary will be pregnant together...keep an eye on each other, can't you?'

She decided that silence would serve her best.

Chapter 59

Meetings, Brawmarsh and Rotherham, April 1911)

Jack had mixed experiences through the next week.

He had met briefly with Mary and Thomas, and the atmosphere between he and his brother-in-law remained tense. Thomas was clearly thrilled by the impending addition to the family. Mary, whilst appearing to be pleased, when congratulated, was more subdued than he had expected. He assumed that this was tempered by the loss of their daughter and possibly, the swiftness of her pregnancy following the recent issues with her husband.

He took her to one side.

'Are you alright, sister? I don't see any great excitement about your news?'

She responded quietly.

'I'm fine, Jack. Just unexpected and so soon after losing Peggy.'

He studied her for a moment.

'And all well with you two now?'

She replied all too quickly and irritably to Jack's mind.

'Look, we're fine. Just leave the issue please…'

She turned abruptly and walked to her scullery, appearing to wipe her eyes.

Jack moved to follow her but was intercepted by Florence.

'An emotional time, husband. Let me deal with her later. She just needs a bit of care, that's all.'

He shrugged and lifted his hands in submission.

***

He faced two meetings within the next few days. A Labour Group meeting and a session with the Executive of the Union. He walked to the former, considering a range of issues he wished to raise.

He was surprised when, shortly after the commencement, the new member, Willy Arthur stood to speak.

'Mr Chairman, I want to register my concern over a few issues. First, the continuing poor performance of our Party at the December General Election. Two members only from this area – both Sheffield. No success for our candidate.'

'Second, the failure of our Party to respond to the increasing problems for the poor in our town. Wages are falling, prices are increasing and we have done little to seek to push for remedies or to support these families. What are our proposals to address these problems?'

Jack sat back with a bemused smile. The man had voiced the two key issues and, for a change, he was not the one raising them.

Chairman Roberts blustered a response.

'What can we do lad? We have provided funds to the election. We have limited money to help the poor. We can only keep driving our Labour message.'

Jack stood to speak.

'I commend Willy for raising these points. The Liberals remain in power both locally and nationally. They are still the choice of the voters in our region.'

Roberts angrily interrupted his comment.

'Bloody easy to demand action! So, what do you suggest we do differently then?'

'We take a more militant approach, Chairman. We strengthen our socialist message. We push our national Party to cease their support of this Liberal Government. And if you are not prepared to change our approach, perhaps it's time for a change in our local leadership!'

'Well, perhaps you Prendergast, should push your bloody Union to do more. If there's a better option than me then vote!'

The other newer member, Malton raised his hand to speak.

'I've remained fairly quiet so far, just observing the manner in which the meeting operates. Seems to me that our message is simply not getting through to our potential voters. Maybe a mass meeting would help. Invite the local people. State our case. Maybe provide a bit of food to tempt them. Listen to what they want and have to say. Build our policies and approach around that?'

Jack sat back nodding his agreement. This man appeared to speak some sense.

The Chairman saw the opportunity to remove some tension.

'Let's get ourselves a beer and carry on after that.'

During the adjournment, Jack took the opportunity to speak to Arthur and Malton in one corner of the room.

'We've not had a lot to do with each other, but your comments suggest we have similar views?'

Malton spoke first.

'Both Willy and I are miners on the Rotherham estate. I've never got meself involved in politics before, but things have changed since the old fella passed away. He was pretty good in his treatment of his workers, but signs are it's changing. His son, George is an arrogant shit. Treats us like bloody servants. Word has it he's after reducing our wages and increasing our rents. We're after some support from this party, if and when – and it's more likely when – it happens.'

'Have you a Union, Joe?'

'No fella. Been some discussion but Harcourt has already let us know that anyone joining or encouraging will be sacked. That would cost both our jobs and our homes, so you'll understand the reluctance amongst the lads.'

Jack smiled to himself before replying.

'I know George Harcourt. I've had my own personal run-ins with him. Nasty piece of work. I think you need some support from other trade unions. Leave it with me.

216

Anyway, let's talk about the idea for a mass meeting. Seems a good idea to me.'

The rest of the meeting was more amenable and concluded with an agreement that Jack and the two new members should be asked to organise the local assembly in the next month.

***

Florence took the opportunity to visit Mary whilst Jack was otherwise occupied at his evening meeting.

'How are you, sister?'

Mary hung her head and clearly upset, did not reply at first. Florence took her in her arms.

'Lass, you've just got to get on with it!'

Mary looked up and shook her head.

'Oh Florence. I'm just so confused. Thomas is being far more kind and considerate now and, knowing what I've done I'm so mixed up. I could be expecting another man's child. How can I deal with that? I wish the baby would just die Florence. I wish I could just die!'

'Bloody stupid lass! Now listen to me. The child has committed no sin. I understand that you're upset but you have to accept the consequences of your actions. I'm being harsh I know.'

She stopped and stepped away.

'Let me be practical with you now. Eddie is tall and dark. Thomas is tall and dark. You have to hope my brother is the father, but to be frank if he isn't no one would know, would they? The only people who have any knowledge are you, Eddie and me.'

She looked up tearfully and nodded.

'But will Eddie remain quiet, Florence?'

Florence thought for a moment.

'Where's my brother tonight?'

'He said he has to meet with the contractor after five o'clock.'

217

'Right, lass. So Eddie will be back earlier. I'll speak to him tonight when he's back from work.'

Mary shook her head.

'Oh Florence, be careful. I don't want any upset...'

'Go upstairs when he comes in. I'll talk with him and make sure he understands.'

They sat over a cup of tea for the next half hour before hearing the back door open. Florence pointed and Mary disappeared upstairs.

'Evening Florence. Are you well?'

She stood hands on hips.

'No Eddie I'm not well. And neither is my sister-in-law. We need to have a conversation.'

He shrugged his shoulders and wandered past her to the scullery taking a drink of water directly from the tap.

'A conversation about what?'

'About the fact that you have taken advantage of my sister and she's now pregnant, mister.'

He smirked and waved her away.

'So, she says. Nothing to do with me if she's expecting. Her husband's back home and sleeping with her.'

Confronted by his smug and dismissive attitude, Florence sought to control her temper.

'Are you denying any relationship with Mary?'

He moved to walk past her. Florence pushed him back.

'Look, woman if she threw herself at me when she was in need of some company, what's it to do with you?'

'She didn't throw herself at you, man. She was vulnerable and you saw an opportunity!'

He laughed in her face and pushed her aside.

'And what about it, lass? Simple to me. She offered me sex and I took it. That's my story.'

'And if her husband found out. If Jack found out...'

He waved her away.

'I'd deny it. And if you really want to make an issue here's what I can do, Mrs Prendergast. I'll write a little note to Thomas and bugger off back to Sheffield. That'd mess up their marriage and her reputation. It would also damage your husband's standing as a councillor, what with his sister being a wanton slut!'

Florence could contain herself no longer. She lunged at him with an open hand but he caught her arm and grasped her by the throat, pushing her against the wall.

'I'm staying here as long as I wish, lady. I believe you and Mrs Davies will say nowt. And if she needs any help in the future I'll do my best.... she's hardly in a position to say much, now is she?'

He pushed her to the chair and leant over her.

'And if you need a man, Florence just let me know...!

He turned and left her red-faced and gasping for breath.

Chapter 60

(Trade Union Meeting, Sheffield, April 1911)
Braithwaite, at the head of the table, opened the session with the usual self-congratulatory comments.

'Gentlemen, our membership is increasing. We are demonstrating our commitment to the membership by our involvement in the new National Insurance legislation proposals. This will allow our members to benefit from sickness and unemployment benefit in the very near future. Under these regulations, we will be forming an 'Approved Society' whereby we will take responsibility for the provision of these benefits. We are delivering a better future for our people...'

Jack tried to restrain himself. *Behave lad – remember you need to remain calm...*

He sat and listened for a further five minutes before raising his hand.

'I'm sorry, Mr Chairman but once again I have to challenge your view.'

Norman Braithwaite sighed and sat looking at Jack with a jaundiced eye.

'Every bloody meeting, Jack Prendergast. What's your point?'

I've a few Norman...quite a few...'

'The Liberal Government is proposing that low paid employees...the majority of our members pay fourpence per week for the benefits. The employers pay three pence...the state pay two pence. How is that a fair policy? So, the poor pay more than the bloody rich...again! In a fair world, the people who have money should pay more in taxes to cover this. We have tried to get our members to pay for this cover and the majority have declined. Now they are compelled to pay. Without our protection'

He drew a breath and continued.

'This is a Poll Tax on the Poor. Look at the benefits, shall we? Unemployment benefit of seven shillings – about a third of their normal earnings. No help for their dependants regardless of number. And selective...and limited to only fifteen weeks. What after that? Back to the poor house mentality. And the 'Approved Societies'. Bloody sickening! Tax collectors for the Government. And employers offering this option and taking a profit for their running of these! Our members are being led astray by this false option. We should resist it, not participate in this fake proposition'

One of the number faked a yawn.

'Bloody hell Jack, crack on a bit lad for God's sake!'

He laughed and held up his hand.

'Just one more thing and then I'll shut up. Well, mebbe a couple.'

He slapped his hand on the table to obtain one last moment of attention.

'We need to think again about recruiting women members. My wife, Florence has done all she can, but as a supporter of women's votes she – and in my view correctly – has said she can do no more unless we allow the female members to have a vote in our Union. Increase their contributions if you must or give them some say. Otherwise, we will lose a large contribution to not only our funds, but our future passion and expertise. We men, are not always as smart as we think – so my wife tells me! Finally...'

A few of the attendees applauded and laughed

'Alright, finally. We – as a Union - have to prepare for future hard decisions on our relationships with the worst of the employers. We also need to be prepared to stand alongside our fellow workers to gain union recognition and support their fight. I'm looking for a commitment to support our friends.'

He sat and returned to his papers.

Braithwaite blew out his cheeks and looked to the room.

'Listen lad, I'll support your point on women members. We need to mebbe give them half a vote for half contributions. Anymore and I'll be hung up by our men members. I agree with you on the need for the rich to pay more for sickness and unemployment and I suggest we adopt this as a future aim. But I still think we need to run an 'Approved Society. If we don't the employers will and our members will not be served best by that.'

He stopped and wagged his finger at the group.

'On the issue of recognition and support for others – well that's for our members to decide, but I caution that if we go down that route, we have to be prepared for the sacrifices that will involve. I leave you to muse on that.'

The meeting voted with the Chairman on his main points.

At least he could take something home to Florence…

Chapter 61

(Brawmarsh , May 1911)

Florence glanced across at her husband. He looked worn and tired. She had decided that she could not burden Jack with the confrontation with Eddie, but had no idea how she and Mary could address this.

Eddie had remained in residence at the house and, according to her sister-in-law, continued to show no remorse or regret for his past behaviour. To the contrary, he appeared to be taking great pleasure in making vindictive remarks when Thomas was not present, and had taken to stroking her stomach occasionally, laughing at her discomfort.

She took some comfort in the fact that – with Seamus' temporary return – Jack had a social outlet. The Irishman had found some short-term accommodation in the town for he and Teresa and, consequently, had become a regular attendee again at the Welfare Club. He and his wife had also visited the house and lifted her spirits with their humour and good nature.

'Will you be having a drink with Seamus this evening, Jack. I think he's good company for you. Takes your mind away from your work.'

Jack broke away from his paperwork and laughed.

'You're a grand woman, Florence. How many men are encouraged to take a beer by their wives? To be honest, I thought we might invite them over for a bit of food on Saturday. I could get a few beers?'

'I'd like that, Jack. Get Emma to bed and we can sit and have a bit of a laugh. Go have a drink tonight and see if that suits?'

He nodded and returned to his documents.

***

Jack and Seamus were joined by his two Labour group colleagues at the Club at Jack's invitation. They were good company and quickly bonded with Seamus.

The conversation turned to the issues around the Rotherham Manor mines and community.

Willy pursed his lips and frowned.

'Not good at the moment. Harcourt has advised his workforce that he can't continue to pay the current level of wages and he's already had his manager visiting some of our workmates at their homes. He's also after putting up our rents. Claims he needs to carry out work and we'll have to contribute.'

'And are the houses needing the work or not?'

Joe added his view.

'They're like all property, Jack. They need a bit of updating, but the increase in rents and him suggesting over a pound a week reduction in our wages will make life very difficult for all of us. We are on the edge of poverty already.'

Willy continued.

'We're not left with much choice to be honest. We could move to other areas for our work but to move our families and then have to find housing would be hard. A lot of other mine owners are looking to cut jobs and costs and they don't have accommodation for their employees.'

Jack nodded his understanding.

'It's similar across a lot of businesses these days. Jobs are being cut in the Steel industry – at least the high earning ones. More low skilled tasks and paying less money. Our union tries to influence, but the workers are frightened of losing any jobs they have.'

'As we've told you before Jack, if we tried to bring in a union Harcourt would sack the one's joining....'

'But if you stuck together, fellas? Harcourt needs the income from his coal. You've some strength there?'

'He'd bring in blackleg labour from outside the area. Evict our families and put them in our homes.'

Jack mused over the issue whilst Seamus brought another round.

'If he couldn't get the coals out, the carts and trains in, the replacement labour in, that would soon impact wouldn't it?'

Willy nodded his agreement but Joe expressed his concern with the idea.

'He'd bring in his bloody thugs from the estate and beyond. He'd evict us if we took any strike action, if that's what your suggesting, Jack?'

Seamus banged the beers to the table.

'Oh, for Christ's sake, men Are we here to enjoy ourselves or talk bloody work and politics? What we need is a song or two!

With that he stood and boomed out the opening lines of his favourite republican song.

A committee man dashed across waving his hands.

'You can't be singing in here lad. Disturbing the peace, you are!'

Seamus smiled broadly at the man and broke into the second verse whilst clutching the man heavily around his shoulders. He paused.

'Aw join in, you miserable bugger.' He continued with a further song better known to the drinkers throughout the Club. Within minutes the men joined with little concern for any harmony or tune.

The committee man continued to wave his hands furiously and was totally ignored as the singing continued, led by the now drunken Irishman.

Chapter 62

(Jack and Florence's house Brawmarsh, 20 May 1911)
'And you've been barred for how long?

Seamus and Jack both burst into laughter.

'Well, ya see Florence, we're not allowed back for a week, they said. But Seamus took the committee man to one side, bought him a large whisky and seems it's now two days.'

Seamus raised his beer.

'Aye, seems he was easily influenced. Mind, I also told him I'd bring a few of my Irish friends from Rotherham over for a drink and they'd be unhappy if they couldn't sing their songs. Seemed to focus his mind, like'

They broke into more laughter and Seamus opened another bottle of beer for he, Teresa and Jack.

'You're not drinking with us, Florence/'

'No fella. Better behave with the baby on the way!'

Well, it's grand that you and Mary ull be having your bairns about the same time though. You'll be looking forward to them growing up together?'

Florence sought to smile and nodded.

Jack attempted to stand.

'I'll get some more beer from the back, Seamus lad.'

Jack stood and swayed, closing his eyes and fell back to his chair. Teresa shook her head

'Oh, for God's sake, Jack. You're bloody gone.'

He fell into a deep drunken slumber.

'Right, I'll get another beer and mebbe look in on Emma. Save you the stairs, lass.'

As she left Seamus held Florence in his stare.

'Now then lass. I may have had a beer or more, but there was no pleasure in your eyes when I talked about you and Mary with the babies, was there now?'

She hung her head and he watched the tears form in her eyes. She hurriedly brushed them away.

'Tell me Florence. You've some issues? Is your baby fine?'

She waved his concerns away.

'No Seamus. I'm fine but...'

She stopped herself and started to move to the scullery.

'Sit back down, lass. You've something to say....'

She broke down and sobbed. She needed to talk to someone. The full story fell from her lips as Seamus watched and listened.

'So, this shit is out to cause problems with Thomas and Mary? And with Jack? You can't carry this secret, lass. It's bloody hurting you. Why have not told Jack?'

She looked at him and shook her head,

'Think what would happen, Seamus. He'd kill the bastard! Even if he confronted him, Eddie would find a way to spill his story to Thomas and he and Mary be finished. Jack has a position in the town. He'd mebbe lose his job and his life – our life - around here would be finished. He can't know...ever.'

Seamus threw himself from his seat.

'You can do nothing. Jack can do nothing then? Mebbe someone needs to take a hand...'

Florence raised her hands in protest.

'I didn't tell you to get you involved, Seamus. Please leave things?'

He waved her away as Teresa returned.

'I'll not do anything, girl. Trust me...'

Chapter 63

A warm late spring day – perfect for people to come and attend the Labour rally, they hoped.

They had built a podium in the town square – despite protests from some opposition councillors – and had convinced a number of local shops to volunteer some contributions for food.

Florence and Mary had produced a large pot of rabbit stew and some cold meat and vegetables. Others had brought some tomatoes, roasted cold potatoes and chopped onions. There was haslet, brawn and tripe.

Cold cooked early vegetables from allotments and a variety of cakes and puddings added to the temptations on offer. Florence had spent much of the morning shooing young boys away as they tried to sample and steal parts of the offering. Eventually Jack had taken a hard stand and told the boys and their parents that, unless they behaved, they would be denied any further food which seemed to influence some of their activity.

'It's like late May Fair, Florence.'

Mary, away from the house, seemed happier than for a while and was blossoming in her pregnancy.

Jack breezed over smiling with pleasure at the arrangements.

'All looking really good. How are you, sister? All fine at home?'

Mary's mood seemed to change as she smiled without any great enthusiasm.

'Grand, Jack. All fine.'

Florence waited until Jack moved on.

'And how are things honestly?'

Mary seemed to shudder and then composed herself.

'I suppose as well as I could expect, Florence.'

'Do you mean he's still giving you problems, lass? Tell me!'

She turned to walk away before Florence grasped her firmly by her wrist.

'Tell me! Is he still bothering you?'

Mary waved her away before turning with her hands to her face.

'Of course, he's still bothering me, sister. He knows I can't object or complain....'

Florence looked hard at her.

'Has he had you again, girl?'

Mary pushed her away and wiped her face.

'Yes he has. What can I do? He's said he'll tell Thomas. I can't lose my husband, Florence. I can't...'

Florence pushed past her in desperation. *I can't let this continue!*

Jack wandered back to her enthusing about the arrangements.

'This is absolutely great; lass I just hope they'll turn up...'

He stopped and pulled her face towards him.

'What's up, girl? Why the tears?'

She waved him away.

'Just pleased it's all good, Jack...that's all...'

They watched as over the next hour or so the numbers increased and the congregation grew.

Over the next hour there was a range of Labour speakers, many simply indulged by the crowd as they took advantage of the food on offer.

How would they measure the success of the event? thought Jack. *Best they could hope for is to pitch the socialist message and prompt discussion and debate.*

He was joined by Willy Arthur and Joe Malton.

'So, gents how do you think it's going? Any interest?'

Arthur waved his hand dismissively.

'Bloody frustrating, Jack. Majority of the men are cynical. They simply don't see beyond the current ruling parties. 'Better the devil you know' thinking.'

Joe nodded in agreement.

'The pity is a lot of the women see our cause as in their interests. They are the ones that have to manage and see more of the poverty. The men seem to close their eyes and hope for the best.'

Jack clenched his fists in frustration.

'I think you've hit the nail on the head, fella. Our party will only succeed and move forward when we get the women voting and that seems no nearer. Mebbe the only way we can get these buggers on board is when more of them see their wages cut and their jobs lost. It's already happening, but these silly sods just think keeping their heads down and falling in line with the Company owners is the way to tackle it!'

'And what is your union doing about it, Jack? Best will in the world, they don't seem inclined to take the businesses on, do they?'

Jack raised his hands defensively and sighed.

'You're right, Joe. I'm more bloody frustrated than most. But I'd throw it back at you two. Your owners are cutting your money, raising your rents but you and your workmates are doing bugger all too! We will make no progress in getting union representation and changing the attitudes if everyone sits back. Sorry lads but you need to help yourselves...'

He watched as the two men stood helplessly and without a response.

Chapter 64

Jack, at the request of Seamus, was on his way to the Welfare Club for a couple of beers. He was deep in thought when he heard a shout from behind. He turned and saw Thomas moving briskly to join him.

Thomas was clearly still uncomfortable in his brother-in-law's company and hesitantly reached to shake his hand.

'Look Jack, I know you are still angry with me over my behaviour. I can't keep apologising. Seamus asked me to join him for a beer and I suspect he's asked you as well. He's trying to get the two of us to settle our differences. Can we do that now?'

Jack reached and took his hand.

'Listen Thomas, we'll put all that's happened behind us for the sake of our wives and families. I need to tell you that if you step out of line one more time, I'm done with you. Understand?'

Thomas nodded and they moved on towards the Club.

'Why was Seamus so keen to get us together tonight?'

Jack mused before responding.

'I believe he and Teresa are ready to go back home. They've had nearly four months here whilst her father's been unwell and I suppose they miss the bairns. He's got to go back to his business too.'

'Is her Da better then?'

'Don't believe he'll get better, Thomas but they can only stay so long. I suspect they may have to be back again in the near future…sadly.'

They arrived at six o'clock to find Seamus already ensconced in a corner table with his first beer drained.

'Your round, Prendergast. Best get em in before more arrive.'

Jack looked at him and laughed.

'Is this a bloody party then?'

Seamus stood and shook their hands.

'Aye lads. Call it a leaving and reconciliation session before I go home.'

Jack brought three beers to the table.

'So, who else is joining us, fella?'

Seamus leaned back and consumed half of his beer in one move.

'If he turns up, I've asked that young Eddie to join us. Told him to be here for about seven o'clock to give us a chance to sort you two out…..'

Jack held up his hand.

'I believe we're sorted, fella. Between Thomas and me now, so you can stop your peace-making. Frankly, a bloody rebel Irishman trying to referee could never bode well could it?'

They all raised their glasses and, without further discussion, agreed to move on, ordering more beers.

***

Eddie left the house, delighting in the continuing power he enjoyed over Mary. He left her earlier indicating that he intended to 'enjoy her company' in the next day or two. He had been told by Seamus earlier that it was a 'bit of a leaving do' and laughed to himself at the thought of a few drinks in the company of Thomas and Jack.

He turned into the quiet and unlit alley way some two hundred yards from his destination and, in the dim light, saw three figures approaching.

'Evening fella.'

The man at the front approached him.

'We're looking for a local pub that would be good for a decent beer. Can you suggest anywhere?'

Eddie relaxed and turned to point and direct them to a couple of options.

The voice, clearly an Irish accent, stopped him with a hand on his shoulder.

'I think we've met before, lad. Are you Eddie?'

He smiled and nodded.

'Aye that's me. Where have we....'

The first punch struck him in his mouth and he felt his teeth break as they flew across the path. The second blow from behind knocked him to the floor. He winced and rolled as the boots rained on his ribs and head. He saw an object raised above him and his face was violently beaten by some form of baton.

'You'll remember this, fella. It's time for you to go back to Sheffield. You'll not be working for a while.'

With that, the club struck him repeatedly and unmercifully on his arms as he heard his bones break. He started to cry out in agony, but his mouth was covered as one man pushed his head to the hard brick paving.

'You're leaving Eddie...tonight. This is a message from Mary. If you name her, we'll find you again and leave you in far more pain fella. D'ya understand, ya bastard? Well, nod if ya do?'

He raised one hand.

'Please no more....'

'No more, you feckin arsehole. You're a shit of a man. Go near Mary Davies again and you're feckin dead. Understand?'

He weakly nodded.

'And one last message, you shit.'

The boot struck him brutally between his legs and he screamed in pain. He was drawn to face the perpetrator.

'That'll put you out of action for a while.....right lads, leave the arsehole where he lies.'

They walked away as Eddie lay bleeding and broken on the pathway.

Chapter 65

(Jack and Florence's house, Brawmarsh , 7 June 1911)
'It doesn't look like Eddie will be back working with Thomas again now. He's moved back to his family in Sheffield.'

Seamus roused himself from the chair.

'Bad job lad. Seems he upset some fella's'

He returned to his drink and sought not to return Florence's stare.'

Jack shook his head and continued.

'Both arms broken and ...well...some damage elsewhere. No one seems to know the men who attacked him. A good lad. I feel sorry for the man. He doesn't remember much. Thinks they were Irish but not locals'

Seamus looked up.

'It wouldn't be Irish lads. Why would they be around here? I think he'd upset somebody given the way he was sorted. Mebbe a woman involved?'

He glanced to his side and met Florence's glare with a smile.

'Aye, probably woman trouble. Usually is...'

Jack completely missed any inference and continued the discussion.

'You're home tomorrow then, Seamus?

He sat back with his third beer before belching and replying.

'We're away tomorrow. She needs to see the children and I've to see to my business. Her Da isn't going to get any better but we can't stay forever, can we? And her mother is doing my feckin head in...'

Florence was the first to comment.

'Will you be back again, Seamus?'

He lifted his head and raised his beer.

'Only if this bastard keeps buying me a beer....'

They laughed.

Florence pointed her finger at him and beckoned him away from the others.

'Come and help me get the food out, fella'

He looked puzzled.

'Is Teresa not fit or what?'

Florence waved her hand.

'Need to ask you something....'

He followed her to the scullery and she turned and thrust her finger to his face.

'I told you not to get involved, Seamus.'

He looked at her and smacked her gently on her cheek.

'You did lass. That's why I did what you asked. When the poor bugger was damaged, you'll recall Jack, Thomas and myself were in the Club for all to see. Seems he crossed the wrong people, Florence...... anyway, the problem's gone now, has it not?'

He smiled and returned to his beer.

Chapter 66

(Trade Union Office, Rotherham , November 1911)

It had been a very quiet six months or so, in some respects. Apart from two new additions to the family group....

A new son, Arthur – the name easily agreed with Florence – and a new niece to Thomas and Mary. Elizabeth – to be known as Beth. Both delivered without any substantial issues for their women. Both seemingly healthy and now exercising their lungs when they met.

Jack studied his papers and sat back in his office chair, deep in thought.

The world was changing so quickly now. It appeared, from his reading, that the European powers were building their armaments and seemed determined on warfare. Germany, under the mad Kaiser, had built their navy and refused to accept any proposal for a peace arrangement in the continent. They, according to the observers, had aspirations to build an Empire. Turkey, and parts of the adjoining countries, had weakened and fallen into internal disputes. It seemed that a war was inevitable.

England too had its own warmongers. His party – the socialists locally and in the Parliament – had totally rejected any proposals that would lead the country to conflict, but others were demanding increases in spend for war readiness.

Additionally, there was further growing problems. The workers across the country were starting to exercise their views and rebel against the constraints of the employers. Wages had fallen, conditions were no better and poverty had increased in the working classes.

There had already been disturbances and withdrawal of labour in a number of industries and places. The national railway strike had achieved better pay and conditions but sadly had resulted in six deaths in Llanelli – two murdered by troops.

And in Ireland – the failure of the ruling parties to agree any resolution of the claims for independence had increased the tensions. Both the Loyalists and Republicans were – it was suggested – increasing their local armies and building towards rebellion and conflict.

Jack had received a short letter from Seamus – couched in guarded terms. He had indicated that *'life was getting a little more uncomfortable back home'* and *'some of my friends are looking for a different approach to their life in the future'*

As he had read this, he understood that Ireland was ready to combust. *God knows how that would go.* he thought. Given some of the characters he had encountered from that country, he knew that the outcome would go far from well.

He was awakened from his thoughts by a thumping at the office door. It was unusual for callers to appear and he walked uncertainly through the corridor.

He was met by his two Labour colleagues, Joe Malton and Willy Arthur.

'Now then, fellas. This is a surprise. What's to do to bring you here?'

They walked through to the office and his visitors perched uncomfortably on the edge of a table.

'We're here to ask for some help, Jack. We need your Union's support...'

They explained that George Harcourt had not only carried out the reduction of their wages and increases in rent, but had also evicted two families of miners who had attempted to drive Miner's Union membership.

'What's happened to them?'

'They have moved to family in the town but that can't continue. Small homes and little space.'

'And no money, no wages...' added Arthur.

Jack sat back and held up his hand for them to quieten for a minute or so.

'What is it you expect us to do?'

Malton was the first to speak.

'You once suggested that stopping the coal getting out would harm Harcourt and his finances. That's what we need to do, but we have limited men and many are reluctant to get involved. They are feared of losing their jobs and homes.'

He mused for a few moments.

'We can legally support you and picket the site. I don't think I could convince the steelworkers to join in a sympathetic strike – I don't believe the union would back me up either, given the loss of jobs in our industry and competition from overseas.'

He picked up the telephone and was connected to the Union Chairman, Braithwaite.

Arthur and Malton could only hear one side of the conversation…

'So, Norman. What's your view? Would our union give some support?'

They watched Jack as pursed his lips, smacked his hand to the desk and responded.

'What's the bloody point of our movement then? If we don't support others in their fight to get recognised!'

They heard a strong response on the other end of the call.

'Fine Norman. I'll do as you suggest and talk to my local members and get their view. I'll wait to hear whether your speaking to the Executive gives us formal permission?'

He threw the phone back to its rest.

'Right fellas, my Chairman tells me we can't support you without the main Committee agrees. However, he also said that we can locally ask the steelworkers in our community to see if they'll get involved. I'll do that and let you know. Meet me on the Welfare on Friday night? Gives me a few days.'

They nodded, expressed their thanks and left.

Christ Jack thought. *I'm out on a bloody limb if it all goes wrong...*

Chapter 67

(Welfare Club, Brawmarsh , 24 November 1911)
Jack had spoken to a number of union representatives at the Sparkgate foundry, and others in the general area in his industry. Whilst they were understanding of the situation, they were unsure as to whether they would get any support from the workforce.

'What will we need to do, Jack?'

'All I'm asking is that we stand as a line and ask the cart and train drivers coming in and out to refuse to leave and enter. If they refuse, we stand back and let them do their jobs.'

A couple of the representatives shook their heads.

'Harcourt has a lot of influence, Jack. We could lose our jobs if he speaks to the Company.'

He accepted the comments with a nod and raised hands.

'Understand, but it could be you lads next asking for help. If the trade union movement is going to succeed we need to stand together.'

He left, with no great expectation of support, but single-mindedly determined to present himself at the picket line.

***

He arrived at the Club and both Joe and Willy sat at a corner table anticipating his arrival.

They exchanged handshakes and both looked hopefully at Jack for good news.

'Look fellas. I'm getting a bit of support from the steel lads, some of them will come and stand on the line with you. But to be honest, not enough to make the difference. Tell me again how the coal gets in and out? And have you spoken to the Miners Union for their help?'

Joe was the first to speak.

'He has two ways of moving the coal. A rail line running to end of the estate takes most of it. Then local cartmen to deliver around the community for their fuel.'

Willy interrupted.

'That's where we need to be careful. If we stop the cartmen, then the town and area ull have no heating fuel. That'll turn people against us. We've talked to the local Miners official and he's said he'll make sure there are some of his members on any picket line.'

Jack held up his hands to stop the conversation and sat back to consider the options.

'Right, two things here. We need the local people with us. I know this sounds bad, but if they lose their coal supply and we can convince them of our case, it will be Harcourt and his cronies who are seen to be responsible?'

'Second, the answer has got to be to get the train unions on board. I've got a way we can sort this, if they'll join you. I'll talk to the local union fella, so leave that with me. Meantime, you need to get your workers ready. We need some at the main gate. Is there any other way the carts can get in and out?'

'There's a couple of rough tracks, Jack on the other side of the estate. Narrow but they could get through.'

'Right, so you need to get as many of your lads to bugger up those roadways overnight. Dig ditches across. Place the heaviest blocks of stone you can find along the tracks. Throw water down to create heavy mud. Block the gates with whatever you can get hold of. Understand? Whatever you can do to stop the carts getting in or out. We'll need a couple of your fellas on those gates to try and convince the carters to stop their activity.'

They both nodded.

'Next, talk to the miner's union fella. We'll need as many as possible at the main gates. And then, talk to the men and women in their homes. They'll be threatened with eviction. Tell them to lock and block their doors – let no one enter and ignore the threats. I'm hoping that Harcourt will have to direct his little army towards the pickets and he'll leave them alone when he sees what's happening at his gates. And tell the women to manage their food. They will face some difficult days...possibly weeks..'

He held up his hands and continued.

'Your men stop work at daybreak next - Friday 1st of December and leave the mine. Everything else happens the night before. If they don't do that we have no strength, no power – do you understand?'

Again, whilst looking bewildered by the fury of his comments, both men confirmed their acceptance.

'Now, it's the railwaymen we need to get to support us. If they say no, then we'll struggle. That's down to me. Right fellas, can you sort what I've asked?'

Willy and Joe looked to each other. This was moving much faster than they had expected. They now had to go back and convince their colleagues.....

Chapter 68

Florence sat and looked across at her husband slumbering
in his chair. She was tired and frustrated. Their new baby,
Arthur, was loud, vocal and seemed unable to sleep for a
full night. She had resolved to deal with the issues, without
involving Jack as much as possible.

He seemed tense and irritable lately, and she knew he
had many problems preying on his mind.

Her own life had become dull and repetitive. Their
eldest, Emma, was approaching two years old and
becoming a real handful. She had been a good baby, but
now was finding her feet and demanding much more
attention.

Florence had been confined and unable to exercise her
views and enthusiasm for women's suffrage. It appeared
there was little progress, despite the increasing rebellion
amongst the Pankhurst group. She had read – with some
discomfort – that the coronation of the new King, George
V, had been disrupted and now felt her loyalties divided.
Always a Royalist, but struggling to balance this with her
passion for her vote.

Now the latest….this bloody Government, despite their
commitments had failed to deliver. Asquith and his Liberals
had been elected with a promise of a bill for women's
suffrage. They had allowed this first to be changed to a
restriction for the vote for women with property, and now
had abandoned the legislation. Worse still, the proposal had
been replaced by a Manhood Suffrage Bill, proposing a
vote for all men and excluding any woman from voting
rights.

Lying bastard, she thought. Elected on a promise, and then following his own belief by reneging on his commitment.

The newspapers had been full of negative reports of the reaction of the suffragettes. London shops had windows smashed, public buildings and post boxes set on fire, even bombs placed in doorways throughout the city.

More frustratingly the British colonies of New Zealand and Australia had given the vote to women. So had some European countries – Finland and Norway.

She felt outraged but equally frustrated, unable to contribute to the protests and anger of her female compatriots.

At the peak of her anger Jack entered the house and she turned her temper towards him, in the absence of any other.

'Your bloody party supports Asquith and you do nothing when he changes his mind to suit his own purpose.'

He stood back from the verbal onslaught.

'Florence, I'm not Asquith, nor am I a Labour Member of Parliament. What the hell has got into you?'

She threw herself to the sofa and folded her arms.

'I'm bloody annoyed, Jack. I sit at home unable to support my women's movement. You are able to follow your political agenda. I can't. I'm just a wife, at home, expected to look after the children. I'm a chattel. Under the current laws I'm still only your wife, not a person in my own right!'

He tried to reach out to her hand, but was pushed away.

'You're going to tell me it will happen, aren't you? Well, not the way the politicians are moving things at this time. I will still have no vote in ten, mebbe twenty years' time, Jack. I need to get more involved...'

He stood away and was lost for words. She was correct. The politics he'd hoped to change remained unhampered. He now needed her help and had hoped to find her supportive. He spoke quietly and tentatively.

'Florence, I will continue to do all I can to get the vote for women, you know I will. But now, I need your help, lass…..'

She looked to him and laughed.

'And what this time, Prendergast? It seems you are full of empty bloody promises, but need my support regardless.'

He sat and stroked her hair. There was no falseness. He looked at her and adored her. She was everything he had hoped for in his wife. Committed, passionate and honest. He was desperate to help her achieve her expectations, but had no way of delivering this, until the mood of the country changed.

'Listen, Florence. Help me again please? We have a strike taking place on the Rotherham estate shortly. I need you – and probably our Mary – to talk to the local shops and people and help to feed them. Will you help me?'

He watched her jaundiced eye on him.

'Now, here's the way Jack Prendergast. I'll help you, and encourage Mary to do the same. Two things. One, you speak at your next your <u>U</u>nion Conference to get women a full vote in your decisions and elections. Two, you kick the backside of your Union Secretary – he was supposed to help with funds for the women's suffrage movement. He's playing silly buggers…we've had ten pounds so far and no help from him…nowhere near enough. Are you listening?'

He smiled and held up his hands in his defence and then leapt upon her.

'Thank you, girl. I love your bloody attitude and I will do what you ask.'

He embraced her passionately as they fell into a tangle on the floor laughing …..

Chapter 69

(Rotherham Estate, 1 December 1911)

Charles Dickens had started one book with *'It was the best of times, it was the worst of times'*

Jack understood – in a different context - how true his words were. It was the best time to call a strike in the coal mine. Industry and people needed fuel in the winter months and would soon become agitated if their supply was exhausted. However, it was also the most difficult time for the community. Cold weather and no heating, a limited source of food from their gardens and Christmas impending. Good for the strike, terrible for the people if the stoppage extended beyond a week or more.

The group of some twenty men stood at the estate entrance, shivering in the very early morning frost. Good to their word, the miners had downed tools at the end of their night shift and no further workers had entered the mine.

He was now hoping that his discussions with representatives of the railway unions would result in their support. If they declined the strike would fail. The official had sucked his teeth and appeared reluctant initially, having only recently taken their own action. He was unsure if his members would wish to risk further confrontation.

Jack had sold his argument strongly.

'You won your fight for better wages and conditions. If we want to make our movement count for the population, now's the time we support each other and use our combined strength. Your strike was about pay. These men are fighting for their homes and the future of their families. They are just asking you not to cross the picket line. They need your help....'

The man had appeared to acknowledge the case and said he would consult with the relevant members without any further commitment....

The men at the gate had already noticed a horseman looking down from the hill above, and then turning quickly, riding back towards the Manor.

'Wait for it, men. They'll be back in numbers.'

Jack nodded in agreement and moved to speak to Arthur and Malton who had now arrived, having visited the railway sidings.

'Not good, Jack. The trains are still coming through and leaving with their stock. We've men on the far side of the track just outside the boundaries, but the drivers are taking no notice.'

They both looked disheartened.

'Fellas, give it time. I'm convinced the railmen will support you. I'm expecting some of the steel men here as well. Early days...early days, lads.'

Despite his attempts at positivity, he was becoming concerned. He had expected some twenty to thirty of his members to present themselves, but no sign.

The pickets were alerted by the sound of horses from across the hill. A group of some fifteen men rode towards them led by George Harcourt.

Rotherham waved his hand to halt his followers and moved towards the gate.

'Move from my land, you bastards! I suggest you return to your work now and we will take no action against you. If not, you will return to your previous homes to watch your wives and families being evicted. I will not tell you again.'

He turned and pointed towards his troop.

'These are here to move you on. I have directed a similar number to the railway to tackle your pitiful attempt to stop the trains. And I have another ten men who are waiting for my directions to commence the evictions. I have also instructed the local police constabulary to present

247

themselves and arrest you all as trespassers. Do you hear me? Return to your work immediately or face the consequences.'

Several of the men seemed cowed by his comments and started to talk nervously amongst themselves.

Jack drew Willy and Joe to his side and stepped forward.

'Harcourt, you are a thug and not fit to wipe your father's boots. He will be turning in his grave to hear you speak to your employees as if they are still some sort of servants. They are no longer your bloody slaves. They are men who have rights and with the force of the trade unions, you will soon come to appreciate that you can no longer tread all over them.'

Rotherham looked down at him and moved his horse closer.

'Ah, the book thief, Prendergast is it? You have no right to be on my land or any involvement with my employees. I suggest you leave now.'

Jack laughed and pointed to him.

'You, Georgie need to understand the law!. We are standing on common land – not your property. These men have every right to protest and take strike action, and to ask others to assist them by not crossing this line. The police have no authority. We have not breached any rules or committed any offence. We are staying here until you remove your threats to reduce their pay and increase their rents. Talk to them. Negotiate sensibly for God's sake.'

Harcourt waved him away.

'I run my mines. I own this land. I'll not be told what I should do by a bloody thief and these rebels.'

At that point, a man ran hurriedly towards the group.

'Willy, Joe. The trains have stopped. We've stopped the bloody trains, fellas!'

Rotherham rode towards the man and threw his horsewhip at him. He fell with blood across his face.

Some of the men at the gate, whilst initially stunned, recovered quickly and threw themselves over the barrier to defend their colleague and, at that point, more of the horsemen joined the charge.

All hell broke loose as Harcourts men threw whips and batons at them. A number of the riders were dragged from their mounts and thrown and kicked to the ground.

Jack stood in shock.

'No, fellas, no! Come back. You're playing into their hands.'

He moved into the chaos pulling men apart, alongside Joe and Willy.

'Back to the bloody gate. They're trying to provoke you all. Out, before the police turn up!'

The groups separated and the pickets moved to return to their stations.

Harcourt, having avoided the brawl, rode back towards them and once more threw his whip, striking Jack across his back and causing him to fall heavily. He was kicked by the horse and rolled in agony before being hauled to safety.

'There ya go, book thief!' he laughed and turned his mount, calling to his men.

'Come with me. Back to the railway and village. Time to show the bastards who runs this manor!'

Jack, bleeding heavily from the blow, stooped and coughed in pain.

'Willy, get yourselves across to the village. Leave a couple here. You are not trespassing. Go now.'

Arthur and Willy gathered their party and set off at a sprint towards their homes. Two of the men stayed behind and immediately attended Jack who lay struggling for his breath.

He pushed them away and struggled to his feet.

'I'm alright. Go back to the gate, fellas.'

***

Harcourt's men rode to the village and slowed as they approached.

They turned to each other in disbelief as they saw two groups walking down the railway tracks. In the lead a band of some thirty women carrying baskets and holding arms. Behind them a further assembly of men – possibly more than sixty or so – holding banners. As they moved closer, the women formed a ring around the properties and held hands.

The men stayed on the railway line and formed a further wall of defiance.

Rotherham turned to his followers.

'Break them up. Ride through the bitches!'

He turned to wave them forward but received no response.

'My Lord, they are holding children in their arms – all of them...'

He turned to the man and cursed.

'If you want to keep your bloody job, you'll do what I tell you.'

His cohort looked to each other. Despite living on the estate, they had family and friends in the community, they frequented the local shops and public houses, they mixed with these people.

One of the men climbed down from his horse and led it to Harcourt.

'I'll not attack women and children. I'll find work elsewhere if that's what's required.'

He was joined by his colleagues as one by one they dismounted and stepped away.

Arthur and Malton arrived with their group and stopped at the scene. They watched as the estate men, as one, walked away leaving Harcourt alone.

It was Florence who moved to the forefront.

'My husband is Jack Prendergast. He has had dealings with you in the past. Trust me you will never beat him when he has the people like these behind him. We will walk back home now, but don't believe we won't be back if you threaten these folks again. I hope you understand, Lord Rotherham.'

She spat out his name and turned to wave the women away.

It was Willy Arthur who moved to the head of the congregation.

'So, Mr Harcourt. Shall we discuss how we resolve our issues?'

***

Florence watched as Jack soaked his badly bruised body in the tin bath. He sank his head back and laughed.

'How the bloody hell did you organise that, lass? You stole the day.'

She rubbed his back and smiled.

'Well, Jack Prendergast, you've still some things to learn about me and women in general. Once I talked to the women folk in the village, I was surprised at their reaction. A lot of them became angry – particularly about the evictions. It wasn't me who suggested we walk to the pit. Another woman did and became very passionate about it. It came from that.'

'But you risked our children, Florence. What if they had attacked you?'

She shook her head and laughed out loud.

'That's why you'll never understand women, you silly bugger! There were no children in our baskets. It was blankets and a couple of our number doing a good impression of infant noises. Other women in the town looked after the bairns whilst we did the protest. Did what was needed though lad, didn't it?'

He looked at her in wonderment. *How the hell did he find this lass?*

'Are you serious Florence? Is that what you did?'

She cocked her head and walked away smiling.

'You'll never know, Prendergast...you'll never know..'

Chapter 70

A week had passed since the Rotherham Estate stand-off. There had been no direct communication from Arthur and Willy, but he understood the men had returned to work. Rumours around the town suggested that Harcourt had withdrawn his wage cut and rent increase proposal but there was no confirmation as yet.

Just as he took a chair in the Club, Thomas bustled in, clearly in a positive mood. He joined his brother-in-law at the table.

Jack looked up and raised his hand to welcome him. The change in Thomas over the last six months or so had been remarkable. He had addressed his drinking habit and returned to his business with energy and enthusiasm. Consequently, the relationship between the two of them had become far more positive.

'And what makes you so bloody chirpy, Thomas?'

'Bloody good news. I've found a good lad to replace Eddie. Fella come down from Newcastle for work with lots of building skills. Sammy Brown. Recently married man. Looking to find some more secure work. Exactly what I needed.'

Jack started to comment but Thomas continued enthusiastically.

'And he's looking for a place to rent so I've offered the place above the workshop at a decent rent. He and his wife, Alice are moving in next week so welcome income, brother. Better still, I've been asked to work on refurbishing some properties down Lower Sparkgate. Old church buildings that some wealthy fella wants to do up and rent. I'm guessing about six months of work. Bloody grand!'

Jack smiled and slapped his shoulder.

Thomas rubbed his chin and seemed reluctant to speak.

'Something else on your mind, fella?'

'Aye, Jack there is. I don't know how you and Florence are coping but both of us are outgrowing our homes. We've both two children and I suspect more to come. Both our properties have only two bedrooms, outside privies, no real washing and bathing areas. The places I'm going to work on have the space for three bedrooms, proper bathrooms and toilets. Lots of space and good gardens. How would you feel about moving to them?'

Jack gave him a hard stare.

'What and live next door to you and my sister? Bloody hell, Thomas. Could we cope?'

He stopped and thought for a minute or so.

'Listen, lad. For once in your life, you've had a good idea. I'll talk to your sister and we'll come and look at the place. Anyway, how's my sister and the bairns?'

'Really good, Jack. Your Mary seems to have come out of her sad mood since the lass was born. I suppose that's just what women are like when they're expecting? She was seeming like she had the world on her shoulders, but fine now. And the children are blooming. Little Elizabeth is coming on well. Grand to have a little lass again....'

His voice trailed off.

'Just wish my Peggy was still here...'

He turned to try and privately wipe his eyes.

'Listen, lad. You're allowed to be upset when you remember her. We all miss her.'

Their subsequent silence was broken by the arrival of the two miners.

Jack and Thomas both greeted them with a firm handshake.

'Fellas, I have to tell you that you served your colleagues well last week. Credit to you both. How are things now?'

Willy Arthur was the first to respond, hammering his fist to the table with a passion.

'As you'd expect Jack, Harcourt was reluctant to talk to us and, even when we eventually met, he refused to remove his impositions. We stood firm and told him that the lads would walk out again if he refused to negotiate and recognise our Union rights. He still claimed that he was short of money. We just laughed!'

Malton continued the story.

'We pointed out that his thugs had refused to support him, and even if they had, we had some fifty lads who would take them on if he came at us again. We listened to his abuse for a while and threatened to walk away and stop the mine again. How bloody quick did he surrender, Jack!'

Jack smiled at their responses.

'And the outcome. Has he backed down?'

'Too bloody right he did. No rent increase, no wage reduction, no evictions. He still refused to recognise the union but that's for another day, Jack.'

'And your Florence. What a woman! Mind I'm glad – best respect – that I don't have to live with her! No offence, fella..'

The group broke out laughing. Jack nodded and stood to buy the drinks, before turning to them.

' Ya think that was a display? You should see her when she's really pissed off lads…!'

Chapter 71

(Trade Union Office, Rotherham , March 1912)
It had been a wonderful end to a traumatic year. Jack and Florence had volunteered to have Christmas at their home and. despite the limited space and the excitement and disputes amongst the children, the day had been the best for many years. They had tired their families with some limited presents and a grand meal and sat to discuss their futures.

Both families had viewed the development Thomas had discussed with Jack and had been enthused by the properties. Bigger homes and situated on the edge of parklands, with space for both vegetable and play areas in the garden space. They had immediately committed to a move, and had secured an assurance from the landlord that they would have an option to chose their house once finished. Inevitably Mary and Florence had selected their homes next door to each other.

Jack had some reservations, but, given Thomas' new attitude he was prepared to deal with the situation.

'Let me tell ya both now. It won't be a bloody open house. We'll meet and enjoy our families but I don't need you every day or evening. If we understand that I'll make the move.'

Florence had given him a dismissive look.

'You are a miserable shit, Jack Prendergast! What a lovely opportunity for the children to grow up together.'

He pointed his finger and laughed.

'Yes, Florence but not necessarily to watch your bloody brother grow up again!'

Thomas had looked concerned until he understood that the comment was spoken in fun, but with a caution.

Jack now returned from his reflections to his paperwork. It was unduly quiet. No great disputes or issues, which given the mood of the country and workers was surprising. The last twelve months had seen massive industrial unrest, and he believed the opportunities for his party were now rapidly increasing. Even in the local community, the defence of the Rotherham miners and the general increasing poverty and costs of living seemed to be gathering a momentum for a different approach to politics.

He was brought from his thoughts by the telephone call.

'Jack Prendergast.'

'Now, how are things ya young bastard!'

He puzzled for a moment.

'Seamus? Is that you?'

'It surely is, fella. I've had to have this bloody device fitted for my business and the only number I have for the people I like is yourself. How things?'

The two men exchanged updates on their lives and families.

'Listen, Jack. How do you fancy coming to see us over here? Me and Teresa have a big place, so there'd be room for all your brood. Be good to see ya and let you have a look at our country.'

Jack, taken aback by the proposal, stuttered a response.

'Come to Ireland? Bloody hell, Seamus…it's a grand offer but I'm not sure. Our youngest is still barely seven months old. I'll talk to Florence. When were you thinking of?'

'Whenever lad. Next month? April's a grand time to visit.'

'And how welcome would an Englishman and his family be in your country at this time?'

Seamus laughed and responded quickly.

'Ya called Prendergast, fella and you'd be in the company of my family and friends. You'll find we're a moderate bunch. Don't tell anyone you love the English Government or the King. Don't mention religion too much. Nod and agree when they tell you that the country will be independent soon. To be honest, the Irish talk so much you'd probably only have to nod now and again in the right places. How's that?'

Jack couldn't stop himself from laughing out loud.

'Listen ya Irish bugger, I'll talk to my wife and give you a telephone call later.'

'Aye, that'll be grand lad. Don't call me before ten or after three. I'll either be asleep or at the pub.'

As they ended the call, Jack sat back and considered the option. Much was in favour. Great company and the family had not taken any holiday. The negatives were taking the young children and his impending commitments. Whilst he was not required to stand for re-election for a further couple of years, he needed to be in the town to support and campaign for the Labour candidates for the May council elections.

And despite Seamus reassurances, the mood in Ireland was volatile. Did he want to be drawn in?

***

By the time he arrived home, Florence had the children in bed.

'They were waiting for you, Jack but both tired.'

He was frankly thankful. Much as he loved the bairns, he needed time to talk with her tonight.

He waited until she had settled next to him and they discussed each other's day.

'There's something on your mind, Jack. You can't ever cover up, fella. I read you like a book!'

He shook his head and drew her closer.

'Nothing serious, girl. A telephone call from our friend, Seamus today.'

She sat up abruptly.

'Are they all fine? Is there a problem?'

He told her the detail of his discussion and the offer to visit Ireland and sat back unsure of her response.

She sat and mused for a while.

'It would be lovely to go and see them, Jack but there's a few issues. You'd need time off from work. We couldn't go for less than a week – it's at least a day to get there. And the cost? But the main problem would be the children. I don't think it would be practical to take them on a long journey at their ages.'

'The time off isn't a problem and we've a bit of money put to one side so no difficulties there. Could Thomas and Mary look after Emma and Arthur?'

She laughed and shook her head.

'For God's sake! It'd be Mary who would have to do the caring with Thomas at work. Four bairns under three with two of them babies. I don't think so. And the main point is that I'm still feeding Arthur. It's a lovely thought but not practical is it?'

Jack nodded and shrugged his shoulders.

'Just an idea but I'll telephone Seamus and say no at this time'

Florence studied him for a moment.

'Why don't you go?'

He frowned and shook his head.

'That would be unfair, lass. I couldn't leave you with the bairns…'

'Bloody hell, Jack! You leave me all day with them. I'd have Mary and Thomas on hand.'

She softened her tone and held his face towards her.

'You need a break, lad. It's been a difficult time and you've more coming with the elections. Go and get from under my feet for a few days.'

Jack sat back and reflected on her suggestion. She was right in that he felt tired and run down. A break – particularly with a character like Seamus – would give him a chance to restore his energy.

He leant over and kissed her.

'You're a bloody treasure, gal. Let me think about it.…'

Chapter 72

How the bloody hell did she convince me to make this trip.

Jack leaned over the side of the ship and lost the last of his earlier breakfast. *Bad move to indulge himself in the harbourside café.*

He had travelled by train to the city and then looked for options to travel to Ireland. He accepted that this was random and risky, but he needed the easiest and cheapest route to Dublin. The main shipping routes were to Belfast from Liverpool.

He had found a couple of men who listened to his request and smiled to each other.

'Listen, lad. We can take you cheap to Dublin but it's a smaller craft and, if you've never sailed, you might find it a tad rough in a boat this size. As long as ya understand?'

He had paid half the cost of the ferry fare but now wished he had not been so frugal. The Irish sea was still turbulent and choppy, and he soon found that he had neither the legs or the stomach for sea travelling. It took them several hours and, as they drew up to the harbour and docked, he briefly thanked his companions and jumped to the side as quickly as possible. His legs were still at sea and he sat to one side to recover.

Seamus had simply said that he should call him when he docked. He had the number but was totally lost as to where he could find a telephone. Looking around the only occupied building he could sea was the Harbourmaster's office. He stood unsteadily and made his way to the door and gently knocked. No answer. He pushed at the open door, and called before walking inside. Still no response.

He wandered inside with some trepidation.

'And who the feck are you!'

Jack jumped and turned to face a very large ruddy faced man, hands on hips. He blocked the exit and waited for a response.

'Jesus, man, you scared the shit out of me!'

'Good. That was the plan, lad.'

Jack decided to simply declare his case and hope.

'I've just landed from England. I need to contact a friend of mine over here. Would I be able to use your telephone?'

The man continued to look at him threateningly before replying.

'And who would your friend be? What's his name? And where's he live?'

He spluttered struggling to recall Seamus' surname.

'Seamus....he's from Dublin..'

'Ah ..that'll be feckin Seamus from Dublin. I'll look at my list .....here he is ...he's one of about three hundred and sixty fellas....'

Jack threw his hands in the air.

'Look fella, I think he's Seamus Murphy.'

The man looked at him with a jaundiced eye.

'You've never mixed much with us fella, have ya? If I look at my list again I'll narrow it down to about one hundred and fifty. Any more ya know about him?'

Jack stopped, and in desperation threw out a thought.

'He's a builder...brother-in-law Conor Rafferty?'

He watched as the man's face softened and burst into a laugh.

'Now then. That's bloody Seamus Murphy – why didn't ya say?'

By now, Jack was completely lost and just nodded his agreement.

After a short telephone call, and an equally brief exchange, the coastguard waved him towards a point at the far end of the harbour. He stood with a small bag of clothes and gazed hopefully.

Within ten minutes a pony and trap arrived at a rapid pace, and a young man threw himself down and held out his hand.

'You'll be Jack? I'm Liam Rafferty, Uncle Seamus' nephew.'

Jack stopped himself from stating that as Seamus was his uncle he was obviously his nephew and simply laughed to himself. He shook hands and climbed aboard. This was going to be an interesting trip...'

Chapter 73

(Dublin, Ireland, April 1912)

It was a wonderful country. Green – inevitably so – given the persistent rain since his arrival – but beautiful countryside. Dublin, a busy city - well populated but carrying a relaxed manner and gentle air. The people friendly, humorous but somewhat guarded. There was an evident and very strong religious belief within the people he had met. The women particularly devout, with the men, in the main, following their faith with a touch of gentle cynicism.

'We go to church and we take the bread and follow the confession, but it lets us feel less guilt when we go on the piss and enjoy the craic. Jesus man, the priest ull generally be at the bar before us but never seems to stand his corner! Richest bloody fella in the pub...'

Seamus had insisted they 'take a drink' on his second night in Ireland. They, along with Teresa and the children had taken a tour of the city during the day, and he had declared that having done his 'family duties', it was only right that he should take Jack for a few beers. Teresa had laughed and indicated that it was not unexpected.

'You'll find the lads a grand group, Jack. They like a drink and a laugh. My only caution is that you try and avoid any politics. If you find yerself in that discussion, either stay quiet or indicate your Republican beliefs. Understand?'

'Will your nephew be present, Seamus?'

Seamus slapped his shoulder and laughed.

'Why, Jack? I think you're missing him, lad! I doubt he'll be joining us, but if he does you can be sure Conor will keep him on a leash.'

They entered a small and dark bar. Nicotine-stained walls decorated with images of racehorses and portraits of men, whom Jack correctly assumed to be past and current nationalist icons. The place was busy and loud, but too early for any music and songs. Just a general hubbub with – at this hour – light-hearted debate and disagreement. The barman was busy drawing pints of stout, taking his time to let them settle before completing the drink. He faced regular abuse, both for his deliberate pace and the lack of volume in the pint.

'Jesus, fella. I paid for a pint. Will ya not fill the bloody glass?

'Watch him Patrick, he'll be taking a drink from that for himself...'

The barman was completely undisturbed by their comments, other than occasionally smacking the complainers drink to the bar, and smiling whilst deliberately spilling the froth, prompting more complaints.

Seamus and Jack joined a group of middle-aged men at a table and he was introduced to the membership.

'So, fella. You're over from England; must be bloody awful beer if you have to come this far for a drink.'

The speaker was a large, thickset man.

'Now Jack, let me introduce you to my father, Michael Murphy – known as 'Mickey' or as some would call him 'the awkward old bastard'

Mickey clenched his fist and jokingly stood to confront his son.

'Aye, you'll abuse me now, ya little shit. Ya think ya are big enough, do ya?'

Seamus leaned over, laughing and kissed his father on the cheek, gently resting him back to his chair.

'He was a hell of a rebel man in his day.'

'Still am, ya cheeky bugger! I still have my principles, if not my capability. Come sit with me, Jack and I'll tell you some stories...'

Seamus tried to intervene, but was dismissed with a wave of his father's hand.

'Go buy the beers, lad. Off ya go...'

Jack spent the next two hours in Mickey's company and listened as the man told him of the history of his country and the reason for his passion for independence. He heard of the story of Cromwell – 'the bastard', the potato famines and the reluctance of the Government to help the Irish people. He heard about the starvation, the migration to America and the subsequent bitterness of those left behind. He felt obliged to quietly challenge the man's prejudice against the English, but was subsequently defeated by the logic and calm explanation of the drive for a separate state.

'Ya see, Jack, I've watched and waited for the London government to offer this country their right to rule their own affairs. Every time we are told to wait. Then we are told that we will have our state but still subject to their rules on our money, our foreign relations, our armed forces. They are offering us the opportunity to be a feckin colony, lad. Trust me, we won't accept that and the shit will fly very soon...very soon....'

He fell into a thoughtful silence and Jack understood that he was not seeking rebellion. He simply wanted to be a citizen with rights, not a subject of a country he felt no connection with. Eventually he stood unsteadily and was immediately attended by his family. He turned to Jack and gripped his arm.

'My time is nearly over, fella. My rebellion will be history. You've listened patiently a long time tonight. I don't ask for your support...only your awareness and understanding. Take care, lad.'

As he was walked away, Jack sat and reflected alone. He found himself completely moved by the discussion, and now with far more awareness of the republican cause and their passion for change.

***

Jack packed his small case in preparation for his departure. The return journey would be far more comfortable as Seamus had found him a place on the ferry to Liverpool at no cost.

'Don't ask, lad. The odd favour is always owed here and there.'

As he picked up his baggage Seamus moved to his side with a large, flat brown envelope.

'Now listen Jack, I'm going to ask ya to do me a favour. Can you drop this to the bottom of your bag and take it back to your home?'

Jack looked to him and said nothing initially. Eventually he took the package.

'Do I need to know what I'm carrying, Seamus?'

'Nothing that will kill ya, lad. Just a few bits of paperwork. A friend of mine in Sheffield will call on you to collect it when you're back home.'

'It's Republican material isn't it, Seamus?'

Seamus raised his hand in acknowledgment.

'Look, it's a few leaflets and letters to our friends in your country. If you're not happy with carrying it, then I'll find another route. I believe you understand and have a strong sympathy with our cause. If I'm wrong then leave the envelope on the table.'

He turned and left Jack alone.

What to do?

He had found himself adopting a very different view of the Irish politics and a significant shift in his sympathies. Indeed, he had reflected for a day or so, and now believed that his overall approach to his beliefs and ideals lacked any of his earlier passion.

It was time for him to move on and commit; to stop accepting the moderation of his political colleagues. It was now time to confront and challenge. With that, he slipped the envelope to the bottom of his case.

Chapter 74

(Jack and Florence's house, late April 1912)
His return journey had been without incident but long and tiring. He arrived home to Florence's embrace and was able to help settle the excited children to their beds before falling to his chair.

'So, Jack. How was the trip?'

As he told her of his time there, he found himself laughing out loud reflecting on the characters and antics of the Irish people he had engaged with.

'A complex people, Florence. Funny, entertaining and friendly on the one hand. Then when you spend more time with them, passionate and frustrated. I'd go so far as to say angry at times. Volatile and easily roused if you speak out of turn. Let me tell you that there is definitely going to be conflict.'

Florence sat and held her tongue for a minute or two observing him.

'Beside all the fun and laughs, husband, there is a bit of a change in you, isn't there? You seem a little more introspect and thoughtful.'

Jack nodded gently and felt the need to stand and speak.

'I've realised that I have either to commit to my beliefs and let people know my views, or else give up on my politics, Florence. I listened to the fellas in Ireland and I've realised that their commitment, their values and principles are much stronger than my own. I need to get off my backside and work to my values and my views. Sell them and hold true to my ideals.'

She considered her response carefully.

'You seem to have become influenced by the Republicans over there?'

'Aye, lass I can't deny that I listened and understood their desire for independence.'

Florence grabbed his hand.

'I can accept your desire to change things. You know I have the same views about the women's vote. All I'd ask you to recognise is that, if what you've told me is correct, the Irish will turn to rebellion and perhaps war. Just be careful, Jack. By all means follow your principles, but not at any cost....'

He nodded quietly, pulled her to his knee and held her tightly.

'And how has your time been whilst I've been cavorting abroad?'

'It's been fine, fella. The children have been good. I've had time with Mary to talk about life and stuff. I went to their house with the bairns on the second night and they'd invited his new worker and his wife, Sammy and Alice. They are a lovely couple, Jack. You'd like them. Good humour and straightforward.....'

She hesitated as she looked into his eyes.

He drew her closer and then led her by the hand.

'Let me show you how much I've missed you, lass....'

Chapter 75

(Brawmarsh, May 1912)

The day was warm and still. Always a good sign to bring out those who could vote. The turnout seemed to be good, more than normal, Jack thought.

The Labour Party had continued their campaign and drive since the May event some twelve months earlier. Whether this would result in any increased enthusiasm for their cause would be demonstrated by today's decision.

He stood with the two new candidates. He had convinced Willy Arthur to put his name forward. The second Labour nominee was a man from Sparkgate who he knew little about – Charlie Betts. He, apparently, was a relatively quiet character but holding strong views about the direction of the Labour movement. In his brief exchanges with Jack, he had repeatedly stressed his beliefs that the party was too moderate and needed to look more towards the doctrines of Marx for their future.

It was clear that the turnout was higher than usual which hopefully bode well for their candidates. They faced both current Liberal councillors and Tory opponents in their wards. His party supporters had come out in strength, touring the town and door-knocking to encourage their potential voters to attend.

When the polls closed that evening, the mood was tense. Jack watched the two Liberals who appeared in a self-congratulatory mood. He presented himself at the count and could see that – as always - it would be a close call for both his colleagues.

The electoral officer, satisfied that the numbers had been accurately collated, strode to the stage.

He first announced Willy's result. Jack clapped his hands and cheered as it was declared that his colleague had a majority of some thirty votes.

This was subsequently repeated as Betts too was elected by a smaller number.

'Bloody hell fellas. Great result!'

He clapped their shoulders and shook hands. Now three Labour councillors – nowhere near enough yet but a significant shift in the political mood in the town.

'Now let's make it count, gents'

Chapter 76

Other than Jack addressing – as committed to Florence – the need for equal voting rights for women members, and the need for the body to more strongly support the Women's Suffrage movement, it was a standard and unexciting session. As he expected, the vote declined to support the right for the women members to have any change in their voting rights. There was an indifferent commitment to pushing the suffrage drive.

He had remained relatively calm, but now found himself becoming frustrated and angry with the continuing conservative approach of the union.

As the Chairman sought to close the meeting, Jack raised his hand to speak.

'Mr Chairman, I stand here both disappointed and disillusioned with this body. Every meeting is repeated. Maintain the status quo. Accept that things are as they are. We are no longer representing the members views. We have to look at the way workers in other industries are fighting. A two month long national miners strike resulted in a minimum wage for their membership. We are not even close to that. We still are struggling for recognition in many of our works. It is time to take a different view now.'

He paused as many of the Committee talked amongst themselves and, dismissively, made clear that they had heard this before.

Jack thumped the table to prompt their attention.

'Each one of you, including you Mr Chairman, depend upon the votes of our members to maintain your cosy bloody positions!. So, here's my proposal. Every one of you should seek re-election in October...even you Chairman! I will lead an alternative group of candidates with a stronger grasp of what is required for our future. Either understand the need for change or retire, gentlemen!'

He threw his papers to the floor and walked from the meeting.

Chapter 77

(Jack and Florence's house, June 1912)

Florence felt she needed to act. Her husband was carrying his political intensity into their home and frankly she was bored with it.

He sat in his usual chair studying the newspapers until she walked across and swept them from his hands.

'You are becoming a sad arsehole, Jack Prendergast. Life is more than bloody politics. You're coming out with me tonight. Mary and Thomas are joining us and they've asked Sammy and Alice to meet up. We're going to the Village Hall for their Summer Party. I've bought the tickets so no argument. Get yourself dressed …and I mean nicely!'

'What about the bairns.'

'I'm leaving them on their own, Jack. A bit of food and drink they'll be fine…'

She smacked him gently around his head.

'You are a bloody idiot, Prendergast. Do you think I wouldn't have sorted that? Mrs Jones is coming around to sit for us. She's a grand woman, and given she's had seven of her own, I think she'll cope.'

She stood and pushed her finger to his face.

'I'm going to put on my glad-rags, fella. I suggest you find your best suit and join me. Listening!'

Jack sat back stunned by the onslaught.

Within the hour Jack had taken the instruction and sat waiting for his wife. She bustled down the stairs and gave a twirl.

'My God, lass. You like bloody lovely. Shall we stay in…?'

She brushed him away laughing.

'Get away, man. Mrs Jones would have a bloody heart attack if she caught us now!

They arrived at the Village Hall to find it already heaving and the local band in full flow. Mary, Thomas with Sammy and Alice had already found a table and waved them over. Jack was introduced to the new couple. Sammy was a dark-haired slim man in his early twenties, Alice, tiny, brown haired and pretty. Both understandably spoke with strong Geordie accents and Jack found himself having to ask that they repeat their conversation.

'It's a bloody different language, Sammy' he laughed.

Normally reticent in new company, Jack found himself easily relaxed with the couple. Both were talkative with a wry sense of humour.

The room was quietened by the band leader.

'Ladies and Gentlemen. Regrettably our singer has developed a throat condition and is unable to continue. We will continue to play our songs but unless we have any singers in the house, it will be music only.'

There was a disappointed murmur across the room. Jack turned to see Sammy and Alice in conversation.

'Ah, go on Sammy. You've a good voice. Give us a song.'

He tried to protest but eventually moved to the stage.

'Bloody hell, can he sing?' Thomas asked. 'If he's rubbish, he might damage my business….'

They laughed and watched as Sammy spoke to the band. He took the microphone and, with a broad smile on his face, spoke to the audience.

'I'll give it a go. Don't throw yer glasses if you don't like my singing!'

The band struck up a popular song from that year. 'Oh! you beautiful doll.'

The room fell into silence as his beautiful tenor voice was pitch and word perfect.

'Has he done this before?' asked Jack.

Alice laughed and nodded.

'Aye, he's done a bit of club singing back home. Semi-professional stuff. He's not too bad is he?

'Bloody good.' Said Thomas in amazement.

Sammy left the stage to applause and calls of 'more'.

He returned to his seat and was congratulated by the group.

He looked at them with a twinkle in his eye.

'So, who's next then?'

'What follow that…not likely, lad..'

It was with looks of surprise as Jack stood and walked to the band.

'Can he sing, Florence?'

'Not to my knowledge.'

'I hope he's not going to give another political speech, lass…'

Florence laughed nervously and watched nervously as her husband took the microphone.

He looked across at her and smiled.

'I've just come back from Ireland and I heard this tune over there. I think it's a perfect song for my beautiful wife. It's called 'When you were sweet sixteen''

When first I saw the lovelight in your eyes.
I thought the world held naught but joy for me…'

His rich baritone voice carried the tune beautifully.

Thomas looked at his friends in shock.

'Jesus, he's got a lovely voice, Florence….Florence…'

He was wasting his words as she and Jack held the others gaze.

'I love you as I loved you
When you were sweet
When you were sweet sixteen….'

He stood down and walked back as the room stood, applauding in appreciation. Florence stood and drew him close with a passionate kiss and whispered in his ear.

'Let's get you home, fella and send Mrs Jones on her way…'

Chapter 78

(Trade Union office, Rotherham, June 1912)
Not unexpectedly, the first call on the Monday was from the Chairman of the Union, Norman Braithwaite. He did not hold back with a torrent of anger towards Jack.

'Well, Jack I have to express my disappointment in your comments at our meeting. I've always supported you – even when you've over-stepped before. Now, you've really put the cat amongst the pigeons. The committee members were bloody furious, lad. And I mean furious. Who the hell do you think you are, demanding resignations? They're demanding your head, your immediate resignation!'

Jack waited patiently as the rant continued and then spoke.

'Listen Norman. I have appreciated your guidance and sponsorship over the last few years and my issue is not personal. I respect you and your contribution. However, if you and my colleagues are determined to continue their predictable approach to our mission, I will not accept that position. I will tender my resignation – given the rest of the Executive are prepared to do the same. I will then put my position to our membership at the October Conference. We need a significant change in our politics, Norman – not the current acceptance of the grovelling to the Liberals and their employer friends.'

Braithwaite returned to his tirade and indicated that his colleagues were declining to resign.

'No bloody chance. Why should they dance to your tune, Jack Prendergast?'

Jack interrupted.

'We are not about to agree, Mr Braithwaite, so I'll repeat what I said earlier. If they choose not to resign, I'll demand that they stand for re-election or appointment at the

Conference. I've already got a team of replacements ready who share my views.'

Braithwaite ended the call without further comment.

Jack sat and mused. He had not yet sought other candidates but it was clear he had to move quickly before others started to send their messages to the members.

He picked up the telephone and started his campaign.

Chapter 79

(Labour Party meeting, Brawmarsh, July 1912)
'*Might as well be hung for a sheep as a lamb*' Jack thought as he sat to the table. Following his confrontation with his union group, he decided a similar approach to this assembly.

Cliff Roberts welcomed the two new councillors who had now been appointed as members of the meeting.

'Well, gentlemen. We are making significant steps forward in our community. Two new council members. Our message is clearly getting through....'

As Jack raised his hand to speak, Charlie Betts stood.

'I'm a new member of this group and newly appointed member of Brawmarsh Council, so I'd like to introduce meself. To be honest, I was elected as a result of the efforts of very few of you. Jack Prendergast and Willy Arthur and their families and friends worked their backsides off to win the elections for Willy and myself. The rest of you are a bloody joke. Lots of noise, no bloody effort.'

He waved a pointed finger to the meeting.

'How many of you went out and chased our voters? How many turned up to encourage? Bugger all! But many of you turned up at the count, at the back. Waiting until you knew the result and then creeping forward to give us your congratulations! You are not fit for the Socialist cause...I'm watching you all! The term 'socialist' seems to cause you bloody pain. I'm telling you that I will not bow to your weak and pathetic efforts to drive our party. I'm determined to drive an agenda which is about dealing with poverty, dealing with the unemployed and distressed people in this town. That's why I was elected. And with you...or without you, that's my aim.'

Jack could do no more than nod. The man had made the speech on his behalf. The meeting, initially quiet after this onslaught, started to grumble amongst themselves.

He stood and held up his hand.

'Let me state…and you will probably not be surprised, that I entirely agree with the views which Charlie has expressed. I have been a member of this insipid Committee for several years, and you all still haven't got the simple message that we need to push a stronger agenda. A number of us went out last year and told our population what we wanted to do. That's why Charlie and Willy were elected. So, gentlemen, the three of us may still be a minority in this group, but I'm calling for your resignations! Let the true representatives of the working class now take control. Stand down all of you!'

Roberts stood and slapped his hand to the table.

'You bastards will ruin the Labour Party in this area. If you're not happy, you should step down!'

Willy Arthur raised himself and thumped his fist.

'I've heard enough over my short time as a member here. I call on the whole Committee to present themselves to the members for election. I'm not a great reader, but as I understand our constitution, it requires three members to call for this. You have the three, Chairman!'

Cliff Roberts scurried through his papers and exchanged hurried and terse comments with his supporters.

Jack spoke once more.

'Don't bother checking your documents, Mr Chairman. Willy is absolutely correct. I therefore demand you present yourselves for re-election at our Annual General Meeting in October. I look forward to your confirmation and communication to our members. Thank you.'

With that he, Charlie and Willy stood and walked from the room.

***

'So, how many people are planning to fall out with, Jack. You have attacked your union group, your Labour Party and no doubt you'll be as bad at the next Council meeting. You are really upsetting a fair few folk.'

'Listen, Florence, my attitude has had to change. You heard my comments some weeks ago. I can no longer play the bloody moderate. I will be true to my beliefs in future.'

'And if you lose your job, Jack...and you could, where does that leave me and your children?'

He frowned and shook his head.

'And what should I do? You have told me in the past about your commitment to the women's movement. Don't challenge me now when I'm only following my principles and my view of our future. I'm confident that my views, my attitudes are right. Just support me, Florence.'

She, hands on hips, stood before him.

'I hope you're right, Jack because I have to tell you that your passion has been delivered in another way. We've another child joining us....'

Chapter 80

This was to be the most difficult time in his life to date. Jack was throwing his job, his future to the votes of the meeting. The mood in the Union had been positively hostile over the last few months. He had faced abuse and slurs – not directly but clearly spread from the more senior members of his organisation. He had been told, from some in the know, that he would lose his position and would not ever return. He was labelled a 'bloody Marxist, a Communist' and therefore not fit for office.

He had collected a small number of candidates to stand – only six. The Committee was eleven members and therefore he and all his nominees need to win their votes to give a majority on the Executive.

As he arrived at the session, the mood was uncomfortable. He was ignored by some, welcomed by others. He understood the attitudes. Disrupting the past status quo. Threatening the positions of a number of longstanding members.

Bugger that. He thought. *Stay true and confident in your belief, Jack.*

Braithwaite declared the conference open and undertook the usual required procedures at the commencement.

He – almost reluctantly – turned to the proposals from the floor. There were a number of routine corrections to the previous minutes and various challenges on funds and spend. Eventually he turned to the membership, sighing.

'Right members, from Jack Prendergast. A proposition that the entire Executive Committee stand down and submit themselves for re-selection. As I understand this, there are alternative candidates for these positions. I wish to declare my personal opposition to this proposal. I believe, we

280

represent the majority of the membership and do so very well. I do not agree with Mr Prendergast's desire to move our union to more socialist principles. Indeed, I have a concern that he wishes us to become a more Marxist organisation leading you to more strikes and confrontations with your employers. I ask that you reject this attempt to seek rebellion and agitation.'

He moved to one side with a reasonable level of applause.

Jack moved to the podium. He was nervous. His future, and his income. depended on his capability to convince the audience. He faced them seeing a number who had already turned their backs and seemed determined to ignore his remarks.

'Members. Despite our Chairman's comments I do not seek to create disruption. Let me declare, that I do not share the attitudes and views of the current Committee and, frankly, have found their approach for some time to be unrepresentative of the membership. I am approaching this conference with different ideas. I have some six of our members who will stand to support these views.'

He watched the congregation and recognised that they had not been inspired to date by his comments. There was a need to send some simpler thoughts. He put his papers to one side.

'It is time I sent you a simple message. You are all here to represent your membership. Go back and tell them you voted for no change, for the easy option. To keep the employers running their lives, cutting their pay, their hours. Playing free with their jobs. Next week unemployed. No representation, no safe working conditions, a life dependent on the rich men who rule their lives.'

He stopped to take a drink and noted some stirring in his audience.

'I'm standing here representing not just you. I'm for your wives and your children. For you and their future.

281

Think, members. Do you want your families to have your lives or a better chance with their time? My colleagues and I think we need better opportunities for your bairns. Not scrambling for food and rent, being subject to the owners offering work at their whim. If you hold with the current body, the current politics, your children will repeat what you have now!'

He paused and felt a more positive response.

'We want a better life – a time where you have the right to look after your future and that of your families. Yes, it will cause some pain and suffering for a short while, but what do you have at this time?'

'I'll shut up shortly. You'll either understand what the future holds and go with us or accept what you have. This is your choice – for you and the rest of your – and your children's life. Our Chairman has me labelled a Marxist. I doubt he has even read what Marx stated. If it means that I believe that the people of this country should share the benefits of their labour and have a better quality of life as a result, then yes I'm a Marxist.'

He stopped and looked across the room.

'Support my proposal. Vote for the new candidates. Move our union away from their slumber and move yourselves and your families to a better future.'

Jack moved back to his seat. The conference appeared stunned and many entered into private and heated debate amongst themselves. All the current Executive members and their opponents stood to make their call for support – some more convincing than others.

The conference dealt with standard and routine issues before the vote was taken. With only around one hundred delegates, it would be established relatively quickly whether the call by Jack had been answered.

After an hour or so, Norman Braithwaite took to the lectern to announce the results. Jack listened intently as the votes for each candidate was declared. The outcome was that Jack and four of his colleagues were elected, leaving the current committee with a narrow majority. However, the shock result was that Braithwaite lacked the support, and was not re-elected.

Jack could not help but feel some sympathy for the man. He had held his position for many years and had been a mentor for him in his early days.

He moved towards him and thrust out his hand in a gesture of reconciliation, but was rebuffed.

Braithwaite waved him away, clearly shocked and angry with the conference decision. He turned and pointed.

'You'll destroy this bloody union with your extremist views. I hope you're happy!'

Jack shook his head in disappointment and chose not to respond, walking instead to join his newly elected group to extend his congratulations.

His first battle had resulted in some success. Now to tackle the local Labour party hierarchy.....

***

One week later the local party meeting was well attended, with membership having increased significantly following the local miner's strike, and as a result of increasing deprivation in the community.

Once again, with Willy and Charlie, Jack had convinced a number of men to stand against the current ruling committee.

Cliff Roberts and others amongst his group had undertaken their speeches and. Jack approached the makeshift stage in the Village Hall.

'I'm not about to give you a long, drawn-out speech, as you'll only listen to the first minute or so...you've already enough from Mr Roberts and his friends to send you to sleep '

This drew laughs and cheers from the audience.

'So, here's the message. The current Committee have been around for too long. They don't choose to understand the poverty, loss of jobs, reduced pay and poor working conditions you experience. They cuddle up to the local Liberals and are led by the nose. Sadly, we now have Ramsay MacDonald as our national leader. Another bloody moderate cow-tailing to the Government. Time for a change, members. Vote for some passion, belief and energy. You have committed your fees to the party. It's time you saw action to return your contribution. Thank you.'

Roberts and his cronies smiled to themselves, having expected a more substantial attack.

The vote for each candidate was to be a show of hands to elect the nine Committee members.

Roberts, as current Chairman, led the call for votes. As he called each name, it was clear that the current members were lacking support. By the conclusion, six of the challengers – including Jack, Willy and Charlie were voted to the Committee. Roberts retained his seat.

It was Charlie who stood and thanked the membership.

'The mood is changing, members. You have given us your trust. Now, prepare for true socialism to prevail. Thank you!'

The meeting erupted into cheers and shouts of support.

Willy raised his hands in appreciation and turned to Jack.

'Right, lad. We've upset the bloody apple cart. Better be ready to show we mean it!...'

Chapter 81

Mary had left a message that Thomas would be in the Club tonight and suggested Jack join him for a 'celebratory beer'.

He arrived at around seven o'clock to find the Club room quiet with just the usual snooker players and domino men in attendance. He bought a drink and took a seat musing over the last month. He'd had enough politics over the last few weeks, and desperately needed a time to relax and devote attention to Florence and the family. She was, once again, blooming in pregnancy, and appeared to be more relaxed than previously in bearing this child.

As usual his brother-in-law, accompanied by Sammy, burst energetically into the room.

'Why do you always turn up after I've bought my beer, Thomas? Are you lurking outside so I bloody pay?'

Thomas gently slapped him on the cheek.

'That's because, fella you'll be buying me a couple of beers tonight!'

Jack shook his head. He tended to be concerned when his brother-in-law became enthusiastic – it inevitably had a bloody downside at some point. He sighed and waited.

'The houses, Jack. Finished them today. Ready to move in, fella. That's bloody grand isn't it?'

In the last few weeks, Jack had put the house move to the back of his mind. Florence, inevitably, had referred to it with a substantial and costly proposals for decorating and furnishing. He had sought to nod in agreement to maintain the peace. He responded with an attempt at enthusiasm

'Aye, wonderful, Thomas. Pleased you've got finished. When are we thinking of a move date?'

'Next week'

'You're having a bloody laugh, fella! We can't just up and move in a week. I've to give notice and we'll need to pack up and sort a whole raft of stuff.

Thomas initially looked disappointed, but his enthusiasm soon returned.

'So, give your notice tomorrow. Your Florence ull get things moving...'

He heaved a further sigh in response.

'Listen, you daft bugger. Florence is now coming four months pregnant. No way am I having her stressing and lifting.'

Thomas smirked and smacked his hand hard against Jack's shoulder.

'And your sister too, fella. Due next June or July.'

Jack sat back and threw his hands in the air.

'Jesus, Thomas. It's not a bloody breeding competition! Can you not keep it in your pants...!'

'Says he, with his third child on the way.'

Sammy watched the exchange bemused and interrupted.

'Just for consolation, me and Alice aren't joining this race.'

Thomas punched him gently on the arm.

'Well, lad if you need any tips we're your men...'

Sammy laughed briefly and hung his head.

'Aye, well mebbe that's the case, fellas. We've been trying for a bairn for some time. Alice seems convinced that it's cost we haven't married.'

Thomas – his character ever lacking any awareness of the feelings of others – burst in.

'They'll always try that one, lad. Don't fall for it...!'

Jack gave him the hard stare.

'Not a bloody clue, Thomas, have you?'

He turned back to Sammy.

'If it's any help, fella Florence and I had to wait. We lost one in pregnancy. Just trust that your time will come.'

286

Sammy gave a gentle smile and nodded in appreciation. Jack decided he needed to lift the mood.

'Right, Thomas. Your round. And let me remind you that – despite living next door against my better judgement -you are not bloody welcome at my house unless you ask!'

He turned to Sammy.

'You're not moving in are you? He's not offered you the house on the other side of us?'

'No, Jack. Fine where we are' he laughed.

'Thank God. Couldn't cope with you bloody singing all day long!'

They were interrupted by a call from the bar.

'Telephone call for Jack Prendergast.'

He jumped to his feet. Every thought went to his mind, but particularly Florence. He ran to the telephone.

'Hello fella! Tried your office earlier but needed to speak to you soonest.'

'Bloody hell, Seamus. You had me panicking – thought my lass was in difficulty with our child!'

'Ah, sorry, lad. So, you've another on the way then?'

Jack drew a calming breath and went to reply before the Irishman interrupted.

'So that's both of us, Jack. Teresa's due next May.'

Jack laughed, now more relaxed.

'We're due April or so. And Thomas and Mary. Due June or July. Welcome to the bloody competition!'

Seamus stopped speaking and seemed to be uncomfortable in his mumbled response.

'You alright, Seamus?'

'Well, no problems but...the papers I gave ya...the fella's not able to pick them up for a while. Been arrested and jailed. Sorry lad. Are you OK to tuck them away for a spell?'

Jack blanched and responded uneasily.

'Shit, fella! They are not the sort of thing I want in my possession. From what I read things are getting more difficult over there?'

He waited for a response and could recognise that Seamus was struggling to reply. After a long pause the man replied.

'Look Jack, these papers are important to our cause. I can't tell you more but don't destroy them, lad. Things are not good at all. You'll hear more in the news, no doubt. Without saying too much, the armies are forming. Not looking too good at all. Sorry fella, need to go....speak soon...'

Jack stood with the receiver in his hands. *For Christs sake, Seamus what shit have you left me in...?*

He returned to the bar room and sought to appear unruffled by the discussion.

'All OK Jack?'

He nodded briefly and settled to his chair.

'We've been talking about the problems overseas. Do you think we've a war coming?'

He brought himself back to the conversation.

'Mmm. I think that it's likely, Thomas. There are issues with the Turks and Serbia, as I read it. The papers say that the Germans are building their arms. The bloody Kaiser is as mad as a hatter. I'd say it's likely.'

Sammy leaned across to speak.

'Well, I'll defend my country, fellas. I'll be there in a shot to sign up. Won't take us long to sort them buggers out, will it?'

Thomas drew himself up in agreement.

'And me, lad. I'd be there. King and Country.'

Jack sought to restrict any comment but failed.

'Are you bloody serious? You'd go and fight for nothing. What value to our country? We don't need a war. It's a way to distract our men from their suffering. And to reduce the population. Many will die for this bloody pointless cause. We'll be left with widow's and fatherless children. Who will look after them? The warmongers like Churchill and others will enjoy the battle sitting back in their warm offices in London. They are not thinking of you and the other men. Only land, status and their positions. For God's sake, stop your bloody silly patriotism!'

Both Sammy and Thomas reacted to his comments. Sammy first.

'I love my country and if they call me I'll go! It's about our nation, fella. I won't sit back as a coward!.'

'And me, Sammy. I'll fight for my children and my country!'

Jack shook his head and moved to leave.

'I'm no coward. But I'm no bloody fool either... I'm away.'

Chapter 82

'So, you've had enough fall out with my brother? Are you determined to take on the world, fella?'

'Because he's being bloody stupid, Florence. Both him and Sammy. They're being led by this build up of phoney patriotism. He insists that he'll join up, volunteer if war is declared. A married man with two children and another on the way. Just bloody daft.'

Florence sat and studied him.

'Do you think we'll go to war, Jack?'

'I hope not, lass but I think the Austrians and Germany have got their eyes on parts of the Turkish Empire…and more.'

'But why would we need to get involved? It's a long way from us. Why should we do anything?'

Jack sighed and struggled to explain his reading to his wife.

'It's a bloody mess, Florence. Germany falls out with Russia, then back off. They support Austria and then don't. We support Russia because we have an alliance with France. Bluntly, it's about greed and opportunity. The Tories are looking for war, the Liberals are not in favour. Our party – the Labour Party – whilst we are led by MacDonald are adamantly against it. Our previous leader, Henderson is more sympathetic towards supporting our so-called allies.'

He continued now in flow.

'And that's not the worst of it, lass. Ireland will be a big problem very soon, according to Seamus. Each side are building small armies. Our government is playing silly buggers over Home Rule. If the fires don't start in Europe, they will in Ireland – or both.'

She looked at him with concern.

'Tell me you didn't get involved when you were over there with Seamus?'

He paused before waving her away.

'No lass. I'm not involved at all...'

She smiled and disappeared to attend to a crying Arthur.

What the hell can I do? I'm compromised thanks to Seamus...

His immediate inclination was to throw the Irish papers on his fire. At least, he decided, he would not open the envelope. Better he knew as little as possible....

***

Florence and he were occupied by the impending house move, assembling their furniture and belongings for the move. She had committed to a move on the Saturday 30th of November. Consequently, he had been required to strike an agreement for their departure with the current landlord. It had been agreed that they would be required to pay two weeks rent over and above their occupation. Jack, whilst uncomfortable with what he regarded as an unnecessary cost – caused by the short notice from Thomas in his view, accepted that this was only fair and reasonable, given their past good relations.

There was further spend on a cart to transport their possessions and to fit the new property with flooring and curtaining. He suspected there was more money required to satisfy Florence's plans. On a minor level, there was a few beers for Sammy and Keith, who had volunteered to assist with the heavy lifting on the basis of a free session with Thomas and Jack in the not-to-distant future.

The move went reasonably well, other than the initially strained relations between Jack, Thomas and Sammy. The mood warmed as the men threw themselves into lifting and placing the furniture in several locations, until both Mary and Florence were happy. Both he and Thomas grimaced as their wives exchanged their opinions on the future requirement for re-decoration and the plans for the gardens.

Jack left the group in further debate and walked to the rear of the property. A garden…space for vegetables – if he ever had the time, and still room for some grassed area for the children's play. Behind was open countryside and a small stream. It was a different world from their last house on terraced streets with only a paved area behind and overlooking the neighbours with little privacy. He moved inside – a real toilet and bathroom! Their own, not shared. Three bedrooms – bloody hell, three…Plenty of space downstairs with a nice living room and a decent size kitchen cum scullery.

He stopped himself for a moment and felt some guilt.

My God, I'm representing some of the poorest families and I'm standing revelling in my good fortune.

He felt an arm around his shoulder.

'I can read your mind, husband. You are thinking we are lucky getting all this. Well. Let me tell you we are not lucky. You and I have worked for this house. It's not your fault that others don't have this yet.'

He embraced her and then looked again at the garden.

'I understand, Florence but this should be the way for all the poorest in this country. A home to accommodate their family, a garden. Inside toilets, avoiding having to share the bloody awful outside privies. Bathrooms with hot water rather than cold washes in the kitchen. That should be what our Government and councils should be seeking. Not bloody war and more suffering.'

She held him close.

'Follow your dream, Jack. Follow your belief and passions. It will happen, lad…it will happen…make it happen…'

Chapter 83

(Labour Party meeting , Brawmarsh, December 1912)
'Time to stand aside, Mr Roberts.'

This opening remark stopped the meeting.

Willy Arthur stood and read from a pre-prepared script.

'I've read our constitution in detail. You have to subject yourself to a vote. The numbers have changed, fella. You no longer have majority support on this Committee.'

Roberts threw his hands to the table.

'You silly buggers have the numbers to vote me down, but you'll regret it! I'm still a member with a lot of support. Vote me from my role – I'll be back with the more sensible councillors once they see how you mess up. Trust me!'

Willy gazed at him almost pitifully.

'Thank you for your token resignation speech, Cliff. Let's do the vote. I'm nominating Jack Prendergast as our Chairman.'

The hands were raised and he was formally declared to the senior position. Jack stood and spoke to the group.

'Gentlemen, I'll thank you for your confidence. I don't propose to hold this role for too long. I have many demands on my life and I believe there are others who can drive our new agenda. I will be breaking away from our cosy association with the local Liberals. I will demand that our movement leads the battle against poverty and unemployment. I, and my colleagues, have other priorities. Time for change..!'

***

He returned to the new house, exhilarated but pensive. He shared with Florence the outcomes of the meeting.

She was clearly unhappy.

'You have enough responsibilities, Jack Prendergast. Now one more. When will your bloody family come anywhere in your first considerations! I'm getting angry and upset....another child that won't have your time and attention, is it?'

Chapter 84

(Christmas , Brawmarsh, December 1912)

It had been a wonderful and relaxing time for the family. Despite their spend on the house they had saved sufficient money to deliver gifts for the children – tops and whips for Emma and a couple of soft rough, dog shaped, cuddly toys for their boy.

On Christmas Day they were joined by Thomas and Mary and their brood, and Sammy and Alice, who had, with a deal of prompting, joined the day.

They enjoyed a substantial meal. From somewhere – they didn't ask – Sammy had delivered a large goose.

'It was wandering down the road and died in front of me…mebbe it was a bit tired..'

Given the bird was enormous, it appeared unlikely that it had suffered its demise in that way but no one chose to ask any further questions.

Inevitably the night developed into singing and dancing, with Sammy attempting some recent and new songs. Much as they sought Jack to perform he declined.

'I've done my one time. I've no other songs I know. Leave me be.'

He drained another beer, now feeling the effects, and turned to Thomas.

'So, brother-in-law. Are you still going to fight the Germans?'

Florence gave a fevered look towards him.

'For Christ's sake, Jack! Don't bloody start another argument…'

Thomas, recognising the potential for discord, simply smiled and took Jack's hand.

'Time to call it a night, fella.'

***

The mood the following day was tense and uncomfortable. Florence spent the morning banging pots and pans in the kitchen, alternatively playing with their children and, to all intents, refusing to speak with her husband.

Eventually he broke the silence.

'Are you going to be a misery all day?'

It was as if an inferno had been lit.

'A bloody misery, you sodding arsehole! You get yerself drunk, start to cause trouble with my brother and contribute next to bugger all to the day. We have to talk, Jack. Your temper and aggression might be fine for your politics but you're bringing it home! Something has to change…your workload is making you irritable and unreasonable. You need to put some time into me and the bairns.'

He chose not to respond, recognising that any comment would simply inflame the issue and agitate his wife to further argument. He reflected on his commitments and struggled to understand how he could step away from any of these.

After allowing Florence some time to cool down, he asked her to sit down with him.

'Listen to me for a while. You are right. I have far too much on my plate at the moment, but I don't know how to reduce my commitments. The Union is my job, our income. Having just challenged both the Union Executive and the Labour Party group, I can hardly now walk away. My position on the council is important to me – it's the way we advance our case in the community. So, Florence, I'm struggling with my options…'

She was determined that Jack had to move on and chose not to concede and sympathise.

'Your choice, husband. I'm telling you that I have had to give up things in my life. You need to understand that your politics can't be all-consuming. I cannot continue being the mother and father to our children!'

He had not seen her so angry throughout their life together. If she ever discovered his link to the Irish cause, she would kill him....

Chapter 85

(Labour Group meeting, March 1913)
The industrial strife in the country continued. Strikes in abundance as the trade unions increased their membership. The Tories and Liberals had founded a new alliance recognising the threat and deciding that, at the next election, their motives must be to hold back the growing influence of the socialist movement amongst the working classes.

The situation in Ireland grew progressively worse. The promised Home Rule Bill was continually dragged through Parliament, with the House of Lords – despite their more limited authority – continuing to find ways to delay and frustrate.

Jack had spoken on several occasions to Seamus by telephone. He had been unable to obtain any clarity on the collection of the material he held.

'It'll be right, lad. I'll sort a pick up as soon as I can. Bear with me...'

It was clear from their conversations that both Catholics and Protestants had continued to prepare themselves for impending rebellion and conflict. He had learned that, amongst the nationalists particularly, unemployment was increasing and that poverty and infant deaths were substantially higher than in England. The resentment was increasing.

'The Loyalists have declared that Home Rule will be determined on the streets of Belfast, Jack. If that's their attitude, then it will be also fought on the feckin streets of Dublin...'

His home life was still not harmonious.

Florence seemed increasingly bitter and resentful towards Jack. He had not reduced his workload or commitment, despite his promises that he would do so. His time with her and the family remained limited – another meeting constantly demanding his attention.

Her anger was inflamed more by the lack of progress to allow women their vote. She had read that one of the Pankhurst sisters, Sylvia, had been thrown from the Woman's Social and Political Union due to her drive to attract support in the working-class women from London's East End.

Ejected for attracting working class lasses. They are not the body I can continue to recognise as leading our cause. A middle-class movement chasing votes for certain cliques of their female friends....

Jack was attending another Council meeting. She lay back now close to her term and then, venting her anger, moved to their bedroom and threw her clothes into a case. She wrapped herself in a coat, woke the children quietly, wrapping them in covers as best she could.

She placed the children on the settee whilst she left the house.

'Mary, are you there?'

As the door opened, Mary in her nightdress, Florence bustled past her.

'Throw the bairns to bed somewhere. I'll sleep on the floor if I have to. Mebbe this will make him bloody listen now!'

***

He found himself unable to concentrate and on a few occasions lost track of the meeting. His predecessor, Cliff Roberts, took great pleasure in his loss of attention.

'Mr Chairman....' The voice was dismissive and sneering. 'Are you awake...are you with us?'

Jack struggled to return his thoughts to the discussion.

'Sorry, gents. A bit on my mind, carry on.'

Even his colleagues longer-standing colleagues, both Willy and Charlie, glanced at each other with concern.

Where was the man with his passion now? He seemed subdued and completely distracted.

The meeting concluded with no significant resolutions ; disappointing for the new members who expected some more energy and drive.

They watched with some puzzlement as Jack closed the meeting, collected his papers and left without any exchanges with the members.

He returned to an empty house. He knocked on his sister's door.

'She's not coming home, fella. Not at the moment. Go to bed....'

Chapter 86

(Brawmarsh, April 1913)

She had returned with the children on the following day, still irate and cursory in her exchanges with her husband.

Their relationship remained strained for some weeks until she announced, in the middle of the night, that their third child was 'on its way…now..!'

Jack leapt from his bed, threw on some clothes and ran to his sister's door, raising Mary from her bed, and then sprinted to the house of the local midwife.

Within two hours their new daughter was delivered.

As Florence embraced their new addition, he approached them both.

'Mebbe a new start, Florence. I understand your frustration. I will stand away from some of responsibilities. I'm sorry…..my family will now become my priority, but I will still need to deliver on my other commitments. I'll try to sort this quickly…I honestly will…'

Tired and still in pain she pushed herself upright in the bed.

'I hope so, Jack. Life has to change for us.'

She turned her attention back to the new-born.

'We haven't talked about a name for this little flower, have we?'

'A flower, Florence. What about Rose?'

She shook her head.

'No, fella. Look at her complexion. Pale and creamy….. like a lily'

They both nodded and wrapped their arms around each other.

'Lily…'

Chapter 87

(Trade Union office, Rotherham, June 1913)

The birth of their new daughter, following their period of discord, had a significant impact on Jack. He had to acknowledge that he was over-committed in his trade union and political responsibilities.

He had advised the local Labour group that he could no longer continue as their Chairman, given his domestic and other obligations. This was accepted. Charlie Betts was appointed to the role. Jack was satisfied that their political views were similar and felt that the drive for change would be maintained under their new head.

He had sat with Florence and explained that he simply could not stand down from the Steelworkers Executive. He had led a challenge – albeit unsuccessfully - to change their direction. To leave the Committee now would appear like 'sour grapes' and would lose the impetus they had within the movement. Additionally, his full-time role was vulnerable to people like Braithwaite, who had clearly taken against Jack since the conference.

'He can manipulate the Executive, if I'm not there even from outside the Committee, Florence. It could cost me my job. He'll be looking for ways to move me out...'

Equally, he coveted his council role. He had fought hard to attract local support and again walking away would have a negative effect on both he and the party for the future.

She had reluctantly accepted his arguments, but insisted that where possible he should not volunteer for any additional duties in either the trade union or party.

As he sat at his desk, he studied how he could break the news to her. He had just concluded a difficult, but entertaining call from Norman Braithwaite. In terse tones, the Chairman had taken pleasure in breaking some new information.

'So, you are aware, the trade unions have been invited a conference in August to meet with employers' groups in London, seeking to resolve the current difficulties...strikes and confrontations and other disputes. We considered you as a delegate, but soon recognised that you're too volatile and extreme. I've been nominated to represent our Union.'

Jack could almost visualise the smirk on the man's face. He took great pleasure in his response.

'Well, hardly democratic, Norman but not surprising really, is it?' You've never left bloody Sheffield so how will you travel to a big city...have they given you a map?'

He heard the man start to bluster and swear.

'Now, stay calm Norman. The reason I ask about your plan for travelling is that I've been nominated by my local Labour group to attend. We can travel together, fella...lots to discuss?'

The telephone went dead. Jack smiled as he gently replaced the receiver.

Mmm, mebbe we won't be sharing a carriage on this trip...

However, he had another bridge to cross...Florence...Given, they now had three children under four and one of them, a young bairn to cope with, he was clear that she would not be entirely happy that he planned to be away for two days.

***

He practiced his speech to her on the bus journey to Brawmarsh. He decided he needed both more preparation and some form of liquid support.

'Bloody hell, Thomas. How have you got away with being here, lad?

His sister had delivered a new son, Frederick – to be known as Freddie - some four days earlier.

303

'Listen, Jack. Much as I love your Mary and the bairns, sometimes I need to take a spot of courage before going home. A break …just a bit of my own time.'

Jack nodded, tapped his glass against Thomas's and drew heavily on his pint.

'Jesus fella, you think you've got a hard night. I've to tell her I'm away for two days in London to a meeting…'

Thomas looked up from his beer.

'Are you bloody serious?. Well, one consolation lad is they'll be no more children to bother you…she'll cut off your balls…all the best with that one. And bear in mind we're next door so I don't want to hear you suffering….!'

They clapped glasses together again and both laughed.

'If you hear me in pain, lad for God's sake come and help me!'

***

They limited themselves to the two beers and arrived at their doors.

'Good luck, lad . Don't send my bloody sister to mine again. I've enough pain without her and three more!'

Jack entered to silence. Florence eventually came down the stairs and raised he finger to her lips.

'Hush! They've all gone off so quick tonight. Mary and I took them to the park and they ran around like idiots. Tired themselves out completely. I've done a grand stew and dumplings for us. Be nice to just sit and relax, fella won't it?'

Jack decided tonight was not the time to raise his issue with her…

Chapter 88

(Jack and Florence's house, June 1913)

'So, what have you got to tell me, Jack Prendergast?'

He sat up abruptly and nervously gazed at her bemused face.

How the bloody hell did she do that...how could should she know what was going on in his mind?

'What do you mean, Florence? I've nothing concerning me...'

She laughed out loud and, hand to her face, shook her head.

'You are so bloody easy to understand, fella. You've something to talk to me about. I can read you like a book!'

He looked at her and hesitated.

'Listen, Florence. I've left the Chairman's role with the party – I'll still have meetings every month or so. I'm only bound to attend quarterly meetings of the Union. My council meetings will still be every month or so and I still have to do my work and visits in the community as an elected member. Other than my day job, that's the best I can do with my commitments.'

She chose not to reply awaiting his next comments.

'I've been nominated to attend a meeting in London in September. Trade unions and employers to try and sort our current issues. That will be two days of my – our time - together. If you want me to decline I will, but not without any great feeling that I'll be failing my party and my prospects of driving my union forward. We have a chance to confront the owners of businesses and promote our case. I, honestly am so bloody confused at the moment, lass. I don't want us to fall out, but I need to be true to my beliefs.....'

She took his face in her hands.

'Jack, you are a total bloody idiot. I understand your indecision…I really do. Your passions are what made you so attractive to me, so I can hardly continue to debate and disagree with you, can I? I've also thought about my attitude when we fell out. I was frustrated by your disregard of me and the bairns, but I understand it was what you were born to do. If I don't accept that, we'll never stay together. You must go to this meeting and tell them your views. Go with my blessing, lad.'

Chapter 89

(London Conference, September 1913)

Before his departure, Jack had held another telephone conversation with Seamus. It appeared that the Irishman was reluctant to participate in the discussion, but Jack insisted as he sought to clarify the contents of the package.

'Aw, look lad. I'll get it picked up. Been busy with the new addition – little Sinead – grand girl, she is…'

'Pleased Seamus, but you're not answering my question. It seems that things are really heating up over there. I've heard that the workers have been locked out of their employment..'

Seamus interrupted quickly.

'Docks and railway workers have been on strike and they are bringing in rogue labour. They've sworn to stay on strike for as long as it takes. There's no bloody money and bugger all food, Jack. It's bad and the armies are building. Your government is dragging it's arse on home rule so my friends are becoming very angry.'

'And what am I holding, Seamus?'

'Don't worry lad. Just tuck it away and I'll arrange collection…'

The phone went dead.

***

The journey to London would take some six to seven hours, joining the mainline from Doncaster, after a slower train from Rotherham. The trade unions had proved competent in organising the route and return tickets for their delegates. Consequently, Jack along with some thirty members from the north were assembled at Doncaster, including men from the North-East. The introductions amongst the group were relatively brief. There was some unease – who were the senior delegates? And who amongst them were the strongest characters, the one's likely to raise their voices?

Jack settled into a carriage alongside one or two of the representatives from his union. Unsurprisingly, Norman Braithwaite chose to join an alternative party and ignored Jack's presence throughout the entire trip. The conversation was loud and passionate with a number of men declaring that they were there to 'tell the bloody employers their fortune'. The mood was in keeping with the confrontational approach of their body over the last two years and an air of militancy and aggression was in evidence.

The men had brought their packed meals and many exchanged parts with others, commenting on the regional variations.

'What the bloody hell is this?'

'Way, a singing hinnie, lad. A bit of a cake like. Eat it, won't bloody kill ya!'

Much of their food was standard fare. Bread and dripping, cheese and fruit. Totally in common was bottles of beer – they swapped drinks to test the flavour and strength of their local brews. Regardless, all seemed to be acceptable and there was none left by their arrival at St Pancras Station.

They left the train and, as a group, walked with some trepidation towards the exit.

One man – a representative from Newcastle – claimed to know his way around and led the body from the station and onto the external concourse. He stopped and scratched his head and faced robust comment and abuse from some of the contingent.

'Bloody hell, we've Dick Whittington leading us. Turn again lad...tha might make Mayor!'

'He's never left bloody Ashington – he'd get lost in the tarn, he would!'

Eventually a short, stocky man appeared and waved the group to a halt.

'Ayup, fellas. Is it Ramsay MacDonald?'

'No bloody chance. He wouldn't recognise a working-class bloke all day long!'

By now the men, influenced by their beer consumption, were laughing and slapping each other on their backs.

One of them broke into song and was quickly joined by others.

Oh me lads, ya shudda seen us gannin...

They were soon challenged by the Yorkshire contingent.

Wheear ast tha bin sin ah saw thee...on Ilkla Mooar baht 'at

As the competition became louder, the passing local people stopped in amazement and some disgust at this sudden outburst. The little man ran around waving them to silence.

'Gents....gents. Please compose yerselves. Yer supposed to be a respectable representation of the working class, not a bloody gang of ruffians...'

The men cheered each other and continued to throw gentle abuse towards him before calming.

'If tha knows the way, lead on Captain...if there's a pub on the way, make sure tha stops there...!'

The men laughed and jeered, but followed the man along the narrow pavement, continuing their songs and chants. He led them down a busy road until they arrived at a large and ugly building down a short street bordering along the railway line.

'This is your accommodation, lads. Two to a room so pair up with yer mates.'

They looked at the hostel in dismay. The external paint flaking, the windows covered in grime.

'Bloody hell lads. I'd have brought my paint brushes if they'd asked!'

'Are the employers staying here, fella?'

'Will we be joining our bosses for dinner at the Ritz then?

He raised his hands defensively.

'Best I can do with the money your unions coughed up. It's one bloody night...'

The grumbles continued as they trooped inside to be met by an elderly lady who clearly stood no nonsense.

'Right, I'll need your names and who you're representing so don't mess me about, gents. And no, I don't come free with the rooms...'

'Bloody hell that's one consolation ....!'

She glared around looking for the source of the comment.

'Any more like that and you'll be finding yourself another place to sleep...names now!'

The little man danced around.

'Quick, fellas please. Meeting starts at two o'clock and you've about a mile to walk from here.'

Amidst the moans and expletives, they recorded their names and, without much guidance, wandered off to find their rooms. Inevitably, they were poorly furnished with one moderately sized bed, thin mattress on each. A small, rust ensconced sink. A shared toilet between ten rooms.

Jack found himself sharing with a large man from Newcastle, at a guess mid- forties. He was well over six feet and approaching some sixteen to seventeen stone.. Jet black hair and stubbled ruddy face. They looked at other and laughed. The other man shook his head.

'Bloody hell fella, I hope you don't move about much in your sleep...I'm Billy Wells, representing the Miners Union from Durham.'

Jack reached out and shook his hand.

'It'll be cosy, Billy. Yer a bit bigger than our lass!'

They sat on the bed and exchanged their respective views on the forthcoming meeting. Billy was clearly a passionate socialist and surprisingly to Jack, had read Das Kapital cover to cover. He had met very few men who had done so. They found they had a lot in common. Eventually they moved to join their colleagues at the hotel doorway.

The little fellow re-appeared.

'Sorry gents. In the confusion I didn't introduce myself. I'm Harold Hankey. I'm a full- time officer with the dockers in London. Now then, just follow me, will ya?'

They trooped in the afternoon sun to the venue, a large hall with – as they soon found - small and uncomfortable seats set out in rows. In front of them was a podium and, before it, a further group of more comfortable chairs clearly for the benefit of the employer's representatives who had yet to arrive.

Billy and Jack looked at each other and smiled. Billy was the first to speak.

'Follow me lads.'

He guided his group to the front of the stage and waved his colleagues to the reserved seats. Immediately Hankey dashed towards him.

'Can't sit there, fella. They're reserved they are...'

'Aye Harold. They are reserved for me and my friends. First come...first served...'

He settled back in his position and waved two fingers in the air.

As they waited, they watched the other side appear. They walked dismissively past, an air of brandy and cigar smoke from their long lunch. One of the group approached them.

'I think you'll find you are in our seats, gentlemen...'

Billy sat and crossed his legs.

'Has it got your name on it, fella? If not, then bugger off elsewhere.'

The portly man turned to look for support from his entourage, but to no effect. He moved on to a seat at the rear of the hall.

Eventually a team of five arrived and mounted the stage and seated themselves.

'Do you recognise any of these, Jack?'

Jack shook his head, causing Billy to rise and address the podium.

'Can I ask who the fuck you are and what gives you the rights to sit, like bloody God's above us? This is a conference about our future relationships...not a good start is it?'

The conference fell immediately into silence awaiting a reply.

'I'm Stanley Jordan, the Chairman of the Employers Association. These are my four colleagues from our body..... '

Immediately Billy stood again.

'So, you're all owners and employers. All taking your positions on stage. Looking down on your peasants. Well, I'm not prepared to continue this meeting unless you stand down from that platform and sit amongst the other delegates.'

He waited whilst they talked amongst themselves and then he waved his hand to the congregation.

'Right, members. We're leaving....'

As some twenty of the members rose to leave, Jordan raised his hands and spoke.

'Right. My colleagues will vacate the stage. I need to stay here to guide the meeting. Does that suffice?'

Billy turned and waved his party back to their seats without comment.

Over the next three hours, there were various speakers from both employers and trade union leaders. The message was strikingly similar. A need to find a way to reduce conflict, strikes and improve future relationships. There seemed to be no great support from either of the conference delegate groups. The employer representatives saw no scope for concessions ; the trade union members heard nothing to convince them that they should weaken their resolve to deliver their agenda for worker's rights and conditions.

The conference concluded their first session at around 5 o'clock with a proposal to meet again at 8.30 in the following morning. As the delegates departed there appeared to be no great optimism, or enthusiasm for any further debate or speeches.

Billy Wells turned to Jack.

'Bloody waste of time so far, do ya think? What's your plan for the evening? Do ya want to join me and some of the lads for a few beers?'

Jack shrugged his shoulders.

'I didn't arrive with any great expectations, Billy. Aye, I'm up for a few beers.'

They were joined by a number of other shop stewards and Labour delegates. One man from the London Dock contingent invited them to visit a local pub and try some typical East End food that evening. All agreed that there was no great benefit in returning to the hostel and walked as a group towards the pub.

***

Jack woke up, blurry eyed and staring at a large pair of Geordie feet. He was in possession of about one quarter of the bed and determined that he should vacate his space quickly. The room had an unpleasant odour – a combination of sweat and the after effects of the beer and last night's food.

He took a swill in the small sink, dowsing his head several times to seek to clear his early morning haze. From what he could recall, the party had moved to several drinking holes and finally had been encouraged to try pie and mash by the local lads.

'The mash and pie are fine. What's these bloody things at the side?'

'Eels, sunshine. Bloody grand aren't they?'

Several of the men either spat them to the floor or pushed them gingerly to the edge of their bowls. A number declined to participate and found a nearby fish and chip shop to satisfy their appetite.

Jack heard Billy start to stir and watched as he roughly rubbed his face.

'What time is it, lad?'

'About six o'clock, fella. How are you feeling?

The man grimaced and then groaned loudly.

'The beer was shit...'

'That'll be why you had six or seven pints then?'

'And that bloody sauce stuff on me pie. What was that?'

'They said it was liquor....some sort of parsley sauce...'

Billy groaned again and sat upright.

'Feel bloody sick. My stomach is churning like a cement mixer...'

Jack stood to one side as Billy pushed his way to the door.

'Toilet.....'

God help anybody who follows him....

Eventually both men sorted themselves out, dressed and knocked on the doors of their colleagues to wake them. The responses suggested that the others were in a similar state.

'Right, Jack. Better seek out a spot of breakfast then...'

Jack shook his head. The constitution of the man was unbelievable. They shouted to let the others know their plan and wandered out onto the street. They walked for some five minutes and found a small café offering cheap cooked breakfasts and entered. Within ten minutes Billy was tackling a full English. Jack chose a bacon sandwich.

'This is bloody grand.' said Billy as he slurped on a mug of builder's tea.

'You must have the constitution of an ox, fella...'

'Need to build meself up for the challenges of the day, young man.'

They were joined by their colleagues who took up a range of breakfast alternatives. When all had finished, many still clearly struggling with the after-effects of the previous night, they set off on a steady walk to the Conference Hall.

'What's your thoughts, Billy?

The man made a cutting motion across his throat.

'I've heard nothing I can take to my lads back home. No movement from the owners and employers. I'd be hung out to dry if I conceded anything so far.'

Jack nodded and replied.

'You're right. All about the unions behaving. I don't see the benefit of the meeting so far. And, to be honest, I'm really bloody annoyed that there are no Government attendees and, more to the point, no Labour leaders showing their faces. You would have thought Keir Hardie or Ramsay MacDonald could have got their arses down here for a spell, given they're only sitting up the road.'

They arrived alongside a number of other union delegates and joined the general debate amongst themselves. It became clear that the conference was regarded as a pointless exercise, called to present the employers viewpoint and carrying no significant purpose for the workers.

The morning continued to follow the theme of the previous session, and many of the delegates were now becoming both bored and irritated.

Jordan moved to the stage and held up his hands to quieten the audience.

'Gentlemen, you have heard the proposals for our way forward. We cannot continue to fight and have division. Your futures and ours depend on a mutual understanding and a better way to more calmly address our issues. I think we have made a considerable step forward through this meeting....'

Jack could hold himself back no more. He stood and moved to the podium.

'I've listened patiently over the last two days. I'd like to comment.'

Stanley Jordan looked at him in shock. He was clearly unused to being interrupted or challenged.

'I think we've heard all the contributions we need, my young man. I was about to close the meeting.'

'Aye, well two things. One, I'm not your or anyone's young man and two, you haven't closed the meeting so I'll say my piece.'

He jumped to the stage and waved his hand for attention.

'Won't keep you long. For those who've not met me, I'm Jack Prendergast. I'm here representing my Labour Party, but I'm also a Full Time Official with the Steelworkers Union. Now I've listened – as you all have – to the 'so called proposals' from our employer's group. I came here not expecting much, but prepared to look for a way in which we can take our relationships forward. I'll ask my workers delegates...have you heard anything that changes your view from when you arrived?'

The delegates applauded his comment shouting 'No', 'A bloody sham'....

He held up his hands to invite them to quieten.

'So, Mr Jordan and your associates, I suggest you listen...You and your friends have given us nothing. You have treated the meeting as an opportunity to socialise and enjoy the best the place has to offer. My colleagues have been accommodated in slum hostels, offered no food and no regard from you.'

He waved his hand towards the union delegates.

'Shall I explain what these fellas wanted to hear? Some acknowledgement that, in future, you would accept that your workforce has joined our body because you treat them poorly. A recognition of the right for us to represent them in dealing with their issues and grievances. An understanding that you – in future – have no automatic right to reduce their pay and increase their hours. An appreciation that wages are not paid at a level determined by your whim, but in negotiations with their

316

representatives. And finally, an awareness that their working conditions, their safety and health is not an optional consideration, but a right to ensure they don't lose their lives and become too damaged to work and support their families'

He paused as he was drowned out by applause and cheers.

'So, there you have it, Mr Jordan. Close your bloody meeting and frankly, don't bother proposing another one of your bloody one-sided events until you have something to tell us, something that will take our people forward and improve their lives. Until then, bugger off....!'

He stood down from the stage and, followed by the entire employee's delegation, walked from the room.

Chapter 90

(Jack and Florence's house, September 1913)

Jack had travelled back to Doncaster with Billy Wells and his friends, where his group had changed for their onward journey to Newcastle. They held a long discussion about the future, not least the implications for their union movement with the likelihood of a war in Europe.

They agreed that, inevitably, there would be government legislation to control their activities and, given the need to take men to the conflict, a change in the make-up of the workforce. Women would need to take up industrial tasks. Men unable – or unwilling - to fight would be compelled to work in the stead of those called to arms. They parted – now allies and friends – and exchanged their telephone numbers and agreed to keep up their discussions.

He arrived home, feeling totally exhausted at ten o'clock that night. The children by now fast asleep. Florence was dozing on the sofa when he arrived, but awoke and immediately embraced him.

'How has it gone, Jack? God, it's been strange without you.'

'Aye lass, I'm shattered. I'll talk with you tomorrow, Florence, but not good….'

***

The following weeks and months offered no great change in the climate between employers and their workers. Strikes and lockouts continued to disrupt their working life. There was little of this in the steel industry to date, and Jack found himself frustrated by the inaction from his union. The new Committee's attitude remained moderate and defensive, given that he and the new members were a minority and could not exercise any change in their direction.

The threat of war was increasing and seemed almost inevitable. There was talk of some industries being turned over to the production of armaments and the possibility of the younger unmarried men being conscripted to the army.

The Labour Party remained adamantly against any conflict, but as a minority in Parliament were substantially outnumbered by 'war-mongers'. At least MacDonald had declared his position as anti-war but still, in Jack's view was not the competent and far-sighted leader they required. Great Britain had formed a supportive alliance with both France and Russia over the recent years. Austria-Hungary and Germany had agreed a similar position. It appeared that Serbia – and her future – was becoming the major area of dispute and potential for any increase in tensions.

Ireland continued in ferment...and Seamus was constantly not responding to his requests to address the documents in his possession. He had thought again of disposing of them but decided to hide them away for the time being.

God knows what would happen in the next year....

Chapter 91

(Welfare Club, Brawmarsh, March 1914)

Jack and Thomas were joined by Sammy for an evening beer or two after leaving their work. Their mood was sombre as the news from both home and abroad had become increasingly concerning.

It was reported that Germany had increased its armed forces and was now building warships at a pace. The British government had equally commenced to build up their forces. It was understood, from the better-informed newspapers, that the exchanges between the various countries had become increasingly negative and more hostile.

'It's coming fellas. I think we'll be at war this year.'

Thomas sat back almost triumphantly and looked for their response.

Well, count me in, lad. I'll join whether I'm asked to or not.'

Sammy drew on his beer and slapped his hand to the table.

'It's required of any fit man, in my view. Fight for my King and Country!'

Jack narrowed his eyes and moved to change the subject.

'I think you'll find there'll be a different fight, gentlemen. The papers say that we've moved troops to Ireland. That will be the next battlefield.'

'Aye, well they need sorting as well. Bloody rebels. Time we put them in their place!'

'And what place would that be, Sammy.'

Sammy again smashed his hand down.

'Bloody Catholics causing the problems. Trying to break up our country. Need a bloody sorting to tell him who rules, they do.'

Jack laughed and looked him in the eyes.

'You know bugger all about Ireland, fella. And I mean bugger all! You listen to ignorant men who know nothing about their situation. They're in poverty, locked out of their work. No representation, no support from our government. You need to pick up a book or two and read about Ireland's history. I'm pissed off with ignorant comments like yours. Get your facts right or shut up!'

Sammy rose from his chair and pointed towards Jack.

'Don't speak to me like an idiot, fella. I've seen what's happening. Bloody rebels they are. Don't know when they are well off, they don't! You're a bloody Republican supporter – with your Irish mates...'

Jack rose from his chair and pushed Sammy's hand away.

'I'm away. I've better things to do than listen to shit like this. I'll tell ya this. Yes, I support their cause because they are in the right. The English have treated the Irish badly – from the early days until now. Do you know that when they had a potato shortage many decades ago – a famine – no food? We sent food abroad and sent them bugger all. That's the way we deal with people who are supposed to be part of our countrymen. You need to look at the history, but you won't. Easier to take your bloody ignorant view.'

Sammy leaned across to grab at Jack but was pulled back to his seat by Thomas. Jack turned to leave.

'Two things fella. Join up and get yerself killed for no reason, if that's your choice. Secondly, if you ever raise a hand to me again Sammy, you'll find out how to fight...and you'll not enjoy the outcome. Trust me.'

He stormed home and slumped into his chair.

Florence looked at him with contempt.

'Another bloody temper tantrum, Prendergast! Well, don't bring it home. I've three other bairns to deal with...I don't need your sulks and moods...I deal with it all day long with the children!'

He sighed and held up his hands in apology.

'Sorry lass. It seems like everyone I listen to thinks the war is an adventure, a chance to prove their masculinity. It's all 'we'll sort them out in no time'. Fact is, Florence the Germans, in particular, have been planning for this war for years, for Christ's sake! We are unprepared. On top of this the Irish problem will draw our attention and forces away. They don't realise how bad it will get.'

She stopped him and thrust her finger to his face.

'That's your view, fella. Not everyone's. You have to stop finding bloody confrontation at every corner, for God's sake. What's with the Irish thing now? You seem really concerned when it's raised?'

He felt himself redden and moved away.

'There's something you're not telling me, Jack.'

'There's nowt, woman. Stop giving me bloody grief, will ya!'

They took their dinner in semi-silence, before Jack, still uneasy, left her for his bed....

Chapter 92

(Labour Party meeting, Brawmarsh , May 1914)
There was no denying that he had entered the meeting feeling aggrieved and frustrated. Here was one group where he and his colleagues were in the majority.

The initial discussions were dull and routine. Charlie Betts had proved to be a competent chairman and the meeting ran to the agenda over a couple of hours.

Jack was conscious that he had been strongly advised by his wife that he should – once again – control his temper and comment. He rose to the meeting, determined to remain calm.

'We are approaching a war, colleagues. Our party at national level is against any conflict. I believe that we should also declare our position locally. I am bluntly against any dispute with countries and empires across the sea. They are simply looking for territorial gains – most of which are in territories fractured by previous minor wars and so-called peace settlements.'

'This is not our concern, members. Our position should be clear. Do not volunteer. Resist any demands for conscription. Continue to drive our rights as union members and workers.'

Cliff Roberts stood and addressed the group.

'I am no longer your Chairman, but I tell you this, Jack Prendergast. Your comments do not, from my understanding, represent the views of the men in the community. They wish to fight. They recognise that our country is under threat…'

Jack rose and aggressively pointed his finger at the man.

'How the hell are we under threat! The conflict is a thousand miles away and if we choose to resist, it will not affect our lives. The bloody leaked propaganda from our Government is appalling. There is no risk to our country. The greater risk – which you're choosing to ignore continues - to be poverty, infant deaths and the loss of decent jobs and pay'

'We are a party of the working class. Your view will send these men to be killed in some pointless bloody war. It will not change the lives of the survivors if we win. They'll come back to the same shit employers, the same conditions, the same bloody awful life. They'll just be less of them.'

He took no consolation that their majority confirmed their dissent against any war. From what he had observed, Roberts seemed to be correct. The men were revelling in the thought of a fight....

Chapter 93

(Brawmarsh, June 1914)

The tensions were mounting in Europe, but, more concerningly, Ireland was now becoming the chief threat to the country's peace. In addition to further troops being posted to the Ulster border, the Government had now chosen to place battleships in the River Clyde. This only antagonised the Nationalists and, it was reported the Catholics were now building an army and finding access to arms from across the sea.

In England, and particularly London, the women's movement had increased their protests with violence on the streets, threats of bombing and the breaking of windows in public buildings. It was only one year earlier, that one of their number had been killed at the Epsom Derby after throwing herself in front of the King's horse. Their aggressive behaviour had seemed to escalate since that time.

Whilst Florence was unhappy with their methods, she still held her early beliefs and remained totally frustrated by the lack of progress. Some changes in the law had affected improvements in the minimum level of pay for women and some rights in regard to divorce and inheritance, but the right to vote remained unchanged. There continued to be an impasse between the ruling parties and, consequently no enthusiasm to deliver the required legislation.

She had other things on her mind these days. Her time was totally occupied by the three bairns with the eldest, Emma, now four and proving a real handful. She had a strong will and fierce temper when upset – not unexpectedly given her parentage....

Arthur, coming up three was a quiet character and happily occupied himself. The baby of the family, Lily, remained demanding but was generally a happy little soul.

Florence sat, at times, reflecting on her life. She had been determined to follow her nursing vocation, now disrupted by her family commitments. Would she ever have the opportunity to return? She wondered whether war – if it came – would present any use for her?

She worried about Jack. He remained steadfast to his political beliefs and these, and his full-time position, still committed a substantial amount of his time. She had relinquished her pressure on him to reduce his obligations – it seemed that this would be the pattern of his life and she understood that it would be her life too.

She remained close to Mary and her brood. It had been a real advantage that they had children of similar ages and that they enjoyed each other's company. Her sister-in-law appeared to have put the past behind her, at least on the surface. She had not touched on the issues with Elizabeth's birth for some time and the young girl carried Mary's colouring and features.

A bigger concern was Jack's relationship with her brother. Thomas had remained quiet and subdued in any family meetings over the weeks since the fall-out with Sammy. He had not mentioned any enthusiasm about a call-up to the army in their discussions, but Mary had stated that – despite her protests – he was determined to follow that path, if required to do so.

***

Jack continued to worry about the 'Irish' documents. He had taken them out to throw away but could not bring himself to do so. His loyalty to Seamus and his remote support of the Republican cause still held his hand. He knew that, at some point in time, when he could get Seamus to respond, he would take the appropriate action.

His working life was uncomfortable. His relationship with Norman Braithwaite had not improved. Despite the man being removed from the Executive, he continued to carry significant influence within the Union. He had made it very clear that he believed that Jack had spoken out of turn at the London Conference.

'You weren't there as our representative. You'd no right to speak on the Union's behalf. And you misrepresented our position...

'What position was that, Norman? Sitting on our bloody hands! And I did not speak for the Union – I spoke as a Labour nominee. If you don't accept that, so be it. I'm not about to apologise or change my stance.'

His council work remained frustrating. He had decided that he and his party colleagues could not exercise much authority as a small minority. Consequently, he had spent his time with the people in the town, listening to and seeking to address their issues. He enjoyed the work, and gained some satisfaction when he was able to assist those struggling with employer issues and hardship. He was fully aware that he would face an election later in the year, and any positives drawn from his contribution would help his cause.

He was aware that Florence had her hands full and, whilst she enjoyed motherhood, she felt under-utilised and unfulfilled. Whilst he sought to contribute to the family life he was very conscious that his other commitments regularly demanded too much time away from them. He believed Florence understood....he hoped so...

Chapter 94

(Welfare Club, Brawmarsh, July 1914)
Jack had not frequented the Club much over the last couple of months. He felt that he needed to spend more time with Florence and the children, but also – almost subconsciously – he felt it better he avoided Sammy, given their last encounter. He was only present now, as Thomas had conveyed a message, through Florence, that Jack and he should have a drink.

He arrived to find Thomas already in situ, enjoying his beer.

'Only just got here, Prendergast. Don't suggest I've been here all day!'

Jack – given Thomas's past form - had to laugh.

'Listen lad, your sister has signed my pass this evening, so you must have some influence.'

They raised their beers and sat quietly for a minute or so, watching the other attendees and listening to the standard abuse and exchanges between them.

'What's on your mind, Thomas?'

'It's getting very serious, Jack isn't it? This war is coming.'

'Aye, it is lad. We'll be at war soon I suspect. The papers are full of the shooting of the heir to the Austrian-Hungary Empire in Serbia. That gives them the ammunition.'

'Where is Serbia, Jack?'

He looked hard at his brother-in-law and laughed out loud.

'Do ya know Thomas, that's my worry. You, and thousands more, will volunteer to fight in a war for a country that means nowt to you. Do you know why we're getting pulled into this?'

Thomas shook his head as Jack continued.

I won't bore your arse, fella but here's the facts. Austria wants Serbia, Germany is happy to support them because they want other territories and need Austria's support. Russia has their eyes on Serbia and have an alliance – for some bloody daft reason – with France and us. So, if Serbia get's invaded, we get involved. The murder of Franz Josef by Serbians gives Austria the way to confront and demand from the Serbians. That's why the war will start.'

'So, we have a need to get involved then? We need to support our allies and friends…?'

Jack had to stop himself from beating his head to the table.

'Whatever I tell ya will make no difference, lad. I've given up. You're my sister's husband – the father of three children. For God's sake, get your priorities right, Thomas.'

He watched his brother-in-law muse over his comments, but knew that he would be influenced by others….

***

He managed on the following day, at last, to speak to Seamus. After the initial pleasantries, he once again asked about the documents.

'Jack lad, they're nothing to worry yerself about. I've a fella who's agreed to collect them in the next week or so. You'll have heard the latest news about here?'

Jack declared that he hadn't.

'Your bloody troops have fired on the workers protests in Dublin. Appears there's three been murdered and tens wounded. That, lad will light the fire. Stand back and wait….'

Chapter 95

(Brawmarsh, August 1914)

The dam had burst in Europe. Austria-Hungary had declared war on Serbia and as expected Germany had confirmed their support. The Kaiser had wasted no time in pushing his country's plans for expansion moving to invade Belgium, and consequently threatening France.

On the 4 August, Great Britain had declared war and the passions in the country had been aroused. Posters with Lord Kitchener's face had already been circulated demanding that 'Your Country Needs You'. The Labour Party and many other politicians had declared their opposition. but to no avail.

In the following week, Parliament had agreed a draconian 'Defence of the Realm Act'. A short piece of legislation declaring any dissent by any individual to be a treasonable offence. A number of leading opponents of the war were arrested and imprisoned. Newspapers were now to be subject to censorship. The opening hours for public houses were restricted and beer was to be watered down. Even kite flying and bonfires were deemed illegal. Factories and other businesses were now subject to acquisition by the armed forces for 'war work'.

By the first weekend of August, some three thousand men each day were volunteering for military service. There was an initiative to place further pressures on the locality – the formation of 'Pals Regiments' seeking to build enthusiasm for local men to join together from their towns and enjoy the 'adventure of war' alongside their community colleagues.

Jack sat at home despairing of the situation. On top of all these changes, the Home Rule Bill was suspended – this would inevitably inflame the Nationalists in Ireland. Britain would soon be fighting its war on another front....

It came as no surprise when Florence announced that her brother had wasted no time in volunteering, alongside Sammy. She told Jack that the local cadre would be assembling in the park on the following Saturday morning to be marched to the trains towards their basic training camp. Within weeks, they would be transported to the front in Europe.

Reluctantly, Jack joined his wife and sister with their broods to see the recruits take their leave on the day. There was an assembly of some fifty men, all appearing to glorify in their commitment.

He wandered across to the group with his family to reluctantly pass his best wishes to his brother-in-law. He exchanged a cursory nod with Sammy. To his surprise he recognised another face amongst the men.

'Eddie. Surprised to find you here?'

Eddie shook his hand.

'Seemed the right thing to do, fella. Are you not joining us?'

'Not in a million years...I think the war is a bloody nonsense..'

Eddie looked at him with a dismissive smirk on his face and turned away to call to Thomas.

'Is your lovely wife with us today, lad?'

'Aye. Over there. Go and say hello.'

He walked over to Mary who was standing with her children.

'Well, long time since we met, Mary?'

She stood in shock and looked around for an escape. Eddie reached out and pulled her close, to all intents greeting an old friend. He whispered leering in her ear.

'So, which one is mine then?'

Mary attempted to pull away but he held her tightly by the arm.

'How about that then, lass? Me and your husband in the same group. I do believe we could have a lot to talk about, eh?'

She wrenched herself free and pushed him away.

'Perhaps I'll get some leave whilst your man is at the front. I'll mebbe drop by and see ya when I'm home?'

He stroked her face and walked away, laughing out loud....

Chapter 96

(Jack and Florence's house, Brawmarsh, Late August 1914)

Jack and Florence sat quietly in their sitting room, having settled the children to bed. It was approaching ten o'clock and Florence rose.

'I'm away to bed, fella. Don't be long will you.'

'No lass. Just finish reading the newspaper and I'll be up.'

He settled back and was stirred by a heavy beating on the door.

Who the hell would be coming around at this time?

As he unlocked the door, it was thrown open and he was pushed to the floor. He found himself looking up at three police officers.

'What the bloody hell....!' He started to raise himself.

The man, who he took to be the senior man, swung a truncheon striking Jack across his neck.

'Shut your mouth, fella. You'll be Jack Prendergast?'

He nodded his confirmation.

'What's going on...?'

'I'll tell ya what's going on, lad. You're being arrested under the Defence of the Realm Act. We have information that you're in possession of Irish rebel propaganda and Communist literature.'

'We're carrying out a search of your property. If we find what we're looking for you'll be facing a possible charge of treason. That'll result in your imprisonment and possibly worse. You're in serious trouble, fella!....'

Printed in Great Britain
by Amazon